The clock chimed midnight.

Nate could almost hear the Fates laughing as he crossed the room.

To think that he'd risked getting pulled over for speeding on his way into town. He'd been worried that the nurse waiting for him at the bus station might take a look around, get disgusted and leave on the next bus out. Bitter Creek, Texas, wasn't much to look at in the daytime. At midnight, it looked like the back end of nowhere.

There hadn't been much point in hurrying, though, had there? She wasn't going to stay anyway.

Hannah McBride, the woman he'd hired on the basis of a phone interview and a friend's hearty recommendation, was the sort of woman who belonged in the glossy pages of a magazine, not a dingy bus station, and certainly not at his ranch.

She was everything Nate had ever wanted in a woman.

Once.

* * * *

Dear Reader,

Once again, we're back to offer you six fabulous romantic novels, the kind of book you'll just long to curl up with on a warm spring day. Leading off the month is award-winner Marie Ferrarella, whose *This Heart for Hire* is a reunion romance filled with the sharply drawn characters and witty banter you've come to expect from this talented writer.

Then check out Margaret Watson's *The Fugitive Bride,* the latest installment in her CAMERON, UTAH, miniseries. This FBI agent hero is about to learn all about love at the hands of his prime suspect. *Midnight Cinderella* is Eileen Wilks' second book for the line, and it's our WAY OUT WEST title. After all, there's just nothing like a cowboy! Our FAMILIES ARE FOREVER flash graces Kayla Daniels' *The Daddy Trap,* about a resolutely single hero faced with fatherhood—and love. *The Cop and Calamity Jane* is a suspenseful romp from the pen of talented Elane Osborn; you'll be laughing out loud as you read this one. Finally, welcome Linda Winstead Jones to the line. Already known for her historical romances, this author is about to make a name for herself in contemporary circles with *Bridger's Last Stand*.

Don't miss a single one—and then rejoin us next month, when we bring you six more examples of the best romantic writing around.

Yours,

Leslie J. Wainger
Executive Senior Editor

Please address questions and book requests to:
Silhouette Reader Service
U.S.: 3010 Walden Ave., P.O. Box 1325, Buffalo, NY 14269
Canadian: P.O. Box 609, Fort Erie, Ont. L2A 5X3

MIDNIGHT CINDERELLA

EILEEN WILKS

Silhouette®

INTIMATE™MOMENTS®

Published by Silhouette Books

America's Publisher of Contemporary Romance

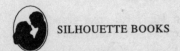

SILHOUETTE BOOKS

ISBN 0-373-07921-4

MIDNIGHT CINDERELLA

Printed in U.S.A.

Books by Eileen Wilks

Silhouette Intimate Moments

The Virgin and the Outlaw #857
Midnight Cinderella #921

Silhouette Desire

The Loner and the Lady #1008
The Wrong Wife #1065
Cowboys Do It Best #1109
Just a Little Bit Pregnant #1134
Just a Little Bit Married? #1188

EILEEN WILKS

is a fifth-generation Texan. Her great-great-grandmother came to Texas in a covered wagon shortly after the end of the Civil War—excuse us, the War Between the States. But she's not a full-blooded Texan. Right after another war, her Texan father fell for a Yankee woman. This obviously mismatched pair proceeded to travel to nine cities in three countries in the first twenty years of their marriage, raising two kids and innumerable dogs and cats along the way. For the next twenty years they stayed put, back home in Texas again—and still together.

Eileen figures her professional career matches her nomadic upbringing, since she tried everything from drafting to a brief stint as a ranch hand—raising two children and any number of cats and dogs along the way. Not until she started writing did she "stay put," because that's when she knew she'd come home. Readers can write to her at P.O. Box 4612, Midland, TX 79704-4612.

First, this book is for Glenda, whose friendship is one of the cherished constants in my life. In addition, I want to thank the people who patiently answered my many questions: Teresa J. Clingman, Assistant District Attorney in Midland, Texas; Sherry Crane, who allowed me to draw upon her years of experience as an orthopedic nurse; and Evetts Haley, Jr., a gentleman of the old school whose knowledge of ranching in general, and of ranching in the Texas Panhandle in particular, is as wide and varied as the land his cattle graze.

Chapter 1

It was ten minutes until midnight, according to the cracked clock on the wall. Hannah looked at it and frowned. She didn't like being without a watch, and she didn't like waiting. Her old, dependable watch had stopped working two days ago and her new employer wasn't here yet. Her choices were limited.

To some people, midnight meant the witching hour. To Hannah Maria McBride, reared on the Brothers Grimm and other fantasies, it meant the moment Cinderella's beautiful clothes turned back into rags. Unfortunately, the people sharing the bus station's waiting area with her bore even less resemblance to Prince Charming than her worn jeans and bulky parka did to Cinderella's ball dress.

She tightened her grip on her backpack, scooted her suitcase a little farther under the bench she sat on, and looked around. The bus station hadn't improved in the hour she'd spent waiting there. The walls were still dirty, the floor was still dirty and she was still the only woman in the place.

The old man sleeping on the bench in the corner didn't

worry her. The three young men who'd just come in, passing a bottle of Mad Dog 20/20 between them, did. Especially the scrawny one, the one with long hair the color and texture of twine. His empty eyes followed her like the sights on a rifle.

She was also bothered by the condition of her wallet. Thirty-four dollars and seventeen cents wouldn't go far if her new employer didn't show up. He was supposed to have been here an hour ago. Nor was she happy about the slimy smile on the face of the ticket agent.

All in all, she was beginning to feel a bit uncertain about what to do next. The feeling was as unwelcome as it was unfamiliar.

Hannah was a rare combination of haste and patience. The way she saw it, action—any action—was bound to be better than sitting around worrying to death about her problems, and if this attitude led her to rush her decisions at times, she shrugged and refused to regret the consequences. But she was a practical woman. Life had taught her the difference between dreams and reality, and working as a nurse's aide the past three years had underlined that lesson. So she was capable of great patience…when she had to be.

Traveling by bus suited her fondness for efficiency, since she could do other important things, like sleep or read, while the driver did his job. The main reason she'd come here by bus tonight, though—the one she preferred not to dwell on—was money.

Money annoyed Hannah. She didn't intend to let it control her life, and she never used it to measure a person's worth. But she couldn't get around the fact that she did need money to survive, just like everyone else, and she couldn't help thinking that one or two of the ragged people who shared the bus station with her tonight were a bit…disquieting.

Yes, she thought, pleased with herself for remembering today's word, that's exactly right. *Disquieting: causing anxiety or uneasiness; disturbing.* Maybe, to pass the time, she could look up tomorrow's word. She glanced at the cracked clock again. Four minutes until midnight. Technically it wasn't quite tomorrow yet, but it was close enough that it wasn't really cheating to peek ahead. She pulled her word-a-day book out of the pocket of her backpack and turned to the page for February 23rd.

Enigma, she read. *A puzzling occurrence; a puzzling or contradictory character.*

An unpleasant giggle distracted her. The scrawny youth with the twine hair was still watching her, but it was his friend with the droopy mustache who was giggling in that nasty, high-pitched way. Hannah frowned at them. She knew better than to let them realize they were making her a teensy bit nervous. Not scared, not really, not with the ticket agent right over—

She glanced behind her at the counter. No one was there.

He must have gone to the men's room, she told herself, or on some other very *brief* errand. Something that wouldn't keep him away long at all. No doubt he would be right back. All the same—

There was that giggle again.

All the same, maybe she would try calling her employer. Maybe he hadn't gotten the message she'd left on his machine when she first arrived. She stood and dug her hand into the pocket of her jeans for a quarter. Right away, she wished she'd zipped up her coat first.

Hannah wasn't a beauty. She knew that, but she also knew that beauty intimidated men, while looks like hers… Well, it was true that some men were put off by a woman who stood a hair under five foot ten inches tall in her stocking feet. Some didn't like redheads, or care for long hair so curly that it looked like she'd stuck her finger in an electric socket. And there were men who didn't like a woman with an old-fashioned, hourglass shape.

But not that many.

The giggler stared at her chest. He grinned like the idiot he was, puffed out his own chest and strutted toward her. His friends fell into step alongside him.

Hannah didn't consider it safe to turn her back on any wild or feral creature. She stood her ground.

The giggler stopped right in front of her. He looked at her, but he talked to his friends as if she weren't there. "Whatcha think, Sammie? You been starin' at her tits, haven't you? I gotta say, those are some mighty fine tits."

Hannah's lips tightened.

"You think she's sellin' it, Mario?" That came from the tall one. The scrawny one didn't say a word.

"Sure she is," the giggler said, spreading his mustache wide in a smile that showed off his yellow teeth. "Why else would she be hangin' out here? Hey, honey, I got twenty bucks. You got a place, or you wanna use the back seat of my car?"

Hannah shook her head. Looking disgusted was easy; looking calm took more effort. But she'd dealt with creeps just as obnoxious during her stint as a bartender. "You boys ought to know better than to talk trash to a woman you don't know. What if I were an undercover cop?"

He snorted. "An undercover cop? In Bitter Creek? Not likely. You don't look much like the sheriff or any of his boys."

"But I'm not from around here, now, am I?" she said patiently. "I just came in on the bus."

His brows puckered in sudden—and probably painful—thought. "Cops don't ride buses."

She lifted one eyebrow, a trick she'd mastered in the eighth grade to irritate her sister. "Know a lot about undercover cops, do you?"

The tall one snickered. "Ooh, Mario, I think she likes you."

Giggles flushed. "I know how to handle a smart-mouthed—"

"You boys need to leave now." The new voice was deep, male, and as coldly confident as winter.

Hannah was startled, but nowhere near as startled as the "boys." They jumped, jerked and moved hastily away, giving her a clear view of the man who'd entered the bus station, unnoticed, while she was surrounded.

He wasn't a man who went unnoticed often. She would bet on that.

"She with you?" Giggles spoke with more respect than she would have expected him to show anyone who wasn't holding a gun.

Her champion was a big man. That was the second thing she noticed about him—his sheer size. He was unusually tall, yes, but it was the entire, oversize package that drew a woman's attention, not just his height. In his sheepskin jacket and dark brown cowboy hat, he looked larger than life, as if he could have stepped down from some billboard advertising saddles or cigarettes.

But his size wasn't the first thing she'd noticed. No, because first she'd heard his voice, that cold-as-death voice. She'd heard it once before. When he hired her.

"Does it matter?" he said at last.

"Not a bit," the tall one assured him. "We was just having a little fun, but—*oomph!*"

The last sound was a reaction to having Mario's elbow jabbed in his ribs. "C'mon, you idiot. No harm meant, Mr. Jones. We were just on our way out."

"Then go." He stepped aside to let Giggles & Friends make their exit.

Hannah wasn't one to hold a grudge. She smiled at her new boss, prepared to forgive him for making her wait. "Thanks for getting rid of those idiots. You're Nathan Jones, right? I'm Hannah McBride."

Nate could almost hear the Fates laughing their heads off as he crossed the room. To think that he'd risked having Jessie Ramirez—proud of his new deputy's badge—pull him over for speeding on his way into town! He'd been worried that the nurse waiting at the bus station for him might take a look around, get disgusted and hop on the next bus out of here. Bitter Creek, Texas, wasn't much to look at in the day-

time. At a quarter past midnight, it looked like the back end
of nowhere.

There hadn't been much point in hurrying, though, had
there? This woman wasn't going to stay.

Hannah McBride, the woman he'd hired on the basis of a
phone interview and a friend's hearty recommendation, was
the sort of woman a man usually sees in the glossy pages of
a men's magazine, not a dingy bus station. And certainly not
at his ranch. Actually, he realized as he drew near, her face
was nothing special—nice, but average, and peppered with
freckles. And young. *Too* young. Her chin had a stubborn
look to it, and her eyes were a friendly brown. But what man
was going to notice her eyes? Any male who summoned the
strength of mind to look above her shoulders was just going
to get trapped in all that hair.

Lord, that hair.

She was everything he had ever wanted in a woman. Once.

Whatever lingering thoughts Nathan held of the placid,
practical creature he had thought he'd hired evaporated when
he stopped in front of flame-haired reality. He shook his head
in disgust. If he weren't desperate, he would put her on the
next bus heading back where she came from.

He raised his voice. "George!"

The door behind the ticket counter opened and a small,
prematurely balding man came out. "Who the—oh, it's
you."

"What did you do, run and hide in the office when Mario
and his friends came in?"

"No," Hannah said. "He waited until they started hassling
me to disappear."

"I don't like trouble," the little man muttered.

"You think I do?" Most of her hair was pulled back in a
loose, sexy ponytail, but one strand had worked its way
loose. She brushed it back impatiently.

Desire flicked him on the raw. Obviously his body had no
more sense at thirty-two than it had at twenty-two, but his

body wasn't in charge. And the rest of him knew better. "Women like you *are* trouble."

"If you'd been here when you said you would be, there wouldn't have been a problem." She stuck the paperback book she'd been holding in the backpack, hefted it and reached for the suitcase by her feet.

He grabbed the suitcase before she could, and scowled. "How old are you, anyway?"

"Twenty-four," she said, straightening. "Not that it's any of your business. So why weren't you here on time? Did you forget about me?"

He hated being late. It put him at fault, and the only thing he hated more than being at fault was having things go to hell so thoroughly that he was never able, afterward, to sort out how much of the blame was his. "I had a cow that needed doctoring. I'm here now."

"Do you often ignore your phone? I called."

"When I've got both hands up a cow's ass, I do." He shifted the suitcase to his other hand. The damn thing was one of those old-fashioned, hard-sided sort that weigh a ton even empty. And this one sure wasn't empty.

"Isn't your brother at the house? I know he's injured, but surely he's able to answer the phone."

"I keep the ringer turned off on the phone in Mark's room so no damn fool female can call and wake him up after he finally gets to sleep."

"His pain meds should help him sleep."

"He doesn't like to take pills."

"Ah." She nodded. "One of those, is he? Well, unless there's some outside reason, like substance abuse, that he shouldn't—"

"I said he doesn't take pills. Not even aspirin."

"I'll get him to take the pain medicine, though. He needs the sleep."

He paused, frustrated because she was right. Mark's hang-up about drugs was keeping him from getting the rest his body needed to heal. "You won't be here long enough to talk Mark into anything." He would see to that.

"Nonsense. It won't take me the entire two months to have him taking his pain pills."

"You won't be here that long."

Her eyes narrowed. "Our agreement was for two months."

The ticket agent broke in. "*This* is the nurse you hired to replace Mrs. Grimes?"

"Nurse's aide," Hannah corrected.

Nathan glanced at the ticket agent. George had always been a nosy little runt, even back in grade school. The little man's eyes bulged with astonished speculation. "If I'd known this was who you was waiting on, ma'am…if I'd known—" He broke off, fairly quivering with all the things he didn't dare say.

"You want to explain to me why it's any of your business who I hire, George?"

"It isn't, no, of course it isn't." He licked his lips. "I was just curious. You understand. I want you to know that I don't believe all that stuff Ben Rydell has been saying."

Nate felt a distant twinge of curiosity about what kind of garbage Rydell was spreading this time, but he didn't have time to care. "Then you don't have anything to be nervous about, do you?" He turned to the woman he had to take home with him. Temporarily. "Come on."

She didn't budge. "I want to know what you meant about me not being here for the two months we agreed on."

"You aren't right for the job. Damned if I know why Harry didn't warn me what you looked like when he recommended you. But I'm a fair man. When I find someone else, I'll give you an extra day's wages for your trouble."

"You call that fair? One day's wages, instead of two months?" She propped one hand on her hip and scowled. The backpack swung from her other hand. "And just what is wrong with the way I look?"

"There are six of us out at the ranch right now—three hands, my foreman, my brother and me. All male. Six men to one woman might be just the way you like things, but I don't have time to sort out whatever trouble you stir up.''

''Now, you listen here! I don't know what your problem is, if you're a woman-hater or something, but I intend to be treated with respect, Mr. Jones.''

He started for the door. ''Nathan,'' he said.

''What?'' This time, at least, she was following.

''Call me Nathan, or Nate,'' he said, shoving the door open. '''Mr. Jones' makes me think someone wants my father.'' Or that the bailiff wanted him on his feet. Some memories didn't fade, no matter how much time passed.

Nathan Jones was not a simple man, Hannah decided when she saw that he meant to hold the door open for her. It was obvious he'd taken one look at her and made assumptions, and while this was hardly the first time someone had leaped to those conclusions, it still smarted. Yet there he stood, holding the door for her.

She couldn't decide if his display of courtesy was more intriguing or irritating.

The moment she stepped outside, wind slapped her in the face with air shipped direct from Canada, courtesy of the huge wind tunnel of the Great Plains. She tucked her chin down and tried to think of a way to connect with this aggravating man with the bad attitude. ''Does your father live nearby?''

''No.'' He headed for a big, white pickup truck near the door. ''He's dead.''

''Oh, I'm sorry.'' While he tossed her suitcase into the pickup's bed, she tried the passenger door. It wasn't locked, so she climbed into the cab, chucking her backpack in the space behind the seat, glad to get out of that wind. She pulled the door closed, shutting herself up in darkness and the smell of the past.

Leather and machinery. Horses and tobacco. The mingled scents were too intimate, and far too familiar.

The bridle she'd glimpsed behind the driver's seat explained the mixed leather-and-horse smell; the oily scent of machinery must be from the mysterious mechanical part that sat on newspaper on the seat beside her. The stubbed-out cigar she'd seen in the ashtray accounted for the smell of tobacco... And the dozens of ranches and highways and goodbyes of her childhood explained the motionless way she sat, waiting for the onslaught from the past to fade.

How many years had it been? Eight, nearly nine? She hadn't lived on a ranch since she turned sixteen and decided she'd rather get married than follow her cowboy father to yet another town. Of course, she'd been convinced it was love, not a hunger for roots, that had made Barry so irresistible.

Now here she was, closed up in what was every bit a rancher's work truck, and planning to live on a ranch once more. Temporarily, of course.

Her new boss opened his door, and the overhead light came on again. He was so tall that he had to take his hat off and set it on the seat when he slid behind the wheel. What a strange, closed face he had. She liked his eyebrows, though. The rest of his face was regular enough to be considered handsome, which she thought rather boring. But those eyebrows! They had personality. They didn't match, for one thing. Both were thick and dark, but one was straight, a frowning slash above his right eye, while the left one had a built-in quirk that gave it a quizzical look.

She wondered what he looked like when he smiled.

"What the hell are you staring at?"

If he ever smiled. "Your eyebrows."

He stared. "What does...no," he said, pulling the door closed and recreating the darkness inside the cab of the truck. "No, if I ask, you might tell me." He started the engine.

He was certainly a big man. He took up an unreasonable amount of space, making the cab of the truck feel suddenly crowded. "Your ranch is about thirty minutes away, I think you said?"

He grunted, looked over his shoulder and started backing up.

She let him get the pickup out of the parking lot and tried again. "Is it near the canyon?"

He gave her an irritated glance. "What canyon?"

"The lady who sat beside me on the bus said there's a canyon on one side of town, with a creek in it. She said that's how Bitter Creek got its name."

"It's an arroyo, not a canyon, and the creek's been mostly dry for the last fifty years."

She wasn't sure what an arroyo was, but damn if she'd ask the man beside her. "I guess you'd know about that. Your family has lived in the area a long time, I understand."

"Yeah." He drove the way he moved, like a man who was at home in his body and used to having it do what he told it to do. She'd seen that sort of casual physical command before, in people who earned their living with their bodies—athletes and dancers, cowboys and carpenters, a waitress at a truckstop—and it always fascinated her. Though she was nowhere near as self-conscious as she had been as a teenager, she hadn't felt entirely comfortable with her body since puberty hit her right between the breasts.

They pulled to a stop at the lone traffic light the little town boasted. It was quiet as only a small town late at night can be quiet, with no small sounds to disturb the hush. Hannah decided to wait and let him break the silence.

He wasn't exactly a chatterbox. They had passed the run-down motel on the edge of town with the blinking Va'ancy sign, and were headed out into the darkness of the countryside before he spoke again. "Harry spoke highly of you."

She smiled. "Harry and Livvy are something else, aren't they?" She'd enjoyed working for them when she took care of Harry's aunt last year after the old woman's hip surgery. They'd kept in touch after Hannah moved on to other towns, other patients.

"I assume Harry told you about me."

She glanced at him, puzzled. The glow from the dash lights was too dim to give her a clue to his expression. "He said you needed someone to take care of your little brother, who'd been in a motorcycle accident.''

''Is that all?''

''Well…he said your family has been in the area a long time. And that I could trust you. You were the one who warned me your brother was a bit irritable.'' About as irritable as a grizzly woken early from his winter's nap, from what she could tell. The first two aides he'd hired had quit.

''Dammit,'' he muttered. ''He didn't say anything else?''

''No, why?''

''He was supposed to.''

Now her curiosity was itching. ''Are you on a special diet or something? I'm a good cook, but I'm not a nutritionist. You'll need to give me instructions if that's the case.''

''A diet?'' He was grimly amused. ''No. I guess it doesn't matter. You won't be staying, anyway.''

''Yes, I will.''

He gave her one of those cool, level looks he'd given the three thugs. Hannah ignored it. She was too busy noticing the sensation in the pit of her stomach, an electric tug as unmistakable as it was unwelcome. Good heavens. She had goose bumps on her arms, too! What a peculiar way to react to his voice. She frowned into the darkness. It was a good thing he disliked her. She needed to focus on her goals, not on a man—especially not a man like this one. Nathan Jones obviously didn't have a tender, caring bone in his body. And heartache was such a *distracting* emotion.

Not that she thought he could actually break her heart, but he could probably deliver a bad bruise. She was going to be living with him for the next two months, after all. Oh, he might not think she'd stick, but she needed the job too much to let him growl her out of it. Besides, she was good at what she did, and his brother needed her. So did her sister, for a very different reason.

Fortunately, Nathan Jones was blessed with plenty of unpleasant qualities, and that should put an end to this ridiculous attraction. No doubt exposure to him would help her unexpected lust to die a natural death. She couldn't imagine continuing to want a man who disliked her.

They rode in silence for several miles. It was inky-dark away from town. The land was as wrinkled as unpressed linen, but basically level and treeless. It was obvious their headlights were the only ones for miles around, yet Nathan Jones used his turn signal when he slowed for the turnoff. The road they turned onto wasn't paved, but it was well-graded and graveled, giving a ride almost as smooth as on the highway. A light flickered up ahead.

The silence was beginning to bother her. When he signaled again before turning into a driveway flanked by the vague black shapes of several large trees, she spoke. "So, are you a belt-and-suspenders type about everything, or just basically law-abiding?"

"What are you talking about?"

"Your driving habits. You use your turn signal even when there's no traffic for miles, and wait politely at red lights even when the entire town is in bed, asleep." She chuckled. "I'll bet you've never had a ticket."

"Not in the past six years, at least."

"What, were you a hell-raiser until then?" She didn't believe it. He was too self-contained, too controlled, for her to picture him as a rebel.

"I don't think anyone would have put it quite that way."

"How would they have put it?" The driveway was long by city standards, but she could see the dark bulk of a sprawling house ahead, along with a scattering of outbuildings.

"You sure you want to know?" he asked.

What an odd thing to say. "If it's too personal…"

"It's nothing you shouldn't have already been told."

"So tell me," she said, but most of her attention was fixed ahead of them, on the house that would be her home for the next two months. She couldn't see much. None of the windows were lit, so she couldn't get a clear idea of the actual size or shape of the place, but it seemed to be a big house. The wall she could see in the spill of porch light on the side of the house was stone. That semicircle of yellow light also showed her a slice of driveway, a small porch and an untrimmed straggle of shrubbery banked against the fitted-stone wall of the house.

The driveway split into two just before they reached the house, one drive heading for a dark building that might be a garage, the other running alongside the house. Her new employer took the straightest road, pulling up near the side porch. She had just about decided that he wasn't going to answer her question when he looked over at her. None of the cheery yellow light from the porch reached his face when he spoke. "I'm careful about how I drive because I haven't been off probation long enough to feel casual about any of the rules."

"Probation?" she said weakly.

"Harry was supposed to tell you about that. Chances are, he could have saved you a bus ride—and me the cost of your ticket—if he had." He turned off the ignition without looking away from her.

Mockery was one of the chilly threads she heard in his voice when he spoke again. Amusement, dark and bitter, was another. "Go ahead," he said. "Ask."

She didn't want to. She hated being predictable as much as she hated being manipulated. That's what he was doing, too—manipulating her, making her respond with a hint of fear and an overwhelming curiosity.

But she couldn't help it. She had to know. "Why were you on probation?"

"Because, six years ago, I killed a man."

Chapter 2

While Nathan Jones got her suitcase out of the back, Hannah sat motionless. He'd killed a man. How? In an accident, like a car crash? It must have been an accident, she told herself. He'd been put on probation instead of serving time. Surely he would have gone to prison if—

Her door opened. She jumped.

He smiled, but it wasn't a friendly expression, and his voice was as coldly courteous as that of the devil inviting a sinner into hell. "You may as well come inside, Hannah McBride. You're not going anywhere tonight."

The ranch house was an old building, particularly for this part of the country, where the white man's passion for walls, roofs and ownership hadn't triumphed until the end of the last century. From what little Hannah had seen of it so far, the central portion seemed to be a combination of brick and stone construction, and the walls were thick. Hannah sat on the wide ledge of the window in her bedroom and leaned her forehead against glass as cold and black as the winter sky outside. A double-zillion stars lit that exterior darkness, shining with a fervor that was always lost in the tangle of city lights. She'd forgotten how splendid the night sky could be in the country.

But it was a cold splendor, wasn't it?

At least she had a nice room. The furnishings were old but of good quality, especially the antique vanity standing against the wall that held the single tall window. Hannah sat on the ledge of that window in her blue-and-white flannel nightgown and hoped the splendor of stars and the feel of winter against her forehead would settle her thoughts.

She sighed once, and wondered about her sister.

Had anyone asked, she would have indignantly denied being worried. Leslie was a McBride, and very well able to take care of herself, thank you, in spite of her current troubles. But sitting here, alone with her thoughts and the pressure of weariness, Hannah would admit she was a bit…unsettled. She didn't like not knowing where her sister was. She was definitely unsettled about that.

Of course, Leslie would be in touch soon. She'd needed to make a fresh start, to get away from the ex-husband who'd been threatening her. That's why Hannah had loaned her the contents of her savings account. Of course, Leslie hadn't asked Hannah to send all her money. Hannah supposed she might have gone a little overboard there, but she'd known she had this job to come to, and it was bad enough knowing her sister was going through hell without worrying about whether she had enough money.

Really, there was very little to worry about, Hannah assured herself as she turned her head to press her cheek against the cold glass. All she had to do was stay where her sister could reach her. Hannah had given Leslie this phone number and address; therefore, Hannah couldn't quit. Or allow her boss to fire her.

Her grouchy, silent, oversize boss. Who had killed a man.

After dropping his bombshell, he'd escorted her politely into the house. The side entrance was through the laundry room and on into the kitchen, which had given Hannah a hint of how hard she was going to work over the next few days getting this house back in shape while caring for an invalid. Dishes were piled in the sink and on the counter, and she'd walked across something sticky on her way to the hall.

Her bedroom was in the west wing, next to her patient's room. She didn't know where Nathan Jones slept.

Hannah shivered. She rubbed at the chill bumps on her arms, then surprised herself by yawning. It was too late, too cold, and she was too tired to get everything straight in her mind tonight. Time for bed.

The only light in the room came from a wall lamp with a hobnail glass globe. She turned that off and stood on the rag rug by the bed, listening.

Hannah had slept beneath so many roofs that she had her own ritual for her first night in a new place. First she set out her special things—the photographs in the hinged frame, the little wooden horse her father had carved, her books. Then, before climbing in bed, she listened. Every building had its own set of creaks and groans, so she stood there in the dark, accustoming herself to the sounds this particular house made late on a winter night. As gradually and inevitably as snow drifts down from overburdened winter clouds, her thoughts drifted once more to Nathan Jones.

What had he meant when he said he'd killed a man? Maybe he meant that he'd caused a man's death. That would be a terrible thing to live with, she thought—the knowledge that his carelessness had caused someone's death.

But that wasn't what he'd said, was it?

He expected her to leave now that he'd told her. And maybe, she admitted, hugging her arms close to her body, leaving would be the smart thing to do.

But Nathan Jones *expected* her to leave.

Obviously, he was trying to make her as eager to leave as he was to have her gone. She hated being manipulated. He didn't think he had to offer any explanations, any other facts about himself, to make her hightail it out of there. He assumed she would jump to conclusions about him as fast as he'd jumped to them about her.

Hannah sneered at the idea as she turned down the covers on the bed. There was the flatness of her wallet to think about, too. She contemplated it. She hadn't been this broke since Barry walked out on her the day before she turned seventeen. Not that she regretted loaning Leslie the money— not for a second—but if she left this job sooner than she'd planned, she would have to ask for help. And she did have friends who would help if she asked, but…

But she was a McBride, and she hated the idea.

No point in worrying things to death. The sheets she slid between were cold, but the blankets and quilts were piled comfortingly high. She'd be warm again soon enough.

Tomorrow, she decided, she would meet her patient and decide for sure about the job. On the whole, though, she thought she would stick it out here. Two months at the wages offered by Mr. Tall-Dark-And-Scary Jones would get her back on her feet financially. She'd be able to enroll at Tech for the summer semester. Or she might work this summer and start back in the fall. She wasn't giving up on her dreams, she assured herself. Maybe she'd had to postpone them a bit, but the university wasn't going anywhere. It would still be there when she had the money again.

The two bed pillows were thin. She bunched them up together into a comfortable shape. The mattress was firm, the sheets clean. All in all, she thought, letting her eyes drift shut, she could have done a lot worse for herself. She'd be fine as long as she stayed away from Nathan Jones, with his tricky ways and dangerous past, not to mention his mismatched eyebrows and that cold, wicked voice.

Oh, that voice…

Desire danced along her skin—a quick, prickly charge that brought her eyes wide-open. She frowned, rolled onto her other side, bunched the pillows up beneath her head again and stared at the black rectangle of the window.

Damn. It didn't seem fair, but she was going to have to avoid him even when he wasn't around.

Hannah possessed the knack, shared by interns and small children, of shutting down quickly and completely, then waking refreshed from even a relatively short sleep. So the next morning when someone started cussing in the room next to hers, she woke fast and clearheaded.

The voice was male and furious. One or two words, loud enough for her to make them out in spite of the wall between her and the speaker, made her raise her eyebrows as she tossed back the covers. Certainly she had heard those words before, having been raised around cowboys who sometimes forgot themselves, but Patrick McBride had been a chauvinist of the old school. He would have knocked down anyone who he heard using that sort of language around his daughters.

Suddenly the cussing stopped. It was followed by a loud yell. "Nate! Dammit, Nate, get your butt in here!"

Hannah didn't take the time for robe or slippers. She left her room at a run and flung open the door to the room next to hers.

The man in the hospital bed had dark hair and coppery skin. She could see quite a bit of that skin, since he was naked except for two white casts, one on the lower half of his right arm and one that covered his right leg from hip to heel. And he was gorgeous. Absolutely, drop-dead gorgeous, from his scowling face to the bare toes sticking out the end of the leg cast.

He sure didn't look like anyone's *little* brother.

"What the hell—" He made a quick, left-handed grab for the sheet twisted up between his legs, and managed to fig-leaf himself, then turned his scowling face on her.

That face was several years younger than his brother's— about her own age, she thought—and damp with the sudden sweat of pain. He was trapped in a position that had to hurt like hell, his back a couple of inches above the bed and the cast on his right wrist stuck through the trapeze that hung

from the scaffolding over the bed—stuck and caught, holding
him miserably half-up, half-down.

She hurried to him. "Tried to swing from the trapeze with
the wrong arm, didn't you? Hold on." She pushed the button
on the side of the bed, raising it enough to come up behind
him and take his weight, easing the pressure on his broken
arm.

He grunted and tried to pull his arm back out of the trapeze. "I can't—"

"I know. The ribs?" she asked sympathetically as she
helped him get cast and arm out of the triangular device.
Nathan Jones had described his brother's injuries when he
hired her over the phone. The right femur—the long, weight-
bearing bone in his right leg—was broken. So was his right
wrist, so he couldn't use crutches to get around. With a couple of cracked ribs as well, he couldn't yet even use the
trapeze to shift himself around in bed.

"Yeah." He lay back against the nearly flat pillow with a
small sigh of relief. His skin was clammy.

She untangled the covers, which were in a heap near the
foot of the bed. "You must weigh, what—about two hundred?"

"So?" The "make me" expression on his face reminded
her of a little boy caught in some mischief. The face itself
was so perfect that it was startling. That stunning face was
framed by hair as black as a raven's wing, worn long enough
to tuck behind the ears. It was straight as a raven's wing,
too.

Gorgeous. She sighed, envying him his hair.

Footsteps sounded in the hall, moving fast. Her employer,
no doubt, who must have been some distance away when he
heard Mark's last bellow for help.

"What the hell business is it of yours how much I weigh?"
her patient growled.

"Pity your language and temper aren't as pretty as the rest
of you."

Nathan's voice came from the doorway. "What's going on here?"

She glanced over at him. "How many aides did you say his temper has driven off?"

"Two." When Nathan came into the room, he seemed to bring a trace of the outdoors with him. The brim of his Stetson shadowed his eyes the way an overcast sky shadows the earth, and she fancied she could feel the cold clinging to his denim jacket through the two feet of air separating them. He directed his question at his brother. "What's wrong?"

The skin on his cheek would be cold, Hannah thought, if she were to touch it. Not that she would, of course... Good grief, she was *certainly* not going to think about touching her boss's cheek.

Mark's lip lifted in a sneer. "Nothing, now. Your new bimbo did a fair job of playing nurse."

She sneered right back. She'd learned long ago that arguing with men who jumped to conclusions based on a woman's bra size wasn't worth the trouble. "I'm not playing. I expect to be paid." She turned to her boss. "Your brother decided to use his broken arm to lift two hundred pounds of man. He got his cast caught in the trapeze. Not too bright."

Nathan turned his scowl on his brother. "Idiot."

"I'm sick and tired of hollering for you every time I want to turn over."

"No problem," Hannah said, wondering if she was imagining the tension between the brothers. "You can holler for me from now on."

"You?"

His astonishment irritated her. "Why not?"

Nathan spoke before his brother could. Irony tinted the smooth, rumbly voice that did such peculiar things to Hannah's insides. "Mark, this is Hannah McBride, the nurse I told you about. I picked her up at the bus station last night."

"Home health aide," she corrected conscientiously. She was five semesters from being able to call herself "nurse."

A smile started in Mark's dark eyes. "Obviously I'm an

idiot.'' He glanced at his brother. "She's sure easier on the eyes than Mrs. Grimes."

"Don't get used to it. She's temporary."

"Maybe not," she said, looking over the clutter covering the top of the little bedside table. "Mr. Jones—"

"Nate."

"Nate, then. You can go now. Mark and I will get acquainted better if you aren't hanging over us like a storm cloud."

Mark seemed to like that. "Yeah, go away, Nate. Hannah and I want to get *acquainted*."

Her boss looked at her, his face expressionless. "I'll take care of whatever Mark needs while you get some clothes on."

Hannah was abruptly reminded of her bare feet. She curled her cold toes self-consciously and reminded herself that she was covered more completely now, in unrevealing flannel, than she would be when she put on her uniform. *He* was the one with the problem, making it sound as if she were running around half-naked. "I'll change when I shower, which will be *after* I get your brother comfortable, and before I come down to fix breakfast."

"Breakfast isn't included in your duties."

"No, but my meals are included in my wages and I eat breakfast. If I'm going to cook for myself, I may as well fix enough for you and your brother, too."

"I ate with the hands." His eyes were a flat, unrevealing black.

"Suit yourself."

Mark snorted. "Maybe you like Julio's version of pancakes, but I don't. Feel free to cook my breakfast anytime, Hannah." He grinned.

Lord, what a sight. She shook her head. "That gorgeous face of yours is going to take some getting used to. It's as distracting as a train wreck."

Nate made a disgusted noise and turned to go. "I'll take

the intercom to the barn with me, Mark—in case you need me.''

Impulsively, thinking only of getting onto a better footing with her grouchy boss, she reached out to stop him. "Mr. Jones—Nathan—if you want to try my pancakes, you're welcome to." She laid a hand on his arm.

He did stop. So, for a second, did her breath.

Hannah was a toucher. Physical contact was part of her job, of course; she had to touch her patients to help, to ease, to comfort. But one reason she was drawn to nursing was that she had always connected with others physically. She was a confirmed collar-smoother, arm-patter and hug-giver, so touching this man through the thickness of his jacket shouldn't have had any effect on her. Yet she felt as if she'd received a soundless shout into her system—a quick, wordless pulse that echoed inside her even after she dropped her hand, startled.

He turned his head. "I don't like to be pawed."

Pawed? *Pawed?* "Yes, sir," she said frigidly.

Mark's cheerful voice broke the sudden, strained silence. "Go away, Nate. Take your sour face out of here. You're leaving me in good hands." Mark aimed a leer at Hannah that would have been more believable if he hadn't been pallid from pain.

Finally, Nate left. And thank goodness for that, Hannah told herself. She did not need his bad attitude cluttering up the sickroom.

"Well." Mark smiled widely, looking at her chest. "Alone at last."

"A lot of good that will do you. Hey," she said, putting her hand breast-high and lifting it, directing his gaze up to her face. "I'm up here, okay? You may as well know that I have a few rules."

"You may as well know I don't pay much attention to rules."

He was going to be a challenge, all right. "It might motivate you to remember that you're at my mercy. First rule—

looking's okay, but no touching. I've got quick reflexes, and I might hurt you. Second rule—I don't care how bad a mood you're in, no throwing things. *Especially* food.''

He scowled. ''Nate told you about that? Well, did he tell you what that old bat had the nerve to—''

''Doesn't matter,'' she interrupted, picking up one of the pill bottles from the cluttered bedside table and reading the label. ''You can throw a temper fit if you like, but don't throw anything else or I feed you oatmeal for three days. Third rule—don't pull any macho crap with me. If I ask you a question, I want a straight answer. Did you get much sleep last night?''

''Some.''

She wagged the pill bottle at him accusingly. ''Uh-uh. Wrong answer. The truth is that you slept lousy, just like you have every night since the accident, because you don't want to take your pain medication.''

''I don't addle my body with drugs.''

''No, you prefer to lie awake for hours, hurting all over. Well, you and I are going to have to talk about that. Right now, though, I'm going to see if I can make you more comfortable while we talk.''

She pushed the button, lowering the head of the bed again, then she untucked one of the blankets and pulled it off the bed.

''If you'll come closer, I'll tell you how to make me a lot more comfortable,'' he suggested.

She ignored that, rolling the blanket up snugly to make a bolster she could use to prop him partly on his side. ''I know what happened. This morning you couldn't stand just lying there anymore. Only you can't use your left arm to shift yourself because of those cracked ribs, so you tried to use your right arm, cast and all.'' She settled the rolled blanket next to him. ''But why didn't you call your brother? He gets up early.''

''Nathan's already shorthanded,'' he muttered. ''He doesn't need me yelling at him every five minutes.''

Her boss was shorthanded, was he? Well, with an attitude like his, that was no wonder. Especially if he made a point of telling all his employees that he'd once killed a man. Especially if the man he'd killed had been an employee—

Cut it out, she told her overactive imagination. "Let's see if we can't find a position that doesn't offend any of your broken places. I'm going to roll you just a bit onto your side. Don't try to help." She positioned her hands carefully on his shoulder and hip.

He did try to help, of course—the macho idiot—and hurt himself in the process.

"Next time, pretend you're a sack of potatoes," she said when she had him on his side. She used the pillows to elevate and stabilize his broken leg in the new position. "You know, you aren't doing yourself any favors by refusing your pain medication. If pain keeps you awake, your body isn't getting the rest it needs to heal. How does this feel?"

"Better," he said grudgingly, but the lines of his face eased as he shifted into the new position with a sigh. "You're bossy as hell, aren't you?"

"Yep. That's why I went into nursing—so I can tyrannize poor, helpless patients like you."

She asked him a few questions about his diet and listened to his answers with most of her mind—the part that wasn't trying to figure out what that last, warning look from her boss had meant. When Mark said he avoided eggs, fried foods and fatty meat, and that he preferred fresh vegetables, she chuckled. "Now I've heard it all. A health-conscious motorcycle jock with a cattle ranch."

"This isn't my ranch."

"Well, you live here, so I thought—"

"No. Not since I was sixteen."

"Oh?" She paused, two dirty glasses in one hand, a sports magazine in the other. His expression resembled his brother's at that moment—closed, with No Trespassing signs posted. "Does that mean you can get away with being a vegetarian?" she asked lightly.

He relaxed. "If you don't eat red meat around here, they think you've joined a cult and try to debrief you."

"I'll remember that. If you're not a rancher, what do you do for a living?"

"I'm a mechanic."

"Ah. So you're a health nut who fixes engines and won't touch your legally prescribed painkiller, but you don't object to skimming your body across the pavement at fifty miles an hour."

"Forty miles an hour. And the sonofa—the idiot who ran the red light didn't give me much choice."

"At least you had the sense to wear a helmet."

"How do you know that?"

"Because you're alive, and you still know how to speak in complete sentences."

"Good point." He nodded. "As a matter of fact, I always wear a helmet. Leathers, too, which kept most of my surface intact."

"And a lovely surface it is, too. I'm sure women everywhere appreciate the care you take of it." Hannah wasn't surprised to find herself unmoved, except in a purely aesthetic way, by that stunning exterior. He was a patient, after all.

"So, Hannah…why did Nathan say you were temporary?"

It wasn't until that moment that she realized she'd made up her mind. Was it folly or intuition that decided her? Whichever, she was suddenly certain this was where she was supposed to be. Mark needed her.

So did Nathan.

No, she told herself firmly. Taking care of her patient was enough. She had a great need to be needed, but she was not the sort of fool who would try to mend a man like Nathan Jones. "That would be because he's an idiot," she said firmly, collecting the rest of the clutter that needed to go to the kitchen. "I'm staying."

"Are you, now?" For the first time, Mark forgot to leer or flirt. "It's going to be interesting to see which of you is right about that."

Chapter 3

The sun was up, but invisible in the overcast sky. Nate's breath frosted the early morning air as he crossed to the stable with Trixie frisking at his side. The big Labrador loved cold weather. She snapped at the snowflakes that were drifting down and melting as soon as they touched the ground.

It had been a dry year. Every thimbleful of moisture was welcome, but it was hard not to grudge those thimbles when they needed buckets.

He met his foreman in the horse stable for their usual morning consultation. Both men kept an eye on the sky through the open stable doors while they talked. Nate asked Abe to ride out with one of the hands, checking for heifers with a poor sense of timing. The first-timers weren't supposed to start calving for another two weeks, with the experienced cows starting to drop their calves around April first, but you never knew what a heifer would do.

"Thought you was gonna do that. Didn't that nurse show up?" Abe reached for his back pocket and pulled out a round tin of chewing tobacco. Abe Larimer was nearing seventy, but Nate wouldn't have dared call his foreman an old man. Whittled down a bit, maybe, leaving only the toughest scraps of hide and bone, along with the sharp, squinty eyes of a man who'd spent a lifetime resting his eyes on horizons not pimpled by buildings.

"She's here," Nate said, "but I doubt she'll stay."

"No?" He pushed the lid off the tin with one thumb. "She get spooked, then? I thought that friend of yours was gonna fill her in on things."

"He didn't." Nate wasn't going to explain why that woman had to leave. No way was he going to say that he didn't want her around because it hurt him to look at her. It was funny, though. Until he'd seen Hannah in that bus station, he would have sworn he was over Jenny.

Abe selected a plug of tobacco. "Guess you'll be taking her back to town today—if she ain't too scared to ride in the truck with you. *Heh.*" Even Abe's laugh had dried out over the years, so that it came out sounding halfway between a snort and a chuckle.

"She may stay a couple of days—long enough for me to get someone from an agency."

"Thought you didn't like them agencies." The plug went in his cheek.

Nate was an intensely private man. He didn't like agencies and he didn't like having a stranger in his house. He didn't like leaving Mark in the hands of someone he didn't know, either, but between Mark's temper and his own reputation there wasn't anyone local left to try. "I might not have much choice."

"So this gal ain't what your friend said she'd be?"

"Nothing wrong with her credentials," he said neutrally. And she wasn't Jenny, he reminded himself. Similar features and a lush body didn't make her into his ex-wife. "But I'll be staying close to the house today, just in case."

Abe nodded and chewed thoughtfully a moment. "You want Felix and Tommie pouring cake?" He referred to the endless winter chore of feeding the cattle.

"Yeah." The question was unnecessary; Abe knew as well as Nate did where the hands were needed, but the old man's sense of propriety made him phrase his decisions as questions. "Another of Rydell's cows was shot yesterday."

Abe shook his head in disgust and spat a stream of brown juice on the ground. "Them kids today don't know what trouble is," he said darkly, if somewhat obscurely. "I don't s'pose you want to move any of the herd to the south field."

"Not yet." Whoever was taking potshots at cattle was doing it from the comfort of a car or truck, which meant the cattle in fields bordering the highway were at risk. But the gramma grass in the south field had suffered badly in last year's drought, and Nate didn't want to stress it. "Maybe I'll be able to ride out tomorrow—see if we can move a few dozen head over."

After Abe left, Nate headed for the cow barn to tend the animals too ill or hurt or valuable to trust to the open range. It was warm inside, animal-warm and animal-musty. He unbuttoned his denim jacket and pulled his gloves out of his pocket. Work would get his body and mind back under control...though he felt like a fool for needing the control. All he'd seen was her toes, for God's sake, ten perfectly ordinary toes peeking out from under that oversize sack of a nightgown. It was absurd to be aroused by the sight of a woman's toes.

But the woman made him hot. That was the plain fact, however unwelcome. Seeing her bare feet had made him think about how warm and soft and naked she was, underneath all that flannel.

Mark had liked looking at her, too, hadn't he?

Nate forced his mind away from the house, his brother and the woman who was taking care of him right now. There were cows to doctor, stalls to muck out. Work was one of the two things that had never failed Nate. Hard, physical labor settled him, smoothed out the knots in his mind and made the unbearable just one more problem on a long list.

Work was one thing a rancher never ran short of, either,

he reflected wryly as he lifted the latch on King Lear's stall. There had been a possibility of freezing rain the last two nights, which meant the prize-winning Hereford had been shut up in the barn. The enormous bull was in a festive mood that morning, wagging his big head and making a playful attempt to gore Nate when Nate turned him into the paddock.

Normally Nate didn't muck out stalls, not even King Lear's. He was a ranch manager, not a ranch hand. Oh, he knew how to do any of the jobs he called on his hands to perform, and he worked alongside them when necessary, but his time was usually better spent elsewhere. When he could, he took the jobs that got him on a horse, because he loved to ride. And, like every soul who earns his living from the land, he watched the weather.

He kept an eye on it now as he broke open the bale of hay he'd tossed down from the loft. The weather was teasing them today, shaking a few stray snowflakes out of the clouds to drift down like dandruff.

Nate had expected to ride out today, but he couldn't bring himself to go off and leave his brother alone all day with *her*. He'd seen the way Mark looked at her. Nate didn't blame his brother for looking, or for getting turned on by what he saw. How could he, when he had the same stupid reaction? But there was no way he would let a woman like that get her hooks in Mark. No way at all.

Not again.

The portable intercom sat on a shelf by the door. Normally Nate left his end of the unit turned on, and if Mark wanted something he turned his end on. It had been reassuringly quiet all morning. The woman must be taking care of Mark, or he would have heard something by now.

Unless he'd accidentally turned the volume down… That had happened once. Best to make sure, he thought, and reached for the knob.

The aftereffects of arousal had left his senses keener than usual, making him aware of kinetic sensations. Maybe that heightened awareness pried some sort of internal door open.

Maybe he was too aware of the woman back at the house with his brother, and all the possibilities that implied. Or maybe it was the sight of his hand in the gray light of a winter day—just that—that triggered the past.

Whatever the reason, as he stretched out his hand, he noticed the dark hairs on the back of it, the strong lines of the tendons, the thick knuckles and small, healing scabs of a working man. And he remembered....

It was winter. She wore jeans and a pink quilted jacket, and they were in the barn—this very barn—sitting in the loft with their legs dangling over the edge. His hand was on her thigh, his fingers curved greedily around it, and she was warm beneath the denim. She had a pen in her hand, and she was using it to write on the back of his hand. Even then his hand had been dusted with black hair and a few scattered nicks and scrapes.

A moment before, they'd been kissing, and she had straw in her hair. He had just asked her to go with him. She was laughing with delight, her full lips turned up as she told him, yes, she'd go with him. But he needn't think that meant she would go all the way because she wasn't going to do *that* until she was a senior—and they were only juniors. She had always been one to plan things, and expect others to fall in with her plans. As Nate had done.

Her green eyes had sparkled so as she laughed and teased and wrote on the back of his hand with her pen. She'd done that all the time when they were in high school. She'd wanted everyone to know he was hers, so she'd written her name on him.

Jenny.

He'd wanted her so much back then. More than anything, he'd wanted the laughing, lovely Jenny Rydell.

Eventually, he had gotten what he wanted.

Another memory replaced the first, slipping between the cracks in his defenses to coat the present with its oily sheen...

Jenny again, several years later. Still laughing, her glorious red-gold hair hanging straight and shiny down her back. But the laughter wasn't so innocent this time, and it was only her eyes that laughed. At him. Her head had been tipped to one side, her expression gleeful as her eyes met his from across the room, her lips parted and moist from a kiss.

Mark's kiss. He'd been sixteen at the time.

Nate stared at his outstretched hand and tried to remember what he'd been reaching for, but all he could think of was how amazing it was that her name hadn't permanently marked his skin. Over and over she'd traced those letters, but they were gone now, completely gone. Just like everything he'd once felt for her, for his lovely, laughing, lying Jenny.

She was Jenny Jones now—still—though he'd never understood why she'd refused to go back to her maiden name after the divorce. She'd been Jenny Jones when she'd laughed at him from Mark's arms, Jenny Jones when she testified against him at his trial, and she was Jenny Jones still. He wished like hell he could take the name back, but some things, once given, could never be recovered.

His hand moved, closing around the volume control on the intercom, just as something bumped his leg. He looked down.

Trixie had a stick in her mouth, a hopeful look in her eyes and a motor in her tail. The silly dog considered any break in Nate's routine an invitation to play. He shook his head and took the stick. She danced back a few steps, then took off running when he threw the stick out the open door of the barn.

Trixie was the only female Nate really trusted nowadays. He knew that was a skewed way of looking at the world, but a man had to be cautious. Maybe he had no reason to think the new nurse wasn't everything Harry had claimed: kind, capable, nurturing. But he had no reason to think she *was* like that, either. And her beauty put him on guard. Trust was a concept he could consider academically, but it had no roots in him, no way of reaching the places inside where he really lived. Not anymore.

Nate accepted the stick from Trixie and threw it again. He

wasn't going to take any chances. Aside from the discomfort of his own reaction to that centerfold-quality body of hers, this was the first time in years that Mark had come home for more than a day or two at a time. Nate might not know how to go about straightening things out between him and his brother, but he knew damn well that having Hannah McBride around wouldn't help.

So she thought Mark was gorgeous, did she?

Trixie raced back with the stick. "What do you think, girl?" he said, taking the love offering and then ruffling the dog's ears while she sat there, grinning her foolish, doggy grin at him. "You think she's after Mark, or me?"

She wouldn't know that Mark stubbornly refused to let Nate give him part of the inheritance that should have been Mark's, too. No, she probably thought Mark was good husband material, financially. Normally, Nate wouldn't have worried about his little brother getting tangled up with a woman. If anything, Mark was too cynical, too apt to slip from bed to bed. But the woman back at the house now was the hottest thing Nate had seen in years. Any man might take a tumble over a woman like that.

Any man except him.

Trixie butted her head against his hand to remind him of his duties. Idly, he tugged at one of her silky ears, then ran it through his fingers. Her eyelids sagged blissfully.

"I know one thing I can do," he told his dog, giving her one last scratch behind the ears. He could tell the woman the way things stood at the ranch. With any luck, learning that Mark didn't have much money would turn her attention away from him.

Would she focus on Nate then? Hunger drummed in his blood at the thought—a low, insistent summons. He liked the idea. He wanted her hands and her gaze and her mouth on him, and if she had money or marriage in mind when she touched him, what did that matter? He'd make it clear he wouldn't offer the one, and most of the other was tied up in the ranch. Not that he couldn't afford a little jewelry or some-thing, if that was what she wanted. If…

He straightened, scowling at himself, his fingers tightening around Trixie's stick. *If* she were staying. Which she wasn't, not for any longer than it took for him to find a replacement.

He sent the stick flying again and glanced at the house.

The intercom had been silent all morning. Suddenly, that seemed ominous. What was she doing? He'd find out, he decided. He'd talk to Mark and find out just how much he needed to worry.

Hannah was finishing the last of the accumulated dirty dishes when she heard the door open, then close. She glanced over her shoulder. Her boss stood in the middle of the kitchen in his worn denim and dark hat, looking around as if he'd stumbled into unfamiliar territory.

"There's coffee, if you're ready for a break." At least she was properly dressed now, in a uniform tunic and slacks and her white Reeboks. Hannah didn't always wear uniforms when she worked—it depended on her clients. Some people were uncomfortable around uniforms, while others were re-assured. But she usually dressed the part on her first day.

"You've been busy."

He made that sound more like an accusation than a com-pliment. She resumed her efforts on a pot that had once held macaroni and cheese. "There's a lot to do," she said. "Did you know the floor in here is a pale green?"

"Of course I know what color the floor is."

"Well, I didn't. Until the second washing, I thought it was a funny shade of gray." She gave the pot a last swish and held it up to see if she'd gotten everything. It looked okay, so she set it down. "Sure you don't want some coffee? I'm going to have—"

She turned around and stopped speaking, because there was no one there to speak to. He'd left without a word.

Hannah shook her head. Rude man. She picked up the dish towel. He was checking on his brother, no doubt. She would applaud his concern if she didn't think it came from a lack of confidence in her.

She dried the pot and her hands, squirted lotion into one palm, then stood, massaging the lotion into her skin and surveying the room with satisfaction. It did look better than it had when she stepped into it this morning.

The kitchen was a big, square room totally lacking in designer touches, and Hannah's favorite spot in the house so far. The appliances were old, but they had once been top-of-the-line. The solid cherry cabinets could be beautiful again, given a little elbow grease. In that, they were like most of what she'd seen of the rest of the house. As she poured herself a cup of coffee, she wondered if the pervading shabbiness meant that the ranch had fallen on hard times. A lot of ranchers were struggling these days.

Or maybe its condition simply reflected a masculine lack of interest, though Hannah found that hard to understand. If *she* had a grand old house like this one—a home that had been around so long it seemed to have grown right into the rocky landscape where it rested—it would never suffer from neglect. Of course, she would never have such a house. Nurses didn't earn that kind of money.

But Hannah didn't need much. She didn't want much. Just a home.

The kitchen would come first, she decided as she carried her coffee over to the big, round table. She'd get those cabinets glowing, then she'd see what she could do with the living room. Maybe, before she left, she would plant some bulbs in one of the neglected beds outside. There was something about the promises bulbs made when you put them in the ground...

"He's asleep."

She jolted, sloshing some of her coffee onto the table, then frowned at the man standing in the doorway. He'd returned as silently as he'd left. "I could have told you that. You don't have to go sneaking around that way," she scolded, going to the sink for a dishrag.

"He hasn't slept well at night since he came home. I've never seen him sleep in the middle of the day. Not since he was six, anyway."

"I drugged him," she said drily, mopping up the spill, then carrying her cup back to the coffeepot for a refill. "You going to join me in a cup?"

"How did you get him to take his pain pills?"

"Poker." She opened the cabinet, took down a mug. The heck with the man. She was pouring him some coffee whether he wanted it or not. "Cream or sugar?" she asked, turning around, one steaming mug in each hand.

"Black."

Darn him, he'd moved again, just as silently as before. He was close now. Too close. Those dark eyes staring down at her were almost as unnerving as his oversize male body standing so near her own.

"You played *poker* with him to get him to take his pain medication?"

Her pulse skipped a beat as nerves hummed along just beneath the surface of her skin. She handed him a mug. "Yep. Five hands of five-card stud. He accused me of cheating, but I told him that unless he caught me, he couldn't prove anything and he had to pay up. I'm too good to get caught right off the bat," she said cheerfully. "Now, I take a little milk in my coffee. If you wouldn't mind...? You're sort of blocking the path to the refrigerator."

He stepped back and took a sip of his coffee. His eyebrows lifted. "This is good."

She chuckled and took out the milk. "I bet you were expecting city-girl coffee, weren't you? I learned how to make coffee from my daddy. Of course, he's always claimed he liked it best boiled in a pan over an open fire, with the white of an egg dropped in to gather the grounds. I don't go that far, but I do like it to have some body." And then she liked to smooth out that bitter brew with plenty of milk.

"Your father is a cowboy?"

"He sure is." She replaced the milk and closed the refrigerator. The buzzer went off. "Oh, that'll be the coffee cake. Hold on a minute."

Somewhere, she thought as she opened the oven door, releasing a fragrant cloud of steam, there might be a man who was proof against the pecan-topped, caramel-sticky coffee cake that the housekeeper at the Barstow Ranch up in Montana had taught her how to bake—but she hadn't met him yet.

At least, she didn't think she had. Nate stood near the table, waiting, his face impassive.

"Want a piece?" she asked, turning so that she all but waved it under his nose.

"No." He looked at the coffee cake. "Sure. Why not?"

She was getting to him, she told herself as she took out the knife and cut two generous pieces. "So, what did you want to talk about?"

"Sit down, would you? I can't talk to you when you're hopping all over."

Hannah would have liked to think that he just couldn't wait to taste her coffee cake, but a glance at his face told her that food wasn't uppermost on his mind. She sighed. "Here." She set his piece in front of him, and sat.

He sat down across from her. First he frowned at the coffee cake, then he transferred the frown to her. "I can't believe you admit you cheated at cards."

"Oh, that was my last resort. First I tried slipping his pain pills into his food, but he got suspicious and refused to eat, so I tied him down and—"

"Miss McBride—"

"Hannah."

Something very like a smile glimmered in those dark eyes. "Hannah. You don't think I'm being very reasonable, do you?"

"Well…no."

"I'm glad you got him to take his pain medicine. He needs more sleep than he's been getting, but he's very stubborn."

"This wouldn't be a family trait, would it?" She paused,

then triumphantly produced the word she wanted. "Patroclinous, perhaps?"

"Patro-*what?*"

"Patroclinous." It had been her hardest vocabulary word last summer. She'd written it on the back of her hand for three days straight before she could remember it. "It's a genetic thing—*traits that are derived mostly from the paternal parent.*"

That glimmer looked more than ever like a smile. "Ah. Very likely." He took a sip of his coffee, looked at it, and took another sip. "You do make good coffee."

"Try a bite of the coffee cake."

This time the smile got all the way to that hard mouth of his and tilted one corner up. "You trying to soften me up with food?"

"You betcha. I—what's that?"

"I don't hear anything." He looked down and cut a bite of the coffee cake.

"I heard something at the door."

"You're right. This is great coffee cake." He cut another bite.

She frowned. There it was again—a soft, sad little whine. She pushed back her chair. "I'm going to see what's making that sound. It sounds like an animal that's been hurt."

"It's my dog. And she isn't hurt."

"Your dog?" She went through the laundry room to the side door, where that sad little whine came from. "I didn't know you had one. Is she a working dog?"

"Her?" He snorted. "No, that worthless animal would rather make friends with the cattle than herd them."

She reached for the doorknob. "What kind of dog is she?"

"She's not supposed to come—"

A huge brown Labrador retriever barreled through the doorway, all but knocking Hannah down on her way in. Hannah laughed. "Not supposed to come inside, huh? Have you told her this?"

The dog was wiggling all over and licking Nate's hand.

Two faint spots of color appeared high on his cheeks. "Sometimes I let her come in the kitchen. Just the kitchen. Only when it's really cold at night."

He was embarrassed? Hannah watched her grouchy boss turn into a marshmallow. His hand automatically found the spot just behind the ears that the dog desperately wanted to have rubbed, and canine devotion fairly oozed out of the animal.

Charmed, she came close and knelt. "Introduce us."

"Her name's Trixie," he said, not looking at her.

"Hey, Trixie," Hannah said softly, holding out her hand. "C'mere, girl. That's a sweet—*ooph!*"

Trixie, alerted to the fact that someone *wanted* her, had whirled around and lunged at Hannah, knocking her flat on her back. Hannah got a faceful of dog tongue and started laughing, which only encouraged the silly animal.

"Are you okay? Back! *Sit!*" Nate's stern voice said rather confusingly to the two of them. Trixie's happy face and tongue vanished from Hannah's field of vision, replaced by a very different one. This face was human and male, with mismatched eyebrows drawn tight in worry as his dark eyes skimmed over her and his hands fastened on her shoulders. "She didn't hurt you when she knocked you down, did she?"

Hannah's laughter faded. His hands were wonderfully large and warm. "No..." She pushed up on one elbow, which brought their faces closer together. His cheeks were dark. He must have shaved only a few hours ago, but his beard was already growing back.

Would his skin be scratchy?

He frowned. "That was a damn-fool thing to do, getting down on the floor with her. What if she'd been vicious?"

"Oh, yeah," she said drily. "I can see how that dog might turn vicious at any moment." She could smell Nate, ever so faintly—a faint, comfortable scent that made her think of barns and apples. Was the apple scent his shampoo, maybe? If she raised up a little bit more, she could put her face in

the place between his neck and his shoulder and breathe in
that inviting smell, find out how much of it was from him
and him alone...

"Uh-oh," she said. Then she kissed him.

Chapter 4

Curiosity and impulse brought Hannah's mouth to his. She wanted to know why he kept stirring such odd thoughts in her mind—wishful, wistful, hungry thoughts. She wanted to know if his cheeks were scratchy, if his mouth was as hard as it looked, if his frowning eyebrow felt different from the other one. She wanted to know what he tasted like, late on a winter morning.

Her answers came in a rush of sensations. The skin on his cheek was just rough enough to make her fingertips tingle. His lips were just soft enough to surprise hers in the first second of the kiss. As for his taste…

Nate didn't kiss like a curious man. No, he opened his mouth and kissed her as if he'd been fasting for days, for weeks, and she'd invited him to feast. His mouth tasted of coffee—hot coffee, dark and bitter with need. When his hand fisted in her hair, loosening the braid, while his tongue wrote its demands on her lips, passion surprised her into opening for him, and her thoughts scattered like sheep when the wolf comes calling.

His tongue asked questions of her, yes, but he answered those questions as quickly as he asked them—answered them with his clever mouth, with his knowing hands. One hand loosed its grip in her hair to curve around her neck, where it paused, stroking her pulse. His palm was as warm as the syrupy heat that it stirred in her, his fingers as rough as the sudden hitch in her breath.

Her body arched and her hands went tunneling into his hair, knocking his hat off. His hair was a surprise, too. He had fine hair, short and deliciously silky.

Then his hand moved.

Her eyes opened in shock as his fingers slid down over her breast—*inside* her shirt. She tried to break the kiss, bewildered, unable to remember how her tunic came to be unzipped enough to let him touch her this way…unable to understand why she liked letting him touch her this way. She didn't know him. She wasn't at all sure she liked him.

But she liked what he was doing.

He muttered something against her mouth. His thumb and finger moved to tease her nipple through the sensible cotton of her bra—tease it, squeeze it, sending ribbons of heat slicing through her. His hand was firm with her, possessive, as if its owner didn't question his right to touch her. And for one long moment she lay there on the hard, clean kitchen floor and let him do what they both wanted him to do, let him learn what he pleased about the shape and feel of her breast…while other questions rose in her, questions as hard and hot and fierce as the need his hand was building.

It was too much. The caution Hannah had learned so painfully so many years ago woke and struggled with needs and cravings that were too strong, too sudden. She pushed against his chest.

He didn't move, and she pushed harder, but it was like shoving against a brick wall. She couldn't make him move, and she knew a moment's panic mixed with confusion over the way her body was still responding, heedless and helpless, to his touch. She made a frightened sound deep in her throat.

At last he pulled his head back. "I'll make it right," he said hoarsely. "Tell me what you want, and I'll make it right. Just don't get greedy, sweetheart. I can make it worth your while, but most of my money's tied up in the ranch."

Money? Between one breath and the next, Hannah's head cleared. He was bent over her, his mouth wet from hers and his hand hot on her breast, and he was talking about *money?*

Pure, feminine fury powered the fist she swung at his head. She would probably have broken her knuckles if she'd connected, as hard as his head was, but he sat up suddenly. *Really* suddenly.

Her fist landed on his elbow instead.

"Ow!" she cried, and hit him again, this blow landing on the solid muscles of his biceps. "*Ow,* damn you, damn you, you think I want money for kissing you? You think you can pay me to have sex with you?" She pulled her fist back for another swing, but he scrambled to his feet and stood there, looking down at her with dark, wary eyes.

Oh, she wanted to hurt him. She really, *really* wanted to hurt him, but instead she'd hurt herself. Her knuckles throbbed. She pushed to her feet. Her tunic hung open, unzipped to her waist. Embarrassment flooded her, and the humiliation of knowing she'd made herself vulnerable to a man who thought so little of her only made her more angry. Her hands were shaking as she tried to get the zipper up. "You think all nurses are whores, or is it just me?"

"I was wrong," he said stiffly.

Was that supposed to be an apology? "Get out," she said, not caring that it was his own kitchen she was ordering him out of.

His mouth looked as hard as ever, his features just as unrevealing, but there was a hint of color on his high cheekbones, color that could be from anger or embarrassment or both. He bent to pick his hat up off the floor, then straightened, his hat in his hands. "I'm sorry."

She wanted him to grovel. "Sorry doesn't cover enough territory. I tried to stop you."

"I was wrong. I said it and I know it's true, but you're the one who kissed *me*. Are you forgetting that part? Maybe I jumped to some conclusions, but when a woman comes on to a man the way you did, he's apt to make some assumptions about her."

She stood tall because pride demanded it. "You don't think any woman is fool enough to kiss you unless you pay her for it?"

"I prefer women who are honest enough to get me to pay for what I want up front, with cash, to the ones who make me pay later, in other ways." He settled his hat on his head. "Get your things together," he said curtly. "I'll have one of the hands take you into town after lunch. You've still got your ticket back to Lubbock, and I'll throw in a couple days' pay."

He was firing her. Oh, Lord, he was firing her, and he had cause, from his point of view. She *had* kissed him. However badly he'd behaved after that, she was the one who'd stepped out of line first. And she ought to be *glad* to get out of here, away from him—except that she still had only thirty-four dollars in her wallet, and her sister was still missing. She couldn't afford to go.

Hannah chewed on her bottom lip and searched frantically for possibilities. There had to be some way to get him to let her stay.

He slapped his hat on his head and started for the door— and stopped, shook his head and turned around. "I'd appreciate it if you could stay a little longer, though. Until I can get someone else in."

The horse stamped one foot and shifted, crowding the man grooming him. It was time for oats, and the big gelding knew it.

Nate shoved the animal's flank hard enough to make him back off. "Soon," he said, running the brush along Ajax's belly. "You've got to get rubbed down before I put you up, and you know it. But you don't think much of my priorities, do you?''

Ajax craned his head around as far as the lead would allow, looking at Nate in apparent agreement.

Man and horse were in the alley between the stalls, directly beneath one of the overhead lights. Trixie had flopped down near the open door. She was panting, having followed Nate and Ajax all the way to the north field and back.

Outside, the sky was two shades of dark past twilight, yet not quite night. Dusk often dragged its feet in the winter, wrapping the world in ever-darker shades of gray. At least, that's how it was here on the plains. Nate used to go skiing in the mountains of New Mexico, back in the days when the world was a golden place. He knew night could hit suddenly in some places.

Abe emerged from the tack room. ''You about finished there, boss?''

''Pretty near.'' The gradual graying of day into night was the way things usually worked, he thought as he drew the brush across Ajax's speckled shoulder. Most of a man's life was made up of such slow turnings, without clear markers to separate one from the other.

But sometimes the darkness really did fall all at once.

''I guess I'll go get some supper, then.'' Abe said that, but he didn't seem in any hurry. He stood on the other side of Ajax, feet planted like a man who intended to stay and talk.

''You do that. I think Julio fixed chili tonight.''

Abe nodded thoughtfully. ''Julio does okay with chili. I don't know what all he puts in it, but it don't matter. Can't taste anything but them peppers anyway. You plannin' on joining the boys in the bunkhouse for supper?''

Nate grunted noncommittally.

''Just wondered, seeing as how you've got that pretty nurse up at the house cookin' for you and Mark. 'Course, maybe you were wanting to give the two of them some time alone.''

Nate gave his old friend a warning look. "I'll go up to the house when I'm ready."

"It's six o'clock."

"I know what time it is."

"A man might get the notion you were avoiding someone."

"Leave it alone, Abe."

"I don't see no reason to—well, now." His weathered face folded into a broad smile as he looked toward the door of the stable. "Looks like you'll get your supper hot after all."

Nate looked over Ajax's broad back and saw Hannah standing in the doorway. Madly curling wisps escaped from her braid to form a frizzy halo around her face. She wore an old blue parka over her nurse's whites, and held a plate wrapped in aluminum foil in one hand, a glass of iced tea in the other.

Trixie had risen to her feet and was wagging her tail madly, delighted that her new friend had come calling. "I'd pet you if I could, sweetheart," the woman said to the dog, "but my hands are full."

Nate's mouth thinned. Another woman might have looked sexless in that uniform and bulky parka. Hannah looked like sin wrapped up in white and tucked into a faded blue shopping bag.

"Somethin' sure smells good," Abe said, giving her his best harmless-old-man smile. "Any chance that's for me?"

She shook her head and returned his smile. "I'm afraid not. Not unless Mr. Jones—"

"Nate," he interrupted, irritated.

"Not unless Nate decides he doesn't want it."

"Pity," Abe said, glancing at Nate. "Boy, you going to introduce me?"

Nate ran the brush over Ajax's withers. "Hannah McBride, this is Abe Larimer. He used to be my foreman, but I just fired him."

Hannah looked startled.

Abe grinned that sly grin of his. "Fired me last month,

too. Don't do him much good. I've been here longer than he has, and I ain't leaving.''

Her smile was bright enough to warm half the stable. "Me, neither. I'll bet we have some acquaintances in common, Mr. Larimer. My father has cowboyed from the Big Bend country here in Texas all the way up to the sweetgrass country in Montana, and for a lot of years my sister and I traveled with him.''

''Shoot, no one calls me mister around here,'' Abe said, and fidgeted himself closer to that smile. ''I guess you know something about horses, then.''

''A thing or two,'' she agreed. ''It's been a long time since I've been riding, though.'' Her gaze slid over to where Nate stood, brush in hand, on the other side of the big gelding. ''That's a handsome animal.''

His body reacted as if she'd just referred to him that way. ''Ajax? He's a good horse, but he's an ugly brute.''

''Where did he get a name like Ajax, anyway?''

''Oh, Nate here is real fond of them old Greeks they make you study in school,'' Abe said.

''Myths?'' She looked intrigued.

Nate ignored that. ''What are you doing here, anyway? I hired you to take care of my brother, not me.''

''Mark needs time to himself now and then. I left him with his supper and the VCR remote. He's watching one of those action movies where someone gets shot every five minutes.'' She started toward him.

Damn, but that woman knew how to move, as smooth as Eve must have moved in on Adam after she had her little talk with the snake. Trixie frisked along beside her, no doubt entranced by the smells coming from that plate. And it did smell good. A lot better than Julio's battery-acid chili.

She reached across Ajax's back, holding out the glass of tea. Automatically he took it. ''I wouldn't call this fellow pretty,'' she said. ''Not with that big Roman nose of his, and his coloring is…''

''Flea-bitten?'' he supplied drily. ''Muddy?''

"Well, yes... But he's a strong, handsome fellow. Aren't you, big guy?" Her voice dropped to a croon as she reached out to stroke the horse's neck.

Ajax, ever curious and ever ready to eat, turned his head and tried to lip the plate she held. She laughed and held it away from him, and her eyes met Nate's.

She had a husky, pleased-with-herself laugh, Hannah did—a laugh that all but reached out and stroked a man. But there were nerves in her eyes. Everything else about her spoke of sex and confidence, of a woman who understood the power she could wield over a man. Not her eyes—they belonged to a kid who has been double-dared and refuses to back down.

It was those risky, uncertain eyes that finished him.

Hannah held her ground in spite of the way her boss was looking at her, tight-lipped and hot-eyed. If her own heart pounded, he couldn't know that. He had no way of knowing that she had spent the entire afternoon talking to herself— lecturing, really—so she'd have her head on straight when she saw him next. She tipped her chin up another notch. No, he couldn't tell a thing by looking at her.

His voice was dry, giving nothing away. "Which of us did you come out here to feed, me or the horse?"

"You." She was in control, she assured herself. No problem. "At least, I hope your horse doesn't like meat loaf."

"Meat loaf," Abe said wistfully. "With tomato stuff on top? And mashed potatoes?"

Hannah nodded. "And corn bread and green beans."

"Corn bread." Abe sounded like a lost soul gazing through heaven's gates. "And would those be *fresh* green beans?"

"Frozen, I'm afraid. I'll have to make a run into town before I have any fresh vegetables. You like corn bread?"

"Yes, *ma'am.*"

Mark had told her about the man who cooked for the hands. Julio was great with beef, it seemed. He could grill a steak or hamburger to perfection, and his barbecued ribs were out of this world. But beef was all he wanted to bother with. Everything else he fixed came out of a can.

"Call me Hannah," she said to the old man. "I'm glad to hear you like corn bread. I sent an extra pan of it down to the bunkhouse when I found out Julio was fixing chili."

Abe's eyes lit up. "I am damn glad to meet you, Hannah. Damn glad. But I gotta be going now. Won't be none of that corn bread left if I don't hurry." He kept talking as he headed for the door. "It's a good thing you've come to take this boy and his brother in hand. They need a woman around the house."

"Abe," Nate said warningly.

"I'm going, I'm going." But he paused at the door, the mirth in his eyes escaping from his mouth in a series of quick, dry chuckles. "*Heh! Heh! Heh!* We'll have to talk, Hannah. I can tell you a thing or two about Nate here—"

Nate looked ready to do murder. "Abe!"

"I'm gone." And this time he actually did leave, chuckling at the rate of one dry *heh!* per step.

"He's quite a character," Hannah said.

"He practices." Nate started brushing his horse again.

Was he trying to pretend that she wasn't there? Irritated, she gestured with the plate she held. "Your supper's getting cold. Maybe you'd rather have the chili, though."

"No," he said. "I'm almost finished. Set it down on the chair by that empty stall, and I'll get to it as soon as I pick out his hooves."

She held the plate across Ajax's broad back. "Go on, take it. I'll tend to your horse."

"I didn't hire—"

She interrupted impatiently. "You didn't hire me to take care of your horse. Or you. I know. But I hate to see food get cold, and I like horses. I wouldn't mind getting acquainted with this one while you eat." And after he ate, they could talk. Get a couple of things straight. She was not really worried about that, she assured herself. Maybe a tiny bit tense, but not what anyone would call worried.

He shook his head, but his mouth turned up in a reluctant smile. "Bossy as hell, aren't you?"

"Yep." She liked his smile. It eased the tightness around his eyes and mouth. It made his bent eyebrow perk up and look more at home on that rugged face. "Now go wash up."

He set the plate and glass on a straight-back wooden chair that sat next to an empty stall, dug into his back pocket and held out the hoof pick. When she reached out to take it from him, their fingertips brushed. She had the sudden, absurd impulse to drop the pick and grab his hand.

His expression was dark and forbidding. He didn't look as though he ever had any impulses at all.

No, she didn't have anything to worry about, she thought as she watched him head for the sink at the end of the aisle. Maybe he did funny things to her breathing. Maybe she liked his smile a little too much. But she wasn't going to *do* anything about those feelings, and that was what counted. All too often, Hannah had ended up learning her lessons the hard way, but the upside to that flaw was that once she learned something, the lesson was there for good. Never again would she mistake the fizzy rush of hormones for anything important or lasting.

She was perfectly safe. And it didn't matter one bit if she never learned whether his bent eyebrow felt different from the straight one.

Nate left his plate and glass on the only chair in the building, an old cane-bottom chair that had been around the place for years. Flakes of paint still clung to the wood, but the paint was so weathered that it had no more color than the wood did. For some reason he thought about that chair and its flaking paint as he headed for the back of the stable, where a closet-size room held a sink and a toilet.

Several months before she died, Nate's mother had bought that chair and three others to replace the ones at the kitchen table. She'd asked Nate and Mark to paint them, and she'd handed them a bucket of paint in her favorite color. Powder blue, she'd called it. He and Mark had thought it was a sissy color, but they'd taken the chairs out behind the barn and put three coats of that soft, pale blue on each of her chairs. Three coats, so it would last.

Mark had done a good job, too, for all that the kid had only been seven years old. Even then, though, he'd taken pleasure in what he could do with his hands. He'd probably taken extra care because he had wanted to do a good job for the woman who'd been a mother to him—even if she hadn't given him birth. DanaRae Jones had had a way of finding the loving places in people, even people who didn't seem to have much love, like Nate's father. Garwood Jones hadn't been much of a husband. Mark's existence proved that much. But whatever love he'd had in him to give, he'd given to his DanaRae. Nate hadn't understood that until he saw what his mother's death did to his father.

Sixteen years was a long time. In spite of the care he and Mark had taken with their work, in spite of those three coats of powder blue paint, all that remained were some flakes and strips of paint the color of pale ashes clinging to a single chair.

What had happened to the other three chairs? Nate couldn't remember. He dried his hands and tried to think of what he'd done with them, but he just couldn't recall, and it bothered him. It bothered him more than it should have. What did the fate of three worn-out chairs matter?

Yet he was still trying to remember when he returned to where Hannah was grooming Ajax.

Trixie, fickle female that she was, was ignoring Hannah now. She sat by the cane-bottom chair and watched Nate with hopeful doggy eyes as he picked up the plate and sat down.

"Something wrong?" Hannah asked. She stood next to the horse and leaned her knee into his right hind leg in a practiced motion. Ajax shifted, taking his weight off that leg, and she bent and picked up the hoof.

"No." He took the foil off and the mingled smells of meat loaf and corn bread hit him right in the salivary glands. She'd piled the plate nice and high. His stomach growled. "You're getting your uniform dirty."

"It'll wash." She ran the metal pick into the crevices between the hoof and the horseshoe. "I've missed this." She sounded surprised.

"Picking hooves?" he asked drily, and started on the meat loaf.

"Horses. I've missed being around them. It's been…" Her voice drifted off. She straightened and ran a hand along Ajax's side. "Though God knows why. Such big, stupid, stubborn creatures you all are, aren't you, darling?" The gelding responded by nudging her with his nose. She laughed.

God, that laugh of hers! Heat prickled his skin as he turned his attention to another physical need. He picked up the big, square piece of corn bread she'd balanced on top of the potatoes, took a bite and closed his eyes. *Ahh.* Fresh, hot and slathered with butter.

"Getting to you, aren't I?"

He opened his eyes. "Is that why you came down here? So you could impress me with your cooking?"

"Partly." She moved and picked up the next hoof, but she didn't explain further. For the next several minutes, he ate, she worked…and he watched her.

She moved with a casual efficiency that was its own sort of grace. The stark fluorescent light overhead should have drained the color from her, but she was a true redhead. Harsh lighting might rob her complexion of its pink tones, but it left her skin milky-pale and stunning. Her hair looked darker than it had in the daytime, and richly red.

There was pleasure in watching Hannah, but it wasn't a comfortable pleasure. Not when it came so close to craving. Not when he'd spent six years getting his life on an even keel again, without the vicious highs and lows of a marriage made in hell. Nate intended to live the rest of his life alone.

But taking Hannah to bed didn't have to change that, did it? He didn't care about her. He *wanted* her, but he didn't care. Still, it came as an unpleasant shock to realize how much he wanted her. He'd been fooling himself when he'd tried to make her leave. He didn't want to fire Hannah. He didn't intend to let her leave.

Not yet.

Maybe his life had gotten too steady. Too level. Maybe, after six years of taking care of his needs as rarely and efficiently as possible, he was ready for a brief, purely sexual adventure. A man could hunger for excitement without letting it disrupt his solitude, couldn't he? And she was just the woman to give him what he wanted—a hard, hot, fast ride.

Hannah felt him watching her.

She finished with Ajax's hooves, put him up in his stall and, following Nate's terse directions, found his feed and gave him his supper. Then, because Nate was still eating and she had no intention of making casual conversation when the questions she needed to ask were anything but casual, she moved up and down the line of stalls.

He had a magnificent Appaloosa mare and a couple of purebred quarter horses. The other four horses stabled there were as mixed in their ancestry as Ajax. Not as homely, though. She smiled as she came to a stop at Ajax's stall again, reaching over the half door to stroke his nose. She'd disagreed with Nate when he'd called his horse ugly, but there was no denying Ajax wasn't going to win any equine beauty contests.

"Do you want to ride?"

His voice, dark and suggestive, sent a shiver up her spine. She wanted to ignore it. "If you wouldn't mind."

"You're welcome to saddle any of the horses but the Appaloosa mare."

"Thanks." She hugged her arms, rubbing goose bumps away, as she turned to face him.

He bent to set his plate on the floor. Trixie watched him, her ears perked with anticipation. As soon as he told her "okay," she fell on the scraps with tail-wagging appreciation. The whole thing looked automatic to Hannah, as if he always saved the last bite of his meal for his dog.

He hadn't taken his eyes off Hannah the whole time. She frowned. "Didn't your mama ever tell you it was rude to stare?"

"Yeah, she did. But I figure you're used to men staring at you."

"I'm used to getting a runny nose in the spring, too, when the pollen count is high, but that doesn't mean I like it."

He actually smiled. Dammit, that was an unfair thing to do.

"Listen," she said a little too quickly, "I didn't come down here to give you something to stare at. I have a couple questions."

He leaned back in the chair, stretched his legs out and crossed them at the ankles. "Ask."

She licked her lips. "Did you ask me to stay on until you can get someone else for my sake, or yours?"

"Mine," he said tersely.

"Well, that isn't good enough."

"I don't know what the hell you want, but—"

"A week. I want you to give me a week. I deserve a chance to show you I can do the job you hired me for."

Now he seemed amused, his mouth curling up. "You can have your week, Hannah."

She blinked, confused. Surely that had been too easy. "Well—okay, then."

"Nice to find we can agree on something."

Why did she get the feeling, looking at him, that there was some part of their conversation she was missing? "Yes," she said dubiously.

"Why are you so set on keeping this job, anyway? I would have thought you would be glad to see the last of this place, and me. Unless…" He tilted his head to the side, a small gesture that had the effect, almost, of a smile. "Unless you were hoping for a repeat of this morning."

''No.'' She shook her head, flushing. ''Oh, no. That won't happen again. I can promise you that.''

He didn't reply. He just looked at her as if he were waiting for her to say something reasonable. Irritated, she said, ''It was unprofessional on my part. An impulse. I'm impulsive sometimes, but I don't repeat my mistakes.''

''If you're not looking for a repeat, why do you want to stay?''

Her chin shifted a fraction higher. ''I'm broke. I need the work.''

''Harry said you were good enough that you stayed booked up most of the time.''

''Harry also said this job would last two months.''

''Which is it you want—to stay a week, or the full two months?''

She lifted one eyebrow. ''You seem bright enough, even if you are stubborn as a blind jackass. I want you to promise me a week. By the end of that time, you'll realize you've been a hundred-percent wrong about me, and, rather than admit it, you'll quit bringing up the idea of me leaving. So I'll wind up staying two months.''

''You're better at honesty than tact, aren't you?'' Most people looked softer when they were amused. He didn't. ''Tell me, do you sometimes have trouble keeping a job?''

''Not as a home health aide, but I was a lousy waitress,'' she admitted. ''You're not supposed to lecture the customers, but I never could put up with rudeness. And I still don't see what was so wrong with offering people suggestions about avoiding saturated fat. I'm not a fanatic or anything, but the fact is that saturated fat—''

He chuckled.

''It's very bad for you.''

''Bossy.''

''Yeah,'' she said softly. ''I am.''

It was quiet there in the stable, though not totally silent; one horse shifted and another snuffled idly at the straw in its stall. The building itself creaked as the outside temperature fell along with the night. Contentment, like the ache in well-used muscles, seeped into Hannah, softening her defenses. She met Nate's eyes and forgot to look away.

He said he had once killed. She looked at him, and all she saw was a man. Just a man. He was a little too sexy, a lot too pigheaded and scary in ways that had little to do with his record. He was crazy about his dog and had a deep-seated wariness of others, and she thought he was more alone than just about anyone she'd ever known.

And right now, he was looking at her as if she were the one thing in the world he really wanted.

Her heart began to pound.

Trixie, who had been lying companionably by Nate's feet, lifted her head, then stood, a low growl sounding in her throat. Nate laid his hand on the animal's head and looked out the stable door. Hannah turned to look, too.

A second later, she heard a car engine. "It's late for someone to be dropping by," she said. In her experience, ranch folk seldom dropped in without calling first. Their days and their neighbors' days were too full for paying unplanned visits at what might be a bad time. "Maybe someone from town…" Her voice drifted off.

Through the open doors of the stable, headlights cut the darkness as a vehicle pulled up in front of the house and stopped.

"It's someone from town, all right," Nate said, standing. "The sheriff."

Chapter 5

Hannah could hear Mark's shoot-'em-up movie before she reached his room. Arnold Schwarzenegger was angry because the woman hadn't done what he'd told her to do. She'd stuck her nose into his he-man heroics, and he was all bent out of shape about it.

She shook her head. If that wasn't typical of the whole arrogant, high-handed gender! Men. Always telling people what to do, where to go and what to do when you got there. Like Nate, sending her into the house while he talked to the sheriff. Telling her to "for once" go do what she'd been hired to do. *For once!* As if she hadn't been doing her job.

It took an effort, but she managed to smooth her expression by the time she passed through her patient's doorway.

"It's about time," Mark said.

Of course, her patient was a man, too. "Ready for our pain pill, are we?" she asked sweetly.

"Oh, no, you don't. Not until bedtime. That's what we agreed when you palmed that ace this afternoon."

"Did you see me palm an ace?" She came closer, trying

to determine how much of his pallor was due to the poor lighting, and how much to pain.

"No, but very few decks have five of them." He pointed the remote at the screen, freezing Arnold in mid-leap as an explosion hurled flames at him and the heroine. "What did Royce want?"

"Who's Royce?" The hospital-style table beside Mark's bed held the remains of Mark's supper. She pulled it closer and started clearing the dishes.

"Royce Thompson is the sheriff."

She stopped to stare. "How did you know he was here?" This bedroom was at the back of the house, so Mark couldn't have seen the headlights.

He nodded at the portable intercom that sat on the table. "Nate left his end on out in the stable. Now, most of the time all I could hear were horses chewing and farting, but when you and Nate got to talking—"

"You eavesdropped!"

He grinned. "You two were a lot more interesting than the movie."

Just what had she and Nate said to each other in the stable? And—she glanced at the intercom—yes, she could hear a faint hum coming from it. The other unit was still turned on. "We need to turn this off. Nate and the sheriff might go into the stable, after all." But she didn't reach for the switch.

"Why, Hannah, you wouldn't be thinking of eavesdropping, would you?"

"It isn't any of my business." Still, she took her time clearing away Mark's supper things, stacking the dessert plate on the supper plate, then placing the knife and fork on top. One at a time. Just in case.

"I don't know. It might be your business. You and my brother have something going on?"

"Of course not. He's my employer."

"I don't guess you'd tell me if you did. But if you blush like that every time I say his name—"

"I did not blush. I never blush."

"—and get all flustered when I ask you about him, *something* must be going on. Just what *did* happen this morning that you're not looking to repeat?"

She opened her mouth to tell him that it was none of his business, realized that would only confirm what he was thinking, and closed it again. "Are Nate and the sheriff friends? Is that why he came out here?"

Drily, he said, "I don't think Nate numbers any law officers from Bitter Creek among his friends."

"Because of his record?"

"So he *did* tell you about that? I wondered. Is that why you want to know what's going on with the sheriff now?" The mischief in his eyes faded. "I thought you were curious about Nate personally, but maybe not. Maybe you get excited by a man with a violent past. I didn't think you were the type of woman who gets off on that sort of thing, but—"

Her jaw tightened. "You've said enough."

"Not quite. See, I'm not always a great judge of character. I could be wrong about you, and my brother has already been messed around by a woman with a twisted need for attention. So if you're looking for thrills, leave him alone. Come see me instead. I can give you what you need," he said, and the smile on his mouth wasn't a smile anymore when it reached his eyes.

Hannah tried to hang on to her temper. "I like to have a personal relationship with my patients. I'm with them for weeks, sometimes months at a time. But that means friendship. *Not* the kind of sorry substitute you're talking about. If you can't accept that, then your brother will get his wish, because I'll have to leave."

The signs of his tension had been so subtle that she hadn't seen them. She only noticed their absence as his expression eased. "Sorry."

"If that's supposed to make everything all right—"

"I really didn't take you for a woman who's looking for cheap thrills. But I have to cover all the bases, so..." His mouth quirked up at one corner. "I still have to point out that if you're after money instead of thrills—"

"Why are you and your brother so blasted preoccupied with *money*? Do you think that every woman on the face of the planet is for sale, or is it just me?"

His eyebrows lifted. "Did Nate offer you money?"

Uh-oh. Said too much again, hadn't she? "It's a good thing I'm not the sort of person who gets my feelings hurt easily, or I'd be upset. Your opinion of me isn't exactly flattering." She grabbed the stack of dishes and started for the door.

"But it's not *my* opinion that matters to you, is it?" he called after her.

She paused in the doorway and, for once, voted in favor of caution and keeping a few things to herself. "I'll be back to help you get ready for bed after I've done the dishes."

Hannah loaded Mark's dishes in the dishwasher and then attacked the pans she'd left soaking.

Was it her? Did she do her hair wrong, or say the wrong things, or—or just what *was* it about her that made some people think she was cheap?

No, she told herself firmly, rubbing at the outside of a saucepan that hadn't been scoured in far too long. No, she was not going down that road—not again. She'd worked too hard at building her self-esteem to let a rude man with night-dark eyes—make that *two* rude men, she corrected herself, rinsing the pot—neither of whom could see past a woman's bra size, affect the way she thought about herself.

Yes, she'd dropped out of high school to get married, and that was a dumb move, definitely dumb, but lots of people did stupid things at that age. That kind of stupidity didn't have to be permanent, even if sometimes the consequences were. She wasn't stupid or cheap or anything like what her ex-husband and his parents had made her out to be.

Fortunately, the meat loaf pan needed a lot of scrubbing.

* * *

By eight o'clock Hannah had finished the dishes and gone in to help Mark get ready for the night. He didn't want pajamas, he didn't want her to bathe him again, and he growled something about not needing to be tucked in, either. So she made sure he took his pain pill, then left him with a couple of basins of water, a washcloth and towel, toothpaste and toothbrush. She was just leaving his room when she heard the front door open, then shut.

It was Nate, of course. Probably he thought she was still in the kitchen, since the light was on in there, and that's why he'd come in through the front door.

Well, let him avoid her. That was fine with her. She certainly had no intention of asking a bunch of nosy questions. No, she was going to get herself ready for bed early, and then read for a while.

After her shower, naturally she went to the kitchen to get the coffeepot ready to be turned on when she got up in the morning. And on her way back to her room she couldn't help noticing the bar of light beneath the closed door to Nate's office. That wasn't what made her pause, though. There was a creaky board in the hall outside his office, and the noise it made startled her for a moment right outside his door.

She didn't go in. She had better sense than that. She went back to her bedroom, turned on the light by the bed and took out the anatomy textbook she'd bought secondhand last summer. And if the fool man had gone to bed at a reasonable hour for a rancher who had to be up before dawn, she could have kept her resolve, too. It was *his* fault she couldn't sleep. Usually an hour spent on "Muscles That Move the Thigh," from the *psoas major* to the *gracilis,* was enough to put her out for the night.

But how could she doze off when she was listening for that creaky board?

A little after ten she switched to another book: the worn copy of Grimms' Fairy Tales that traveled everywhere with her. She ran her hand over the faded cover and thought about all the nights that her sister had read to her from this book.

She had a dim memory of their mother reading from it, too, but she didn't remember her mother very well. She'd died when Hannah was five.

Because Hannah had been raised on the original stories of the Brothers Grimm, she didn't think of fairy tales as spun-sugar children's stories the way many people did. No, her fairy tales were soaked in danger, treachery and terror, and only those with faithful hearts and great courage prevailed against the forces set against them. In these pages, Red Riding Hood was swallowed by the wolf and saved by the hunts-man's ax. Cinderella's cruel stepsisters ended up maimed and blinded. Justice here was as brutal as life, as certain as death, but true love still healed all ills.

Hannah opened the book to the story of Rapunzel. She read once more about how the handsome son of the king fell in love and ended up grieving and blinded, his love lost and his eyes scratched out by thorns. He wandered sightless in the wilderness for many years, until he found his love again. Even though he couldn't see her, he knew her voice. When they embraced, two of her tears fell on his ruined eyes, restoring his vision.

For some reason, Hannah's eyes tried to tear up when she read that part. Disgusted with herself she gave up, closed the book, threw back her covers and slid her feet into her slippers.

It was five minutes after eleven when she went down the hall. That bar of light still shone beneath the door to his office.

She hesitated for a second before lifting her hand and knocking.

"Come in."

Nate's office was a small, windowless room next to the formal dining room. A large desk on the west wall held a computer, monitor and printer. The chair in front of that desk held Nate, who swiveled to face her. Aside from the desk and the man, the room contained two filing cabinets, an ugly brown love seat, and lots and lots and lots of papers. Files, computer printouts, magazines, canceled checks, miscellaneous papers and newspaper clippings were ranged into tidy piles, but those piles were everywhere.

The room also held a dog. Trixie was curled up near Nate's feet, sound asleep.

So, Hannah thought. He sometimes lets her in the kitchen, huh? But not the rest of the house? *Right*. She glanced at the piles as she stopped a few feet inside the room. It seemed best to look at something other than the dark-eyed man who watched her without speaking. "Chaos by a nose," she said.

He frowned. "What?"

She gestured at his office. "The war between chaos and order? Entropy? It looks like chaos is ahead in here by a nose."

"Entropy," he repeated, looking baffled.

She nodded. It was one of her favorite vocabulary words because it applied to so many situations. "Yes, you know—the tendency for things in a closed system to go from a high-energy state to a low-energy state. From order to disorder. Entropy. Looks like it's happening here."

He leaned back in his chair. "You didn't come here to comment on the condition of my office."

"No." For the first time she looked at him dead-on. Why, he's exhausted, she thought, but then couldn't figure out where that thought came from. His shoulders were straight, his expression unrevealing. Yet she had the impression of a man who was weary down to his bones, but kept on going because it was all he could do. She told herself not to be foolish, yet she had to fight the urge to go to him and hold him. Just hold him.

That urge startled her into blurting out what she'd come there to ask. "What did the sheriff want?"

The straight eyebrow and the bent one conspired to give him a sardonic expression. "Afraid you'll be out of job if I get hauled off to jail?"

"No." She sighed. No, she didn't even have that much of

a reason to pry. "I just want to know, that's all. If there's something wrong, I want to know."

His chair creaked when he leaned back, waking Trixie, who blinked sleepily. "He came out to see if I had an alibi."

"And do you?"

"No."

She waited. "You're not going to stop there, are you?"

The corner of his mouth kicked up. "I ought to. But..." He straightened, and the humor that had briefly touched his hard face slid away. "You'll hear about it sooner or later. Someone has been taking potshots at cattle lately with a .22 rifle."

She winced. "Ouch." It was a problem ranchers had to contend with from time to time—kids looking for kicks who decided to shoot something other than bottles. In this part of the country, a lot of teenagers learned to shoot when they received their first rifle—often a .22. "But why would you need an alibi?"

"The last two cows that have been shot both belonged to Ben Rydell. He thinks I did it. Sheriff Thompson checked to see if I had an alibi for last night, when the most recent shooting took place."

"But that's absurd! Why would this man think *you* shot his cows?"

"Revenge."

Hannah shook her head. It didn't make sense. Taking potshots at cattle was a kid's stunt, and this man was anything but childish. "Why would he think that?"

"Because six years ago his sister got me convicted of murder."

After a moment, Hannah remembered to close her mouth.

His voice—that wonderful, winter voice—was mocking. "Were you imagining that it was all some misunderstanding? That when I said I'd killed a man, I didn't really mean it?"

"You don't—I didn't—" She finally collected enough of her wits to put together a sentence. "I thought it must have been an accident."

Something flickered in those hard black eyes. He didn't speak.

She licked her lips nervously. "Did you tell the sheriff you were picking me up at the bus station last night?"

"I didn't spend the entire night picking you up," he said drily, and the words sounded suggestive.

Or maybe it was the late hour, and the fact that she was in her nightgown, or the hint of heat in his eyes that made her restless. "You shouldn't need an alibi. The whole idea is ridiculous." Hannah tried to imagine Nate setting his alarm for two a.m. so he could get up, get dressed, drive ten or twenty miles and shoot a cow. The image was so ludicrous that she chuckled. "The sheriff didn't take this guy seriously, did he?"

"No," he said slowly. Trixie stretched and went over to Nate, who reached out to pet her. "As a matter of fact, he didn't. He doesn't think I'm stupid enough to own a gun when that would put me behind bars."

She was startled. "It would?"

"Convicted felons aren't allowed to own firearms." He stretched out his legs. "So why were you so sure I didn't do it? Are you such a Pollyanna that you don't think I'm capable of revenge?"

"Oh, you're capable of it." Was it fear, excitement or some other emotion that made her heartbeat so slow and heavy, like the music in a movie just before some silly woman opens the door with the monster behind it? "But this is too petty, too—" she struggled to find the right word "—it's small-minded. No, if you had an enemy, you'd either leave the man alone, or you'd destroy him."

"Thanks," he said after a moment. "I think."

She had asked what she'd come here to ask. It was time to leave. Except that she didn't *want* to go, which bothered her. She started for the door. "I'd better get some sleep. You should, too. You look tired."

She was almost out the door when he said her name. That was all he said, just her name, but there was something odd about his voice, something that made her heart pound in wary expectation when she looked over her shoulder at him, her hand on the doorknob.

The light from the lamp on his desk slanted light and shadows across his face, making him look severe, like a man who had reached some inner limit. Yet his voice was supremely level. "You were right earlier," he said. "It was an accident. I was convicted of murder, but it was an accident."

Relief shivered through her like sunshine. "I'm glad." Her voice embarrassed her by coming out in a whisper. She cleared her throat. "I'm really glad to know it was an accident, Nate. Thank you for telling me that."

She closed the door softly behind her.

Nate sat at his desk staring into space, one hand fondling Trixie's ears. He didn't pretend that he was still working.

How many times had he said those words? *"It was an accident,"* he'd told the deputy who was first on the scene. He'd said it to the sheriff, too. To the DA, eventually. And to God-only-knew how many others.

Once, he'd believed his word meant something, that a lifetime of honesty mattered. He had learned differently. After the trial, Nate had promised himself that he wouldn't say those words again. Ever. People were going to believe what they believed, regardless of what he said. Yet tonight...

He hadn't meant to say that. It had just slipped out. He didn't know why.

It was an accident.

Hannah had said she was glad. She'd thanked him for telling her, as if she had some idea of what it had cost him to say those words one more time.

Had anyone believed him that easily? Had anyone, even once in the last six years, accepted him at his word without doubt edging in to cloud the way they thought of him, the way they looked at him? Even Mark...

Even himself.

"Isn't it true, Mr. Jones, that you hit harder than was

necessary? A great deal harder than necessary, in fact, for simple self-defense? Isn't it true you struck Tony Ramos with all your strength because you wanted him dead?''

He'd answered the prosecutor steadily, but deep inside, the questions—all the questions, those spoken and those lingering in the eyes of people who had been his friends and neighbors—had taken root. And sometimes, when the nights were especially long and bitter, he'd doubted himself.

She doesn't know what happened, he reminded himself. Once Hannah found out more about the events of that night six years ago, she'd lose that stupid, blind acceptance. He wasn't fool enough to believe anything else.

But he sat there for a long time, turning Trixie into a melted puddle of doggy bliss by scratching behind her ears, and he didn't let himself think. He couldn't afford to think about the terrible, brief warmth he'd felt when Hannah had accepted him at his word, with no questions at all in her soft brown eyes.

Chapter 6

It was only one-fifteen in the afternoon, but Hannah had been yawning her fool head off for the last half hour. Ever since lunch, really—which she'd eaten with her patient. Her employer hadn't shown up for the meal.

That was entirely his affair, she assured herself as she measured the laundry soap and dumped it in on top of the load of jeans she was washing. So he hired her to cook and clean for him as well as to take care of his brother; that didn't mean he was obliged to show up for the meals she prepared, did it? Even if that meant that she had to throw out some of the food.

She scowled at the table, where a single place setting sat, pristine and unused. It was her own stupid fault if she'd gone to the trouble of making homemade tortillas for the burritos in a lame effort to impress the man. Why was she so intrigued by him, anyway? No more showing off, she promised herself as she folded the last of the sheets. From now on, he could have sandwiches or leftovers for lunch. *If* he bothered to show up.

Hannah was seriously considering a nap. She was yawning as she carried the laundry basket full of clean towels and sheets down one hall and across the living room, heading for the newest part of the house. She hadn't had enough sleep lately, what with arriving here after midnight, then staying up fretting about the sheriff's visit last night. And then she'd lain awake after talking to Nate, trying to understand what it was about the man that called to her so. Was she a fool for believing him? She didn't know. Her heart didn't seem to care. He'd *needed* her to believe in him, and something in her heart had just opened up and taken him in.

Much as she would take in any new friend, she assured herself as she headed for Nate's room. Or a patient. Or a stray dog, for that matter. Didn't she always want to fix things for those around her? That's why she was going to be a nurse, for heaven's sake. The way her mysterious employer affected her was perfectly normal, and nothing to be alarmed about.

Nate's bedroom door was ajar. She shoved it open with her foot and stepped inside. And stopped in her tracks.

He wasn't naked. Quite.

He took his time about pulling his jeans up, then used both hands to zip them. And he looked at her the whole time, not smiling, but not angry or embarrassed or any of the things he ought to be when she'd walked in and caught him in his briefs, with his whole, entire chest bare, along with his washboard stomach and long, muscular thighs.

And oh, my, but he did have an incredible chest. And stomach. And thighs. And…

He spoke at last. "Was there something you wanted?" His hands paused at the waistband to his jeans without snapping them, and then he *did* smile—the conceited ass.

"I, uh—clean sheets," she said, jiggling the laundry basket. "For your bed. I stripped it this morning and—" poor word choice "—I washed the sheets and was just going to make the bed again, and—and you really should close your door, you know. I didn't know you were even in the house."

"You might want to knock the next time you come to my room." He spoke much too mildly. "If you'd walked in a couple minutes ago, you would have caught me right out of the shower. I'd hate to embarrass you."

Now that he mentioned it, she noticed that his hair was damp—the hair on his head, and the small, silky patch of hair in the middle of that incredible chest. "I'm a nurse," she assured him. "I'm not embarrassed by that sort of thing."

"That's good." At last he finished fastening his jeans. "I guess I don't need to worry about closing my door, then, do I?"

That wasn't what she'd meant. She frowned at him but couldn't think of a way to untangle herself from the situation gracefully, so she ignored it and carried her laundry basket over to the bed.

Nate's bedroom was a large, comfortable room, with lots of wood and not much color. Until this moment she would have said that the most noticeable thing about it were the floor-to-ceiling bookshelves framing the bed. Right now, though, that king-size bed occupied more of her attention than anything else in the room.

Except him.

She set her laundry basket down on the opposite side of bed from him. His sheets were white, as plain as the rest of his bedroom, and might have come from a discount store. His bedspread was a luscious dark blue silk, sinfully silky, and the only evidence of hedonism she'd seen.

There weren't any pictures in here. No paintings, and no photographs.

That bothered her. Something seemed off-kilter. He'd made himself a spacious and comfortable nest in here. Why didn't he have any family photos in his private space?

He was still watching her. She flapped the bottom sheet out over the mattress. "I expected you to come in through the kitchen so you could get lunch."

"Didn't have any time. I had another heifer jump the gun.

I could have used a calf-puller, but we were out on the range, so I had to make do. By the time I finished with her, I was in no shape to go into town without a shower and change of clothes.'' He moved at last, going over to the ladder-back chair with a white shirt tossed across the seat. He picked the shirt up. ''You did say something about needing to go to the grocery store?''

''Yes, but you don't have to go with me.'' And you don't have to cover up that chest yet, she wanted to say, but she kept her eyes primly on the sheet she was tucking in. ''I don't expect you to drive me in when I need supplies. I'll bring you the receipt, of course, so you can see that I'm spending your money properly.''

''I'd be foolish to trust you with my brother and not with my money.'' He disappointed her by slipping one long, muscular arm at a time into the sleeves of a plain western-style shirt. ''It will be simplest if I give you authority to sign on the ranch's account. I have to approve you in person, though.''

The phone on the bookcase next to the bed rang. Hannah jumped. ''Oh—I'll get it.'' It was too early to hear from Leslie, who had said she wouldn't call until she was settled, but Hannah couldn't keep from hoping whenever the phone rang. Of course, most of the calls were for Mark, and they were usually from women.

This call was for Nate, though. She hurried through the bed-making, and she almost managed to escape while he discussed beef prices with someone. He hung up the phone just as she picked up her laundry basket again. ''Ready to go?'' he asked.

He obviously wasn't, not with his shirt still hanging open, giving her a nice view of that incredible chest. Had the man never heard of modesty? ''Why don't we get me set up to sign on the ranch account another time? You must have a dozen things you need to do instead of playing chauffeur.''

''I need to go to the feed store anyway, so it's not a problem.''

Oh, wasn't it? Her mouth was dry and her pulse skittered around like a manic squirrel, and she didn't want to stop looking at him. One of them had a problem, all right. But she didn't think she was going to explain that to him.

"So what's wrong?"

"Wrong?" She frowned at Nate. Hannah had given herself a stern talking-to about the way she was letting this man affect her. She intended to listen to her common sense, too— but it would be a whole lot easier to do that if Nate would quit insisting on being so blasted *present.*

"You jumped a foot when the phone rang earlier. Then, before we left, you asked Mark to be sure and take a message if anyone called for you, and you've been a thousand miles away ever since you got in the truck. Obviously you're expecting an important call." He stressed the word *important* just enough to sound sarcastic.

"I did *not* jump when the phone rang." She certainly wasn't jumpy because Leslie hadn't called yet.

"You're expecting to hear from a boyfriend, I suppose."

"No, my sister. Although I don't really think she'll call for another few days. I just wish she would."

He frowned. "You're worried about your sister?"

"Oh, no," she assured him. "Leslie knows how to take care of herself. Usually. Of course, she's a little bit impulsive sometimes—but that's not the case this time. I just want to know she got out of town safely."

He didn't respond for the next few miles, and when he did speak, the words sounded grudging, as if he resented his own curiosity. "Why did she need to get out of town?"

"Her ex-husband. She left him when he became abusive, but after the divorce was granted he started threatening her. When she came home and found her apartment trashed one night, she was scared enough to be sensible. I don't think she would have borrowed money from me otherwise. She's very proud."

"Is that why you needed this job so much?" he asked, his

voice harsh. "You were broke because you'd loaned your sister all your money?"

Now, why would that bother him? She glanced at him, baffled. "Yes."

He muttered something that she didn't catch. Hannah didn't ask him any of the questions his peculiar attitude raised in her mind. Silence was good. If she worked at it, she could practically forget he was there.

The minutes dragged on in stiff silence as they slowed at the outskirts of Bitter Creek, and he turned off on a side street. Two blocks down he turned again, pulling in to the parking lot of a grocery store. The paint that might have once laid out the parking spaces in the lot had long since worn away. It didn't matter, though. In a town this size, everyone knew where the lines were supposed to be, and parked accordingly.

Nate turned off the ignition. "Hannah," he said, resting his arms on the steering wheel and not looking at her, "I need to ask you something."

She resented that, when she'd worked so blasted hard at not asking *him* anything. "All right."

"Will you let me loan you enough money to replace what you loaned your sister?"

"Good grief! Of course not."

He scowled. "I didn't think so."

"If you're trying to get rid of me again—"

"No," he said, and opened his door. "I have no intention of letting you leave yet." Having thoroughly confused her, he got out of the truck. "I'll tell Ed Jenks to let you sign on the ranch account, then I'm going to the feed store. Get what you need and wait here for me."

Hannah tried not to stare at the clerk who checked her out at Jenks's Grocery, but she'd never seen anyone who looked so much like Jabba the Hutt. Except for the glasses and hair, of course.

"I tell you, honey, I don't know how you stand it out

there," the woman said. Jenks's didn't run to scanners and computerized inventory; this checker actually *checked* the groceries. The fingers of one pudgy hand flew over the keys on the register while she slid and sorted items with the other.

"You don't like it in the country?"

"Huh? Well, no, to tell you the truth I don't, but that ain't what I meant. No, I was wondering how you could handle being all alone out there with *him*. I sure couldn't." When she shuddered, the folds of flesh under her chin quivered. Her fingers never stopped moving.

"Mark's got a bit of a temper, but he's okay."

"Not the young one." She shot Hannah a disgusted look. "The other one."

"Oh, you mean Mr. Jones?" Hannah said coolly. "I can't imagine why that would bother you."

"Oh, you can't, huh?" She smiled and leaned towards Hannah. Her mouth was wide and nearly lipless. Hannah kept expecting her tongue to shoot out after a fly. "You don't know, then. You haven't heard about his *record*." She dragged out the last word, relishing it.

"You mean his prison record?" Hannah smiled sweetly back at her. "Of course I have."

"And you don't mind?" Two pale eyes opened as wide as they could. "You don't mind living out there alone with a murderer?"

"Nonsense. There are five other people out at the ranch, and I find Mr. Jones an excellent employer. He's fair and even-tempered and very pleasant to work for." Hannah perjured herself without hesitation, and it was worth it to see the clerk's face screw up confusion. "Oh, I didn't find any whole wheat pastry flour. Do you not carry it?"

"You'll have to go into Amarillo for fancy stuff like that." Her hands started moving again. "So you find him *pleasant*, do you? Well, I guess he just might be real *pleasant* to someone who looks like you do. Pays pretty good for your...time, does he?"

Hannah reminded herself that ladies didn't punch store

clerks in the nose. "I think you charged me twice for those cherries."

"What?"

"That can of cherries. When you stopped working to gossip, you'd just rung them up. I think you accidentally rang them up again."

The woman gave her a dirty look and leaned forward to peer at the register tape. The phone rang, and she picked it up. "Jenks's Grocery. Uh-huh. Sure, Mr. Jones. No problem." She hung up the phone and smirked at Hannah. "Your employer won't be able to pick you up for a while. He's getting a flat tire fixed over at Joe's. Don't worry, though. I'll put the perishables in the cooler for you while you wait."

Oh, great, Hannah thought. She was trapped here with Jabba the Hutt.

"She what?" Nate said.

"Said she was going to the library. Well, she asked where it was first, and it would've been rude for me not to tell her, now, wouldn't it, Mr. Jones?" Darilee Jenks smiled her wide, lipless smile.

Nate kept his temper with an effort. He got along well enough with Ed, but the man's wife set his teeth on edge. She had an oily respect for money. "Did you tell her how far away the library is?"

"Well, now, how could I do that? Do I drive around counting the blocks between one place and another? And the Lord knows I'm on my feet all day, so what seems like a long walk to me might not seem much of a stretch to a young thing like her, and so I told her. I gave her directions. You go down Second till you get to the corner where the Cut 'n Curl sits, I said, and that's Frisco. You turn right on Frisco, and go straight until you hit Canyon Road, then—"

"You sent her down Canyon?" Nate turned and started for the door.

"But—your groceries! Mr. Jones?"

"I'll be back."

He couldn't decide whether he was more aggravated with Darilee for sending Hannah off clear across town through the only bad neighborhood in Bitter Creek, or with Hannah for wandering off. Why hadn't the fool woman stayed where he left her?

The truth was, he admitted as he slammed the door of his truck, he was aggravated with himself, too. Because he'd misjudged her. Right from the start he'd judged her based on her appearance—all flash and no substance—because he'd wanted to see her that way. Damn, he hated being wrong. He pulled out of the parking lot quickly and headed for Canyon Road.

There wasn't much Nate respected more than loyalty. Hannah had given her sister everything she had, stranding herself in the company of strangers to do it. That kind of unquestioning support was how things should be between sisters.

Or brothers.

Canyon Road was a long stretch of dirt and gravel that skirted the arroyo that some people in Bitter Creek liked to call a canyon. The oversize ravine did get fairly deep where it ran along Canyon Road, the dry creek bed at its bottom hidden in the tangle of stunted trees and scrubby growth that covered its sides. On the other side of the road, faded houses with sagging eaves sat in yards that were equal parts dirt and weeds.

Most of the people who lived along here were unfortunate or unskilled, but decent enough. Some were unpleasant. A few were unsafe.

Those were the ones Hannah had managed to find.

Nate was two blocks away when he saw her bright hair. His blood ran cold. Five punks had her backed up against a big wagon wheel, one of a pair set into the ground to flank a dirt driveway. One of them tried to grab her, and she shoved him. Another one got right in her face—and maybe he did something else, too. Because she slapped him.

He slapped her back.

Nate's blood turned from cold to hot in an eye-blink. He

stomped down on the accelerator. Seconds later he braked to a stop and came out of the truck, fast and quiet.

The one closest to him was just a kid, no more than fifteen, so Nate shoved him out of the way. The next one tried to stop him, so Nate hit him in the belly. That one doubled over. Then Nate was in the center of the circle with Hannah. Two of the other punks stood frozen, staring at him. One of them—the one who had slapped her—was the punk from the bus station. Mario Bustamante.

Mario must have seen too many martial arts movies. He yelled something loud and obscene and launched himself at Nate with a flying kick. Nate grabbed Mario's foot and twisted, stepping to one side. Mario gave one high scream and fell to the ground.

A blow landed in Nate's back, just below the kidneys. He grunted and spun, just in time to see Hannah kick his attacker in the back of the knees. He went down with a surprised yelp, and she grabbed his head in an odd-looking hold he'd seen cops use to subdue drunks, applying pressure just below his nose.

The punk's eyes got big, and he stopped moving.

Nate looked around. His hands flexed. Adrenaline had his nerves jumping, but there was no one left to hit. Hannah had hers under control. The one he'd punched in the stomach was still hunched over, looking green, and the third punk was two houses down and running flat-out. The youngest of them— the kid he'd shoved aside—backed up when Nate's gaze landed on him, his hands held out placatingly. "Hey, I don't want no trouble."

Nate scowled. "You're Victoria Smith's youngest, aren't you? Your mama would be ashamed to see you running with this crowd. She doesn't know you're cutting school, does she?"

The kid looked worried.

Mario muttered something and staggered to his feet, but his ankle wouldn't hold him up. He fell back on his rear end and spat something filthy at Nate in Spanish.

Nate shook his head. Mario Bustamante was the worst of the lot, but he was no threat to Nate, much as he'd like to be. With that realization, the last of Nate's fury evaporated, leaving him feeling empty and slightly sick. He hadn't lost his temper in a fight in a long time. Hell, he hadn't *been* in a fight in a long time. Not for six years.

That time, too, a woman had been involved. "Get in the truck," he growled at Hannah.

She slid him one measuring glance, released her hold on the youth's head, and went to the truck without a word.

Nate bent to pick his hat up out of the dust. He wondered if, at last, she had begun to be frightened of him.

Chapter 7.

" "Chimera." " Hannah sat on the edge of her bed and read the word for Sunday aloud. " "A mythological monster with a lion's head, a goat's body and a serpent's tail; or a grotesque or unreal creature of the imagination." "

"Did you say something?" Mark called from the room next to hers. She'd gotten into the habit of leaving her door and his both open, even when she was off duty, so she could hear him if he needed anything.

"No," she called back. "Just practicing today's word." She liked this one. It sounded like a creature that one of the heros from her book of fairy tales might have fought. She closed her book, set it on the table with Grimms' Fairy Tales and stood, sliding her stockinged feet into her dress shoes.

Mark had behaved pretty well since they'd had that little heart-to-heart talk the night the sheriff came to see Nate. Oh, he flirted like crazy when he was in the mood, and he snapped at her when he was hurting or tired. But both were outlets for the pain and boredom of his situation. Hannah knew it was torture for an active man like him to be trapped in a bed. She didn't object to a little bad temper or flirting under the circumstances.

The next voice she heard wasn't Mark's. "Are you ready?"

Her heart jumped. It had been four days since she'd watched her employer wade into a gang of five ruffians, flatten two of them, chase off another and back down the only one still standing. Hannah was sure she could have handled things herself—well, almost sure—but every time she thought of Nate's quick and certain defense, she got a funny feeling in the pit of her stomach, a warmth that was almost like sexual desire. But it wasn't. She was smiling as she turned to face him.

My, but that man could fill a doorway. His head barely cleared the frame. If he'd had his hat on, he would have had to duck. With his dark hair and dark eyes, and in that blue shirt he had on, Nate was a sight to make any woman's mouth water, Hannah thought. But he would have looked even better if he'd been dressed to go to church *with* her.

That notion was foolishness, so she ignored it. "Sure," she said, smoothing her skirt self-consciously. She wore her favorite cold-weather church dress, a dark green corduroy with French cuffs on the long sleeves and a notched collar. It was ankle-length and buttoned all the way down the front, and she thought she looked rather pretty in it.

If Nate agreed, he hid it. He sounded more impatient than admiring. "We've got to leave if you're going to get there before the opening hymn."

"Okay." She grabbed her purse and followed him, but stopped to stick her head in Mark's room. Abe sat in the extra chair, reading the funnies, his feet propped up on a box that held a pile of old magazines he'd brought Mark. The issue of *Life* on the top of the pile had a cover picture of Mickey Mantle in his Yankees uniform.

"You're sure you don't need anything else from town? Just the ibuprofen?" she asked. This morning, Mark had suddenly changed his mind about taking an over-the-counter pain reliever. After a search failed to turn up the bottle Nate was sure should be in the kitchen, he'd decided to drive Hannah to church himself so he could stop by the convenience store.

"That's all I can think of."

"And you've got everything you need for now?"

"Hannah, this is your day off, remember? Quit hovering." Mark softened his words with one of his grins. She was getting used to them. Sort of.

Abe looked up from the funnies. "You'd better go before Nate forgets himself and tosses you over his shoulder. The boy's looking a mite impatient."

"The boy" was looking downright grim. Hannah waved at the other two and, as instructed, got out of there.

As soon as Nate and Hannah were gone, Abe sat up, moved his feet and took the issue of *Life* off the stack. Beneath it was a pile of vintage *Playboy* magazines. He handed one to Mark. "None of them sad-looking things with their ribs showing in here. Nothing dirty, either."

Mark smiled as he took the magazine. A pretty blonde pouted her lips at him from the faded cover. "I'm going to be real disappointed if these ladies have all their clothes on, Abe."

"They're not dirty," he insisted. "These gals are just showin' off a little bit. Not like those pictures they put in girlie magazines today."

Mark had heard Abe on this subject before. According to him, the people that made men's magazines stopped showing respect for women in 1967. "I'm still not sure why I let you talk me into meddling," he said, opening the first magazine with due care for the fragile paper.

"You need that ibu-whatever, don't you?"

"No," he retorted. "But I'm going to have to take it now that Nate's made a special trip into town for it—since you hid the other bottle."

Abe gave one of his dry chuckles. "He didn't have to go.

Hannah offered to pick some up. He just needed a little nudge, and we gave it to him." Abe opened the cover of a 1957 issue that featured a lush brunette in a filmy negligee. "Fact is, whether he knows it or not, the boy needs a woman, and he is powerfully drawn to Hannah. She's a good woman. She'll do right by him."

Maybe, Mark thought. Maybe Hannah was exactly what Nate needed, though Mark wasn't ready to place any bets yet. "What about Nate, Abe? Will he do right by her?"

Abe shifted uneasily in his chair. "He's a good man."

"I know that. But he's not the man he was. That's not surprising, after all he's been through, but sometimes…"

"Sometimes what?" Abe said testily. "Don't just dangle that word there and not finish up."

"Sometimes he reminds me of the old man."

Abe's weathered face turned stern. "I heard more of that sort of nonsense six years ago than I could stomach. Nate might look like your dad, but he don't have Garwood's nature. He keeps a grip on his temper, and he don't need to make everyone dance to his tune."

"But the ranch comes first, doesn't it? With Nate, just like with our old man, the ranch is what matters. All that matters."

"Now, if that's not the most ungrateful thing I ever heard. He brought you home after you got yourself banged up, didn't he? Stayed with you up at the hospital in Lubbock, then brought you home as quick as he could. And now he's got you the prettiest nurse I ever did see."

And aside from that, Mark thought, he only visits for five or ten awkward minutes every day to ask how I'm doing.

Not that Mark blamed his brother for avoiding him. Ever since he had left home, Mark had tried make things easy on Nate by keeping his visits short. That had worked out okay. Nate didn't seem to mind Mark coming around every so often. Maybe they didn't have a lot to say to each other, but the two of them got along, and Mark didn't want to mess that up the way he'd messed up so much else. Then he'd had the damn accident. Nate, of course, had done the right thing. That was one of the things that used to drive Mark crazy about his big brother: Nate always did the right thing.

But he didn't have to *like* doing it, did he?

Mark found a smile—the nice, easy sort of smile that no one ever looked behind. "Sure. You're right, Abe. I'm just feeling mean after all these days in this damn bed."

"Reckon you're entitled." Abe looked at his magazine and turned a page. "Don't imagine it matters if we meddle a bit. Hannah lights up when Nate walks in a room. All we're doing is helpin' things along."

Yeah, he'd noticed that. He'd seen the way Nate's eyes followed her, too. But while Nate might be looking, he didn't *want* to be. "I don't think she knows about Jenny, or what happened that night."

"She hasn't asked you about it?"

"No."

"She will," Abe said grimly. "After a couple of those folks up at the church finish filling her in on their version of things today, she'll have some questions. Unless she flat-out believes the worst. But Hannah's not like that."

"We'll see if you're right about her soon enough, then, won't we?"

"I appreciate your driving me in," Hannah said, smoothing her skirt self-consciously. They'd just turned out onto the highway.

"No problem. I had to go into town anyway."

Nate had been bound and determined to go into town. She glanced at him. His hat sat on the seat next to the little black patent-leather purse that she carried for dressy occasions. His hands both rested on the steering wheel. He had such strong hands, with long fingers and broad palms. Fascinating.

Hannah dragged her attention away from those hands. "I guess you don't mind an excuse to get into town once in a while."

"Bitter Creek?" The twist to his mouth wasn't a smile.
"If I never saw it again, I wouldn't miss it."

That was a bit of a conversation stopper, but Hannah per-
severed. "I could have brought some ibuprofen back with
me."

"Look, if you were wanting to drive in yourself today so
you could do something after services, you should have spoken up. When I hired you I agreed to let you use a vehicle
on your days off."

Oh, right. Like he would have listened. The man was on
a quest. "There isn't anything I needed to do other than get
to church. You said the grocery store is closed."

"Bitter Creek is a small town. Most places close on Sun-
days."

"It's a good thing the 7-11 is open, then," she said. "And
that it stocks ibuprofen. Or you'd probably have taken off
for Amarillo."

"You have a point?"

She smiled. "You were glad to have the chance to do
something for him, weren't you?"

"I don't mind running to the store. Not much else I can
do to help."

Apparently not, Hannah thought. From what she'd seen,
Nate couldn't eat supper with his brother, or watch TV with
him, or play cards, or keep him company in the evenings.
She sighed. "You shouldn't stay away from your brother just
so you can avoid being around me."

"I don't."

"But you do stay away," she said quietly. Every morning
just after breakfast, Nate stopped by Mark's room. The two
men talked about the weather, the ranch and maybe the news
for five or ten minutes. Then Nate asked Mark if there was
anything he needed, Mark said no, and Nate left.

"That's how Mark wants it." He reached out and turned
on the radio, and the fifties' sound of Buddy Holly filled the
pickup cab, hinting that Nate was ending the conversation.
Yet after a moment he spoke. "I thought you'd be more

comfortable if I wasn't around much, after what happened in town."

"You mean because you chewed me out for ten minutes for trying to walk to the library? I was mad about that, I'll admit, but I don't stay mad forever."

"I mean the fight. You were shook up."

"I was not!" she said indignantly. "I took care of one of them myself!"

"So you did." A small smile tugged at his mouth. "How did you manage that, anyway?"

"My sister taught me." Leslie would have been proud of her, she thought.

He gave her another glance—longer, more considering. "You weren't frightened?"

"Maybe just a tiny bit, until you got there," she admitted.

He didn't reply. Somehow his silence felt lighter now, though. Hannah didn't mind letting the conversation lag. She had some thinking to do.

Nate said he'd stayed away because that's the way Mark wanted it, but he was wrong. Every morning, Mark watched for Nate, as if those few minutes were the most important part of his day. Oh, he wasn't obvious about it. He didn't stare or fidget or anything. He just glanced at the empty doorway every now and then before breakfast…during breakfast…after breakfast. Until Nate came. Then he stopped watching.

As for Nate—well, Hannah hadn't been sure about him. Not until today. Nate was concerned about Mark's health, but Hannah had been forced to assume that either he wasn't aware of his brother's loneliness and boredom, or he didn't care. Then this morning, Nate had asked his usual question about whether there was anything Mark needed.

This time, Mark had said yes.

Nate had nearly turned the house upside down looking for the painkiller, and when he couldn't find it, he'd been impatient for her to finish getting ready so he had an excuse to go into town and get the one thing his brother had asked him for. He was so eager to do something for Mark that it made Hannah's heart hurt. For some reason Nate wasn't comfortable giving Mark his company, and for some reason Mark wasn't willing to ask for it. Or for anything else. Until today.

Men, she thought. They could be such idiots.

The song on the radio switched to a sixties' group singing about stopping in a church on a winter's day. She smiled at the coincidence. "I would have pegged you for a country music man."

He didn't look away from the road and the miles of rough land that surrounded it. "Too many songs about prison and cheating women."

Cheating women? Did that have something to do with what had happened six years ago? Hannah fiddled with the zipper on her jacket. How many questions could she get away with asking? "I can see where you might not like songs about prison. Did you…serve much time?"

"What the hell business is it of yours?"

Apparently one question was too many. "Never mind," she said stiffly.

He was silent for the next couple of miles, then said abruptly, "My sentence was probated. I spent some time in the county jail before my trial, but I never did any hard time."

"I see." She nodded, then sighed. "Oh, shoot. No, I don't see. I don't exactly know what it means that you got your sentence probated. I…didn't finish high school. Dropped out in my junior year. Maybe they talked about it during senior year." Hannah smiled. "It wasn't on the GED exam, either. And the only other person I've ever known who was in prison was Three-Toed Walt. He served twenty years for killing someone in a fight in a bar."

He gave her an odd look. "Three-Toed Walt?"

"He only had three toes on one foot. Frostbite, I think."

"How in the world did you meet him?"

"He lived in a tiny shack on the Bartles' ranch up in Wyoming. He'd worked there all his life, except for the time he was in prison, so the family let him stay on when he couldn't work anymore. He was eighty-two and I was twelve when my dad worked there, and he'd been out of prison for years, so I never thought to ask him anything about probation.'' She paused. ''I'm not sure I would have asked him, anyway. Walt was a mean old cuss.''

''Your father let you be around an old man who'd been convicted of murder?''

She shrugged. ''I'm a McBride. Dad raised us to take care of ourselves.'' She looked down and plucked a bit of fuzz from her skirt, nervous but determined. ''So, what does it mean, being on probation?''

He shook his head. ''You don't know when to quit, do you?

She couldn't. Not when she had this ache inside to know about him. ''You don't learn things if you don't ask.''

His voice was harsh when he answered. ''Sometimes a judge decides that a convicted felon isn't likely to be a danger to society because of youth, the nature of the crime or the lack of a previous criminal record. Then the judge probates the sentence, the felon doesn't go to prison as long as he abides by the terms of his probation, and people write letters to the editor about how our justice system lets killers go free.''

Hannah asked softly, ''Did people write letters about you?''

He didn't reply.

It would be a mistake to feel sorry for a man like this, Hannah told herself. Except what she was feeling wasn't pity, or even sympathy. That funny feeling was back in the pit of her stomach, but this time it wasn't warm. It hurt.

The song on the radio changed from ''California Dreaming'' to ''Tears of a Clown.'' Bitter Creek lay directly ahead, between them and the horizon. Somewhere off to the left, on the edge of the little town, lay the canyon Nate had called an *arroyo*. Hannah had looked both words up. An arroyo was a steep-sided channel dug by flowing water; a canyon was a steep-sided valley. From what she could figure out, the main difference was how deeply the water had cut into the earth.

How deeply had Nate's conviction and probation cut into him? "You said the other night that you weren't allowed to have a gun. That's still true, even though your sentence is over?"

"Convicted felons aren't allowed to possess firearms. Or serve in the military. Or vote, in most states."

The first few houses of the little town appeared, followed by a bar called the Lucky Chance on the right. They drove slowly now.

Hannah's thoughts, like their truck, had slowed. But the obstacles blocking her view weren't as concrete and friendly as the houses they passed.

Nate had been convicted of murder, but it had been an accident. Hannah wasn't sure why she believed him so completely. Maybe it was because he'd tried at first to scare her away. Or maybe it was the look she'd seen in his eyes when he told her that it was an accident. Not hopeless, no—what she'd seen on his face that night hadn't been flat and barren, but charged with emotion. But there had been no hope there, either. Nate hadn't held any hope that he would be believed, yet he'd told her.

It wasn't right. He wasn't a criminal, not really, yet he couldn't vote. He couldn't own a gun, and a rancher *needed* a gun. He might have to shoot a snake or put down an injured cow. What if he ran across a rabid skunk? It wasn't right at all. Her hands clasped each other in her lap, tense with her interior struggle. Dammit, Nate did not want her sympathy. He didn't need her to fight his monsters, and life was *not* a fairy tale where right and wrong were clear and simple choices. And it wasn't up to her to fix things for everyone.

She forced her hands to relax. "What will you do while I'm in church, if everything's closed?"

"Dixie's Café is always open. I'll have some of the radiator sludge he passes off as coffee."

"He?"

For the first time since she got in the truck, his mouth turned up in a real smile. "Dixie Bogerty. How in the hell he ended up being called Dixie, no one knows. I don't think anyone ever dared ask."

They turned off onto a side street, and she knew they were almost there. She could see the steeple rising above the houses around them, glowing white and pure in the late morning sunshine.

Bitter Creek had four churches. Hannah had decided to visit St. Luke's because she thought she'd know the songs there. She did love some of those old hymns. "Amazing Grace" always made her feel close to her mother again. Her mother used to sing it to her daughters at bedtime, or hum it when she was worried or sad. It was one of Hannah's clearest memories of her early childhood.

Hannah wasn't worried. Not exactly. But there was something unsettling about the way she reacted to her enigmatic employer. She couldn't help wishing they would sing "Amazing Grace" in church today.

He pulled the truck up in front of the church. In the parking lot people were getting out of their cars, the women in hose and heels and winter coats, some of the men looking chilly in suits, some looking warmer in windbreakers and heavy jackets. Hannah saw kids in all sizes and shapes and a scattering of teenagers, and a lot of Stetsons and Resistols.

It all looked pretty familiar. She took a deep breath and told herself to relax.

"Hannah."

She turned her head to find him looking at her, his eyes intent.

"You said you liked horses, that you've missed riding." He reached across the bench seat and took her hand. His finger stroked her palm slowly. "The weather is supposed to warm up by afternoon. I'd like to take you riding."

Her heart made a nuisance of itself by beating too hard. As if this was a terribly important conversation. As if the mere touch of his hand was enough to start a ribbon of heat snaking up from her belly. "I don't think that's a good idea. You're my boss, and—"

"Not today. Today's your day off."

"It doesn't work that way," she said, exasperated.

"Think about it."

He let go of her hand. Her fingers automatically curled into her palm, holding on to the sensations his touch had evoked.

"Some of the people here are going to tell you things about me. After you've heard what they have to say, you may not want to go anywhere with me, anyway."

"I don't listen to gossip."

His eyes were serious and dark. "Is it gossip if it's true? Some of what you hear will be." He put the truck in gear. "Think about it," he repeated. "I'll be back to pick you up at twelve-thirty. That will give you a chance to get acquainted. Ask some questions. And make your decision."

Dixie's wasn't crowded on a Sunday morning, but a few of the usual crowd hung around, nursing a second or third cup of coffee. Most of them were male. Most of them were people Nate didn't want to talk to, or who wouldn't want to talk to him.

But Earl Navarrete's big white Cadillac was parked out front, and Nate saw Earl in a booth at the back. Earl was thirty years older than Nate and thirty pounds heavier. His hair was black on top, gray on the sides and stuck out around the ears in tufts that matched his salty mustache. His clothes, from the worn jeans to the battered Stetson, were several years older than his car.

All in all, he didn't look like the richest man in the county.

Nate made his way between the oilcloth-covered tables. "Hey, Earl. You dropped Susie at St. Mark's this morning?"

"That woman is mad for church." Earl shook his head sadly, as if he considered this a flaw. Since everyone knew Earl worshiped the ground his wife walked on, the pose was unconvincing. He bought a new Cadillac every year because his Susie liked them. "Sit down. You gonna let me buy you some breakfast this morning?"

"Not today." Nate slid into the booth opposite one of the few people he still considered a friend. "I might let you spring for some of that poison Dixie brews, though."

The man who waddled up to the table was a foot shorter than Nate and more than a foot wider. His white, short-sleeved T-shirt displayed an intricate tattoo of a sinking ship on one arm. The other arm ended in a hook—which carried the coffeepot. His round face was sweaty and scowling when he spoke to Nate. "You ain't been in lately. You too good to eat here anymore?"

"I've been busy, Dixie, with Mark being laid up."

"So, you gonna eat now and pay for your seat?"

"Just coffee this time." Nate didn't mind Dixie's attitude. Dixie was rude to everyone.

Dixie poured the coffee and left, muttering about freeloaders.

"So what are you doing in town?" Earl asked.

"I dropped Mark's new nurse at church so I could pick up some medicine." He sipped at his coffee and grimaced. "Damn, this hasn't gotten any better since the last time I was here."

Earl grinned. "Some things never change. Listen, Susie has got one of her ideas in her head. She wants me to—"

"I saw your truck out front, Jones," another voice broke in.

Nate turned his head slowly. "Hell." The man who stood near their booth wore a belligerent expression on his narrow face, an embroidered western-style shirt over his narrow chest and an expensive Stetson on his thinning brown hair. Nate looked away. He was not in the mood for a confrontation with his former brother-in-law. "Go away, Rydell."

"You may have fooled Royce and some of the others in this town, but you haven't fooled me. I know who's been shooting my cattle."

Nate shook his head. "You've got an exaggerated idea

about how important you are to me. You sure as hell don't matter enough for me to risk owning a firearm."

Rydell narrowed his eyes. "That's what you'd like everyone to believe."

"I don't give a damn what everyone believes. Especially you."

"No, you think you're above the law, don't you? You and your good buddy here think that because you own half the county between you, you can order everyone else around. But some of us aren't going to knuckle under."

Nate set down his coffee cup. "I should mention that I'm not in a good mood."

"Your kind thinks you can buy off judges, or the sheriff, or whoever else you have to. But I'm not backing down. And if your fat friend here—"

Nate's hand shot out. He grabbed a fistful of Rydell's shirt. "Didn't I say I was not in a good mood? Go away."

"Temper, temper," Earl murmured, spreading grape jelly on his last piece of toast without looking up.

Nate let go of the man's shirt. Rydell stepped back a pace, sneering. "You think I'm afraid of you?"

"Maybe you should be—since, according to you, I can buy my way out of anything. So what's to stop me right now from pounding your face until you bleed all over your pretty shirt?"

"Now, Nate." Earl put down his knife and smiled, friendly as any aging wolf. "You know you're not going to do that. Wouldn't be a fair fight. Why, you could pick up Rydell here with one hand and slap him around with the other one, and there wouldn't be a thing the poor s.o.b. could do about it."

For a minute, Nate thought Earl had pushed Rydell right over the edge, and Nate himself into a fight he needed to avoid. The smaller man's fists clenched. "I'll show you what I can do about it. You want to step outside, Jones?"

Fortunately, Dixie waddled up just then. "Shaddup, siddown and order somethin', Rydell. You're taking up floor space.''

"Outside," Rydell said to Nate.

Nate thought about it. He thought about punching Rydell right in his long, narrow nose. But Ben Rydell, for all his other faults, didn't lack guts. He was like one of those yappy little dogs that take on pit bulls. He wouldn't quit. He'd just keep coming, forcing Nate to do too much damage in order to stop him. And even one fight was one too many, he reminded himself, for a man with his record. "Can't oblige you. I never did develop a taste for jail.''

Rydell sneered. "I'm not going to press charges if you bloody my lip.''

"Dixie will, if I do it in his place.''

For a minute, Nate thought Rydell was going to jump him anyway. But Dixie growled, "Either siddown and order or pay rent.''

Rydell turned his sneer on Dixie. "I guess you like his money, too.''

"I like everybody's money. You want to stay, you got to spend some of yours.''

"I'm going." He turned. "I don't like the way it smells in here.''

"You know, Dixie," Earl said thoughtfully as the door closed behind Rydell, "I think he's right. There is a certain lingering stink. You had this place sprayed for pests lately?''

The noise Dixie made might have been a laugh or the result of his two-pack-a-day cigarette habit. He looked at Nate. "You want some more coffee?''

Coming from Dixie, the offer was a gesture of rare support and approval. "Sure. I've got two kidneys. I don't need both of them.''

Dixie sniggered and went to get the pot.

Earl shook his head. "Thought the man was going to get all mushy on us for a minute, offering you a free refill like that.''

Nate shrugged. "He didn't say it was free.''

"Yeah." Earl grinned. "You're right, he didn't. Now, where was I when that idiot interrupted us?"

"Something about Susie having an idea."

"Oh, yeah. She's wants to give a party next Saturday. A barbecue."

"In the winter?"

"That part's my idea. I like barbecue, and we need to do something with that steer of mine some jerk shot a couple weeks ago. I had it dressed out."

"I'd heard they shot one of yours, but I thought it was wounded, not killed."

"Gut shot. Had to put it down. Mark still stuck in a bed?"

"He is right now, but if everything's mending okay, he can start spending some time in a wheelchair after the doctor checks him on Thursday."

"Good. Bring him, then. Hell, bring everyone—the hands and Abe and that pretty nurse you've hired. She can fuss over Mark and make all the boys threaten to run out and break a bone or two so they can get her attention."

A couple of them might consider it, too, once they got a look at Hannah. "I'll pass the word. Thanks."

"You'll come, too."

"I haven't got much time for socializing right now."

"You haven't had much time for socializing for six years, but you'll come next Saturday."

"Earl—"

"Susie wants you there."

And that was that, as far as Earl was concerned. What Susie wanted, she should get. Nate didn't really disagree. Susie Navarette was special. "Earl, I don't have to go looking for trouble these days. It follows me, like Rydell did just now. I don't want to bring those kind of problems to your party."

"I'm not inviting Rydell, and no one else will say a word. Not in my home. Besides—" Earl leaned forward confidentially "—the party's to cheer Susie up. She's feeling kind of down about her birthday. Mind, she doesn't want me saying *which* birthday it is, so pretend you don't know.'' Earl paused. ''She wants you there.''

Nate grimaced. Sixteen years ago, Susan Navarrete had taken two bewildered and grieving boys home with her from their mother's funeral because their father was too distracted by grief to care for them. Nate and Mark had stayed with her and Earl for three weeks. ''That's blackmail.''

Earl grinned. ''The party starts at six.''

Chapter 8

Nate couldn't pull up directly in front of the church. Too many other cars and trucks were parked along the street. But that was just as well. He didn't much want to meet the people he'd see there—people who had once taught him in school, or in Sunday school. People whose daughters he'd dated, or who had cheered for him at high school football games. People who, these days, avoided his eyes when they saw him, or smiled too much. Or didn't smile at all.

Hannah came sailing out of the church right at twelve-thirty. She'd caught some of her hair up in a twisty thing on top of her head and let the rest of it free-fall down her back in a crazy rush of red curls. The wind plucked at those curls, fingering them around the way Nate wanted to do. She walked towards his truck quickly, her little black purse slung over her shoulder, her hands jammed in the pockets of the bulky parka she wore over her green dress.

Ah, that dress. It should have been as prim as a Puritan's outfit, but Hannah, who was so good at so many things, wasn't very good at prim. Besides, she'd left the last few buttons of the dress undone, giving him glimpses of her legs as she headed for the truck. He looked at her wild hair and the teasing flashes of her legs and thought about running his hand up under that skirt, right up along her warm thighs to the even warmer place between them, and he got hard as fast as a teenager making out at the drive-in.

Then he looked at the stony expression on her face. The heat in his blood collided with the rejection he saw coming toward him with those long, quick strides.

Everyone had done a fine job of filling Hannah in, all right. Nate could see he wouldn't be going anywhere with her today. Not today, and probably not ever. *Damn,* he thought, his knuckles turning white on the steering wheel. Damn, damn, damn…

She opened the door and swung up inside, giving him another teasing glimpse of pale legs. Then she slammed the door, sat down with her purse in her lap and demanded, "Did you do that on purpose?"

"What?" He glanced at her. "Fasten your seat belt."

"All that noble talk of yours about me making up my mind about riding after I heard what people said about you. You must have known what kind of garbage I would hear. Dammit, I *have* to go riding with you now."

"You'll go with me?"

"I said I would, didn't I?" Scowling, she drew the seat belt across and fastened it.

The surge of lust he felt startled him. It was too intense. He could handle that, though. He knew his body, knew its needs and its limits and how to ignore both when he had to. But when he drew a breath, it was shaky. That was bad. "I could answer you better if I had some idea what you're talking about."

"You must have known how I'd react. I don't listen to gossip. I told you that. But it was hard to keep some of those people from gossiping. As if Mark could threaten my virtue when he can't even sit up in bed without help! And as for what they said about you—" She broke off.

After everything Jenny had told their friends and neighbors that he'd done, he wasn't surprised that people had tried to warn her about him. His voice carefully neutral, he asked, "Did they tell you I used to beat my wife?"

She darted him a quick look. "Not in so many words. They hinted around at it."

They'd nearly reached the edge of town, and traffic was thin. He forced himself to keep within the speed limit, when what he wanted to do was stamp down on the accelerator. He never felt like he could draw a full, free breath in Bitter Creek.

"Well?" She sounded irritated, and she was frowning heavily. But her fingers were nervous, fiddling with the strap of her purse. "Aren't you going to say anything about— about what they said?"

"No." He'd tried telling his side in the past. People who had known him over twenty years hadn't believed him—with some exceptions, like Earl. The woman beside him had only known him a week. Why should she take his word for anything? "But you *are* going riding with me."

She sighed. "You are an exasperating man."

They'd reached the edge of town. The speed limit sign on their right sat five feet from the parking lot of the Lucky Chance Bar. As they passed it, Nate pushed down on the accelerator and didn't look at the small, cinder-block building that held too much of his past. He told himself to stop pushing her. She had said she would ride with him, and that was what he wanted—time alone with her. Time to seduce her.

But he couldn't drop it. For some ungodly reason, he had to know. "So *why* are you going riding with me?"

"What else could I do? If you'd heard what they said—"

"I probably have, at one time or another."

"They *told* me not to have anything to do with you. Can you believe it? One woman actually said that if I stayed out at the ranch with you and Mark after I'd been warned, they would 'know what to think.' As if I would be the one responsible if you attacked me!'' She glared at the highway and crossed her arms. ''So, of course, I told them.''

''Told them what?''

''That I was going riding with you this afternoon. I was pleasant about it. I said that unfortunately I'd already agreed to go before they warned me. And I assured them that if you did rape me or anything interesting like that, I'd be sure to call and tell them all about it so they wouldn't miss any of the details.''

An odd little wisp of a feeling tickled at the back of his mind. ''You told them that? In church?''

''I was nice,'' she insisted. ''Well—almost nice. I *tried* to be nice. So you see, I do have to go riding with you. I said I would.''

That odd feeling grew stronger, welling up from some forgotten cavern just left of his soul and far below any conscious thought. He felt himself grinning.

''You said that in church,'' he repeated. He could taste the strange feeling at the back of his mouth now. It tasted like Hannah had when he kissed her as she lay on the kitchen floor.

''Yes, so now I have to do it. I mean, you should always do what you say you will, but if you say it in church, then you *really* have to.''

The feeling rolled right up and out, and he laughed. It sounded rusty.

Hannah stared straight ahead, looking mortified. ''It isn't funny. I just couldn't think of anything else to say.''

''No?'' His laughter wound down to a chuckle. He didn't know what to say, either. So he touched her. Just once, along her cheek—such a soft, pale cheek. Did her breath catch? He prolonged the touch by tucking a long wisp of hair behind her ear. ''Thank you, Hannah.'' He pulled his hand back. ''I'm looking forward to riding with you.''

She glanced at him suspiciously. ''It's nothing personal. We don't have a social relationship,'' she reminded him.

''I know.''

"And this ride we're going on is definitely not a date."

"Absolutely not." He reached across the seat and took her hand. Quietly, he started drawing circles in the center of her palm with his forefinger.

He heard her sharp intake of breath. "You shouldn't do that."

But she didn't pull her hand away, and he wasn't about to let go. "What else did they tell you?" Nate intended to have her, but she had to know the truth first. He wanted her to know who was touching her. Taking her. And he didn't want her changing her mind about him afterward, which she might do if she didn't know the truth before coming to his bed.

She was silent. He glanced at her. Her teeth were worrying her lower lip. "Well?"

"One of them said that—that I look like her niece," she said reluctantly. "Like...your ex-wife."

He released the breath that he hadn't realized he was holding. "In some ways."

"She had red hair."

"It's more blond than red, and straight."

"Her figure is like mine."

"You're taller." And a little bigger elsewhere, he thought, remembering the feel of her breast in his hand.

"That's why you didn't like my looks when we first met, though. Because I look like her. Even our faces are alike, from what her aunt said."

"At first glance, maybe. But the resemblance is superficial." As he spoke, he realized it was true. When he looked at Hannah now, he just saw her, not a more vivid version of Jenny. "You're not like her."

"They said she lives in California now, with her mother."

"Thank God."

"It wasn't a friendly divorce?"

She definitely hadn't heard the story. "No."

"It was kind of weird. No one called her by name. They asked Ona how her poor niece was doing out in California, and the way Ona talked about her, it was as if she were talking about a sweet, delicate child.''

''Delicate?'' A knot of old anger clenched inside him. ''She's a lying, neurotic bitch. Or she was the last time I saw her. But six years have passed since then. Maybe she's advanced from neurotic to delicate by now.'' He waited for Hannah to ask. Sooner or later, she would have to ask what had happened six years ago that ended with one man dead and one arrested for murder.

For a long time, though, she didn't say anything at all. Her hand was warm and strong in his, her fingers slightly callused. She sat quietly holding his hand until they reached the turnoff that led to his house. Then, with a sigh, she pulled her hand back. ''So what is her name?''

''Jenny,'' he said. ''Her name is Jenny.'' He made the turn. His muscles had tensed up. His jaw was tight, and he realized he wanted to shake the woman sitting beside him. He wasn't sure why, but he really wanted to shake her. ''For God's sake, Hannah, is that all you're going to ask me?''

''I think so,'' she said thoughtfully. ''Yes, that's all for now.''

''I was convicted of murder. Don't you want to know what happened?''

''But it wasn't murder. It was an accident.'' She looked at the purse in her lap. ''I suppose if there's anything else you need to tell me, you will. Sooner or later.''

It couldn't be that simple. She couldn't just believe him, just like that. ''Your curiosity isn't going to drive you crazy?''

''Well, yes. It probably will. But what happened is really none of my business, since we don't have a personal—I mean a *social* relationship. Just boss and employee.''

''Oh, yeah,'' he said drily. ''That's right. I forgot.''

She nodded. ''It's best this way. But if you decide you *want* to tell me something, that's okay.''

He would have to, he knew. Since he couldn't have her until she knew at least the bare facts, he would have to tell her. But it would have been easier if she'd let the gossips fill her in, because Nate never talked about that night. Talking about it was too close to…hoping. He knew better than to hope people would take him at his word.

He didn't want to see trust replaced by horror or disgust when Hannah looked at him. He didn't want to reach out to touch her and have her back away—or brace herself, as if his touch were something to be endured. *God.* The thought was almost enough to make him change his mind. If he'd wanted Hannah a little less, he would have abandoned his plans right then.

Maybe she had sensed that, and was using her own ignorance to keep him at a distance.

It wasn't going to work.

It would work out fine, Hannah assured herself as she zipped her jeans up. Going horseback riding with her boss was probably not the smartest thing she could do, but she wasn't an idiot. She knew very well that Nate had something in mind other than letting her get her riding muscles back in shape. She could handle that. She just wouldn't get off the horse. What could he do when she was on horseback? Not much. Not enough to undermine her good sense.

Not unless she was wrong about him, and the people who'd tried to warn her were right.

Her boots were in the bottom of her duffel bag. She knelt on the floor to get them out, then sat back, looking them over. A bit down at the heels, she decided, but basically sound. Habit had made her toss them in the bag instead of packing them away in one of the boxes that filled the storage unit she rented, but it had been a long time since she'd worn them. For a lot of years, though, she would no more have left her riding boots behind than she would have traveled without her toothbrush. Less, actually. She could always buy another toothbrush.

The boxes in that storage unit held pieces of her past and a fistful of her dreams for the future. Hannah might be a rolling stone now, but she wouldn't always be living in other people's homes. She had plans. Over the years she'd accumulated a lot of things for the house she would own someday, and when that day came she'd open all those boxes. It would be like a dozen Christmases happening all at once.

Especially if she wasn't alone when she opened them.

That thought made her frown at her boots. Sometimes when she thought about the home she would one day own, she imagined that someone was there with her. Someone…important.

She stood, shaking off that vague image. She wasn't going to think about that. She certainly wasn't going to confuse those funny feelings she had around Nate with anything as real as forever-after love. She learned her lesson years ago. A practical woman took important things like love one slow, careful step at a time.

There was a small stool in front of the pretty antique vanity. Hannah sat on it to tug on her boots, then turned to face the mirror. Ugh. Her hair needed a major overhaul. She pulled out the twisty and picked up her brush.

Her heart was beating too hard. She couldn't decide whether it was fear or anticipation that had set it to such an unsteady rhythm. Frowning, she started brushing her hair. Maybe she'd been too impetuous this time, agreeing to ride out into the middle of nowhere with a man whose neighbors considered him violent.

Not all of them thought that, she reminded herself, the brush moving faster along with her thoughts. A couple of people had obviously disapproved of the gossip that the others were intent on feeding Hannah, and had helped her to turn the subject. But neither had everyone who warned her seemed spiteful or small-minded. Some of them had seemed genuinely concerned about her, and she didn't know why she'd felt compelled to defend her difficult employer. Good grief, the stupid man wouldn't say one word in his own defense! What made her think she knew him better than all those other people did?

Well...there was the way he was with animals. Her face softened as she thought about him and his dog. There was no fear in Trixie of her master, and surely there would have been if he had the kind of temper some of his neighbors claimed he did—a temper like his father's. From what she'd heard today, Nate's father had been dangerous when he got angry. He had been a man who let his rage control him.

People had tried to tell her that Nate was just like his father. She didn't believe it.

Hannah winced when her brush caught on a particularly nasty tangle. Really, she knew better than to rush through brushing like this. Hair as curly as hers tangled quickly and badly, and she was going to hurt herself if she weren't careful. She took a deep breath and tried to slow down, but her heart was still pounding, pounding, much too fast.

Nate set out the leftover roast, the bread and lettuce and tomato, and began methodically assembling sandwiches. Today was Hannah's day off, which left him with kitchen duty. But he didn't mind.

She was going riding with him. In spite of everything she'd been told, she'd agreed to spend the afternoon with him. He told himself that a single horseback ride wouldn't get her into his bed, but it was a start.

Nate still wasn't sure why Hannah had agreed to go with him, but he knew one thing: she wanted him. That much he was sure of, and when he thought about the way her breath had caught when he teased the palm of her hand, his blood began to pool, low and hot, in his groin. He would have to handle her carefully today. He didn't want her changing her mind about him when he told her what had happened six years ago.

Nate piled the finished sandwiches on three plates, loaded them and some soft drinks on a tray, and headed for his brother's room. He'd already arranged for Abe to stay with Mark this afternoon.

Mark greeted the arrival of his lunch with enthusiasm. "Roast? From last night?"

"Yeah." Nate set the tray on the bedside table and took his plate with him to the recliner he'd moved in here after bringing Mark back from the hospital.

"I sure am glad you've quit making noises about Hannah being temporary," Mark said, reaching for his plate. "I haven't eaten this well in years."

"You have women wanting to feed you all the time." Nate bit into his sandwich.

"Among other things," Mark agreed cheerfully. "But just because a person is female doesn't mean she can cook. Not like Hannah. Even her leftovers taste great." He took a big bite. When he'd swallowed, he said casually, "I hear you and Hannah are going riding this afternoon."

"Yeah."

"So...what did you have in mind?"

Nate frowned. "What's that supposed to mean?"

Mark's usual smile clung to his lips, but his eyes were dead serious. "I just wondered what you have in mind for her. Hannah isn't the sort—"

The phone rang. Nate stood and reached for it, glad for the interruption. He couldn't believe his bed-hopping brother was practically asking him what his intentions were. Apparently Hannah had gotten to him. Nate would have to make sure Mark understood that Hannah had been claimed.

"Jones ranch," he said.

"Hi," said a soft, feminine voice. "Is Hannah there? This is her sister."

Hannah was smiling when she hung up. She'd taken the call in Mark's room, her back turned to the two men who had eaten their sandwiches while she talked and pretended they weren't listening.

"Good news, I take it?" Mark asked.

She turned around. "That was my sister. She's in El Paso.

She's got a job.'' She sighed, more relieved than she wanted to admit.

Mark sat in his bed, of course. He wore a T-shirt and the cutoffs she'd fixed with velcro along the side so they wouldn't have to be pulled up over his cast. He grinned at her and the effect was truly stunning. So why wasn't she stunned? Why did her eyes inevitably drift to the other man—the silent man with the harsh face and the unfathomable eyes that captured hers so easily?

''She's all right, then?'' Nate asked quietly.

Hannah nodded. His eyes flickered with something—relief?—but they didn't release hers, and for some stupid reason there didn't seem to be enough air in the room. She felt as if she were waiting for something important, something…

''That's good.'' He turned away and set his empty plate on the tray.

Disappointment hit her like a fist to the belly, hard and unexpected. She'd wanted more from him. Stiffly, she said, ''I guess I'm ready.''

''Eat your lunch,'' he told her, heading for the door. ''I'll see if I can find you a hat to wear. Only an idiot goes riding without a hat.'' And he was gone.

Furious, she grabbed the two empty plates and stacked hers on top.

Out in the kitchen, she talked herself back into a state approaching reason. It certainly wasn't reasonable to be angry that Nate had fixed her a sandwich and wanted her to eat it, or that he wanted her to wear a hat. She certainly couldn't blame him for her foolish imagination. If she'd imagined, when they were in the truck, that his eyes had hinted at a level of caring and support that his words and quick exit just now had denied her, that was downright dumb.

Hannah ate half her sandwich while standing up and lectured herself silently, then loaded the dishes in the dishwasher. Automatically, she glanced around to see what else needed doing.

Nate had left crumbs and a messy knife on the counter

where he'd fixed their sandwiches. She wiped it down. The kitchen was looking better, she thought with satisfaction. She'd scrubbed and then polished one of the cherry cabinets, and it glowed now with the mellow luster of fine old wood. The floor was old and worn, but it was clean.

But the room still lacked something. There were no sugar bowls, no pretty trivets or pot holders, none of the things you expected to find in a woman's kitchen. Even the plates she'd just loaded in the dishwasher were plain, discount-store porcelain. It was as if she were the first woman to ever cook or clean in this kitchen—as if Jenny had never been here at all.

In fact, she couldn't think of anything she'd seen, anywhere in the house, that seemed as though it might have been picked out by the woman who had once lived here. Everything seemed either too old or too new. The old things were all of good quality, while many of the newer things looked like they been selected at random from someone's going-out-of-business sale.

Had Jenny taken everything with her? Or had Nate gotten rid of everything that had anything to do with his ex-wife? Hannah shivered. Nate's voice had held such venom when he spoke of his ex-wife, and that troubled her. Divorce could bring out the worst in people. Didn't she know that? Heaven knows, if she could have done Barry an injury in the first few months after he walked out on her, she would have. But—

"See if one of these will work."

She jumped. "Good grief, you startled me."

Nate came toward her. He was holding two cowboy hats: an expensive gray one with the sides rolled, and an old straw hat that the sun had bleached nearly white. He was frowning. "You looked a thousand miles away. And upset. Is there still a problem with your sister?"

"No." She shook her head. "No, she's fine. She already got her first paycheck—that's why she waited until now to call. She wanted to use her own money."

He nodded and came into the room, offering her the gray hat. "This one's in better shape. See if it fits."

Hannah looked at the hat he held out. It was a lady's Resistol. Had it belonged to Jenny? "The straw looks more my size," she said, and reached for it.

"The straw was my mother's favorite," Nate commented. "She always said the felt hat was too hot."

Hannah looked up at Nate. Both hats had been his mother's?

"I guess you won't be as hard up for money now. Your sister will be able to pay you back some of the money you loaned her."

He smiled. It was, she realized with a jolt, the first time she'd seen him smile like that—with his eyes, too.

"Maybe that will help you forget I'm your employer while we're riding."

Hannah's mouth opened. And closed again.

"There *is* something wrong, isn't there?"

"Oh, no. No, everything's fine." She took her time settling the straw hat on her head. She just needed a minute to think, that was all. She needed to adjust to the fact that Leslie was settled and would be sending most of her money back as soon as the post office opened tomorrow...and Hannah would be free to leave here. If she wanted to.

Hannah looked at Nate and tried to concentrate, but all she could think about was that she hadn't seen his eyes smile before. She'd seen him cold and she'd seen him angry. She'd seen his face taut with hunger. But she hadn't seen the way his eyes crinkled at the corners when he smiled. She hadn't seen that warmth in them before—a heat as dark and inviting as banked coals on a cold day.

She didn't want to leave. She wanted to stay right here, and it had nothing to do with her responsibility to her patient.

Definitely, she was staying on the horse.

Chapter 9

The sky was a huge, dusty blue bowl overhead, its color filtered by high-flying clouds. Hannah had left her parka unzipped in spite of the chilly breeze. The sun was brighter and warmer than it had been in days, and she was glad to have the straw cowboy hat to shade her face. Her thighs were sore, her butt was sore, and when she shifted, the saddle creaked beneath her.

It was one of her favorite sounds in the whole world, the creak of saddle leather.

"Sure you don't want to turn around?" Nate asked. He rode beside her on the Appaloosa mare, a feisty animal with a mind of her own. He wore a beeper at his belt, an old denim jacket over the blue shirt he'd had on that morning, and his work hat—a black Stetson that looked as if it had been rained on, stomped on and generally mistreated for ten or twenty years.

"I'm fine. Ajax is a real gentleman." Someone had obviously spent hours and hours training him.

"A gentleman? He's a slope-shouldered, pigeon-toed commoner."

She laughed. It was easy to laugh today. The sun was bright, the air was cool and she was out in the middle of land as free and open as God's hand. And Nate could bad-mouth Ajax all he wanted. He wasn't fooling her. Hannah knew who had spent all those hours training the horse—the same man who insisted he only let his dog in the house once in a while...when it was cold...and only in the kitchen.

She had been right to come riding with Nate. She was sure of that. He wasn't dangerous, or violent, or any of those things the people at church had said. "Are we heading for those rocks up ahead?" A large outcropping of rock, higher than a house, broke the earth's skin about a mile away.

"If you're up to it. We've got time, and the weather should hold." He scanned the sky with the concentration of a man whose livelihood depended on the weather. "We'll probably get some wind out of the front that's piling those clouds up to the west, but no rain."

Hannah felt up to almost anything today. "Of course. I'm so glad I came," she said, filling her eyes with sky and horizons and a vastness that seemed to stretch halfway to forever. "It's beautiful out here."

He slanted her an unreadable look. "Most people don't think so."

"It's a hard land." Hard and rough, as choppy as a lake in a storm with its ridges and wrinkles and ridges, with no trees or buildings to break up the view. The dirt beneath their horses' hooves was the color of strong tea, and strewn with rocks. Grass grew in winter-dry clumps, brittle and sparse. A few Herefords grazed nearby, their rusty-red coats the only splashes of warmth in the landscape.

A hard land, she thought, glancing at the man riding beside her, tends to grow hard people. "But the land has its own sort of beauty. This is pretty basic country. I like that. I'm a pretty basic woman."

"Are you?" He gave her another of those unreadable looks.

"Basic to the point of being boring."

He gave her a look so full of dry humor that she laughed again. "It's true, though. I know how I look. Flashy." Her appearance had been a problem sometimes, a pleasure others. Like lots of things in life. "But I really am a pretty basic person. All I do is work and plan my career."

"What are your plans?"

"I want to be an R.N. I've got a ways to go still, but I'll get there." Enthusiasm came easily when she talked about her future. "I've been going to Tech whenever I could for the past couple years."

"That can't be easy, with the kind of work you do."

"I take jobs in Lubbock whenever possible to be near the university. I'm not in a hurry. Lord, I'd better not be, as long as it took me to get up the nerve to sign up for the first course!"

"Had you been out of school a long time?"

"Six years. I was self-conscious about it." Hannah chuckled. "I guess 'self-conscious' isn't quite right. 'Scared spitless' comes closer to describing how I felt the first time I sat down in a college class. I had my GED, and I'd passed the entrance exams, but I still didn't feel…adequate."

"Why did you drop out of high school?" He shook his head. "You seem like you'd have had better sense."

"Who has sense at sixteen? I thought I was in love, and when you're in love, you get married, right?"

"You dropped out of school to get married? At sixteen?"

He sounded angry. She looked at him curiously. "Married at sixteen, divorced at seventeen. I admit it wasn't too bright, but teenagers usually aren't, you know."

"Kids get married at that age because they have to," he said flatly, "or their parents wouldn't sign for them."

"I wasn't pregnant, if that's what you mean."

"Then why the hell did your father sign for you?"

He *was* angry. On her behalf, apparently. That gave her

an odd feeling. "I didn't give him a lot of choice. I told him he could either give me away, or he could wait for me to run off to be with Barry." She felt a twinge of the old guilt. Patrick McBride loved his daughters fiercely, however poorly he understood them. It had hurt her to hurt him.

"He was your father," Nate said flatly. "He should have protected you better."

"How could he? I was set on having my way. And he was there for me afterward." He'd shown up at her door about a month after Barry walked out, all eager to get himself thrown in jail for beating up the heir of one of the town's richest families. Hannah smiled and shook her head. Patrick McBride had a real talent for showing his love for his daughters in ways apt to cause them trouble or embarrassment.

"He quit his job in Colorado," Hannah went on reminiscently, "and started back to Montana, but his truck threw a rod outside of Billings. He left it there and kept on coming, hitchhiking the rest of the way." He'd shown up broke and breathing fire, and talking him out of his revenge had been quite a task. Somehow, in the process, Hannah had lost any lingering taste for it herself. After a while, she'd just plain gotten tired of hating Barry. You had to let go of the hard, hateful feelings, or you kept one foot in the past, dragging it along with you. She had wanted to move on.

She glanced at Nate. She wasn't at all sure *he'd* moved on.

"What was he doing in Colorado if you were in Montana?"

She shrugged. "That's how Dad is—his feet get to itching, and he has to be off. In fact, that was part of the reason I got married instead of just—well, you know. He'd decided he was ready to go, and I didn't *want* to go." Hannah's need for roots had mingled with curiosity and plain old lust to make marriage seem inevitable. Maybe other girls her age hadn't thought they had to get married to have sex, but Hannah's head had been filled with fairy tales and wedding bells.

She expected a ribald comment from Nate, or maybe a

smile. Instead, his eyebrows—both of them, quirky and straight—stayed caught in a frown. "Your father could have stayed there with you. You would have come to your senses sooner or later."

"No," she said sadly, "he couldn't. After my mom died, he just couldn't stay anywhere for long."

He didn't answer at first. When he did, his voice was quiet. "My father changed, too. After my mother died. He wasn't the man he'd been before."

"Changed how?"

"He'd always had a bad temper, but he rarely let it loose when she was alive. Afterward…" He shrugged. "Mark and I got good at staying out of his way when his temper was up."

Had their father hurt them? Physically hurt them? Given what she'd heard in town, it seemed possible. She wanted to ask. She wanted to tell him that he wasn't like his father, no matter what those people had said. But his expression was closed and forbidding again, as if he regretted having said so much.

She let the conversation lapse.

Silence felt natural out here. So many of nature's sounds were small and secret, like the whisper of a breeze that tugged at her borrowed hat, or the panicked escape of a jack-rabbit surprised by their passage. Nature could get noisy at times, of course, like when one of the wild storms of the plains blew in, cracking the sky open with thunder and making the air scream with wind and rain.

As if in answer to her thoughts, as they neared the tumble of rock that was their goal, a low growl of thunder sounded off in the distance. To the west, out near the border between land and sky, long streaks of gray rain arced from dusky clouds to dusty ground.

She grinned. "I thought you said we wouldn't get any rain."

"We won't. Wind's carrying it south. It won't reach us."

The rocks they'd been aiming at were much larger than

they'd looked from a distance. A huge slab of granite poked up through the soil in a flat-topped ridge, with crumbles of stone in all sizes scattered around.

"There's a path to the top. It's enough of a climb to be a good stretch after the ride out here," Nate said, swinging down from the mare's back. He led the horse a few steps closer to the rock and tied the reins to something.

When he stepped aside, she saw that there was a metal ring driven into the rock. "You must come here pretty often."

"Mark drove that in years ago. He…used to spend more time on the ranch than he does now. There's just the one tie-down, but you won't need to tie Ajax. He'll hang around. This lady doesn't have his good sense," he said patting the mare on her spotted flank.

Hannah shifted uncomfortably in the saddle, but she remembered her plan and didn't get down. It wasn't that she didn't trust him…

He raised his eyebrows. "Coming?"

Moving around sounded really good. The rocky ridge looked inviting—but so did the man watching her. "I don't think so."

Humor gleamed in his dark eyes. "I'm not going to jump on you. Not without giving fair warning, anyway."

She grimaced. "Fair warning" might not be enough, not the way her body acted around him. "I think I'm better off up here."

"Hannah, you trusted me to tell you whatever else you should know about me—about what happened six years ago. Will you climb the rocks with me now, and listen?"

She didn't want to. She almost wheeled Ajax's head around and kicked him in the ribs. Her fingers actually twitched on the reins before she stilled them. The urge to gallop away was so startling and so absurd that she sat frozen, staring down at him. Hadn't she decided that it was best this way? She'd stopped those old biddies at the church from giving her their version of Nate's past because she'd thought she should hear it from him first.

That *was* why she'd stopped them, wasn't it?

But she hadn't thought that he would bring it up this soon. And now, looking down at him standing by the granite outcropping, tasting her heartbeat in her throat and with fear ghosting across her mind, she understood that she wasn't as sure of anything as she had thought. Not of him. Not of herself.

But he was waiting. And she couldn't turn away from whatever he wanted to tell her. She swung down from Ajax's back.

"He won't wander," Nate told her. "Leave the reins loose."

The path he had said existed turned out to be a figment of his imagination—or so she informed him when her hat fell off less than halfway up.

Both of her hands lost some skin to the rough rock, and when they reached the top she was breathing hard. It wouldn't have been a bad climb if she hadn't been wearing cowboy boots, but the stacked heels, pointed toes and slick soles that were great for stirrups were more than a little awkward on steeply slanted rock.

But she made it. And maybe something other than exertion had her breath coming quick and shallow when she finally stood beside him on the sloping top. Maybe something stirred inside her just because she stood next to him here, with the wind lifting her hair and the land spread out around them...or maybe that stirring had little to do with the landscape.

She could ignore it. "It's wonderful up here. I can see why you might make the climb often."

"I come when I can, but this is more Mark's spot than mine. At least, it used to be." He moved away, toward a long shelf of rock that ran along one side of the nearly level ridge where they stood.

She followed him slowly.

He stopped where that rocky lip was chest-high to him,

leaned his forearms on it and looked out at the land below. "I can't imagine not living here. Even when things were at their worst, I couldn't give up the ranch and make a life elsewhere. I considered it once—" his mouth twisted up "—for about five minutes."

She joined him. The rock was nearly shoulder-high for her, and blocked much of the rising force of the wind. She, too, leaned on it and looked out at a landscape both sweeping and subtle—a view built of rock and dirt and sky and the way the tiny lives below had woven themselves into the larger life of the land. The sight moved her.

So did the man. For once Nate's expression was easy to read, almost naked as he looked out. The home-hunger she saw burning there brought a lump to her throat. This was a man who needed the land, *this* land, the way some people needed fame or wealth, and others longed for love. "It must have been hard on you, being in jail. Not knowing how long you'd be locked up."

"I made bail," he said. "I had the ranch to stand as surety. But...yes. It was hard." He looked at her curiously. "You don't really have any roots, do you? You moved around as a child, and you're still moving. Harry said you take jobs all over the state."

"Oh, but that's temporary. I know how to handle moving around. Lord, I ought to. I've done it all my life. It's not what I want, but it's okay for now, because I know it won't go on forever."

"You intend to settle down, then?"

"Yes." The wind was picking up. When she turned her head, it blew her hair in her face. She tucked it behind her ear. "I'm going to have a home. It may take me a while— even after I get my degree I won't be earning a fortune—but I'm good at saving money. I know how to be patient."

"Where will you settle?"

She shrugged. "Somewhere in Texas." The wind whisked her hair back in her face.

"So you don't have a place picked out yet." Casually he

reached out and captured a handful of her wind-tossed hair. His knuckles brushed her cheek as he pushed the hair away from her face. "What about a man?" he asked softly. "Do you have a man picked out to settle down with, Hannah?"

"No," she whispered. Her heart was beating too hard. The wind tasted of danger and desire, and she had to swallow before she could speak in a normal voice. Almost normal, anyway. "I need to tell you something."

"Is there a man in your life?"

"No, but—"

"Then it can wait."

"No, it can't. You should know that I have decided not to have a man in my life right now." She spoke firmly, so he would understand and not be misled. "I realize I may have given you the wrong impression earlier, and I wanted to correct that."

His expression didn't change. "I appreciate you setting the record straight."

"I don't want to have any misunderstandings."

He nodded. Slowly, the fingers in her hair relaxed their grip. His hand dropped to his side, and her hair immediately flew in her face again. "I don't, either. Do you understand why I've brought you up here?"

"You want to tell me what happened."

"I want to seduce you."

Her jaw dropped. She had to close her mouth so she could swallow her heart, which had inexplicably jumped up into her throat where it didn't belong. Then she said, very sensibly, "No."

His eyebrow—the bent one—lifted quizzically. "It wouldn't be seduction if you said yes right away. But I won't touch you until I've told you the truth."

She frowned at him, thought about what he'd said, and turned to go. "If that's the only reason you have for telling me, I'll see you back at the ranch." She was leaving. It was the only thing to do. Obviously she'd been a fool to come here with him.

"Don't you want to know, Hannah?"

She ignored him and kept walking. She managed to get four more steps between them before he spoke again and stopped her in her tracks.

"Six years ago, I killed my wife's lover."

She hadn't wanted to know. That was the first, foolish thought that slid through Hannah's mind. Deep down, she'd wanted to keep reality at arm's length, as if ignorance were some sort of shield. Hannah was ashamed to realize that now. She'd been afraid. It was that simple, and that unpalatable. But had she been afraid that the truth would change the way she thought about him? Or had she feared that it wouldn't?

She straightened her shoulders, turned around to face him—and learned something else. She still wanted him.

Nate stood there tall and angry and alone in his blue cotton and faded denim, his midnight eyes daring her to either condemn or forgive him—she wasn't sure which he would hate worse. And she still wanted him. She put one hand on her middle, right where panic swirled and desire clawed, and made herself meet those challenging eyes. "How?"

"In a fight in a bar."

She flinched. "That's sordid."

"Murder usually is."

Telling Hannah had been hard. Harder even than he'd expected. Nate watched her now, standing with her feet planted firmly, her hands clenched at her sides and her spine straight. She looked ready to do battle. The wind whipped her hair in her face again, and she met his gaze squarely through a froth of wild red curls.

"But—it was an *accident*." An erratic gust of wind tossed her hair back out of her eyes for a moment, and he saw them clearly. Please, those soft brown eyes begged. Please tell me again that it was an accident.

Nate had promised that he would never defend himself again. But her eyes looked so sad. "Yes. It was."

"So," she said, and this time she grabbed her hair herself

and kept hold of it, keeping it out of her face, ''how did it happen?''

''Publicly.'' He'd made sure of that, hadn't he? His mouth twisted. ''When Jenny told me about her affair with the two-bit singer who was performing at a local bar, I decided I'd had enough of her games. I dragged her down to the Lucky Chance and gave her to him—up on stage. Ramos didn't like my attitude. We went from words to fists pretty quickly. He was a lot smaller than me, so I held back, but he was still pretty easy to flatten. Then I made a mistake. I turned my back on him.''

''What did he do?''

''He came at me with a knife. I…hit him with everything I had.'' He paused. ''The Lucky Chance had black metal tables back then that were bolted to the floor. It kept people from breaking the furniture whenever there was a fight. When I hit Ramos, he went flying off the stage and fell against one of those tables, and he landed wrong. It broke his neck.''

Her eyes closed for a second, then opened. ''But that's not murder. He had a knife.''

''I threw the first punch.''

She shook her head so vigorously that her hair escaped, whipping itself in her face again. ''But it wasn't on purpose. Why would the jury call it *murder?*''

''Because my wife did.''

''*What?*''

''Jenny told the DA, our neighbors, the jury, anyone who would listen, that I was a madman that night, crazy with jealousy. She said that I went to that bar intending to kill her lover. That I had said so, several times, on the way there.''

Her eyes were wide. ''People say things like that all the time without meaning them.''

''I didn't say one damn word to her once I got her in the truck. I sure as hell didn't threaten her boyfriend's life. I didn't care enough by then.''

''She lied,'' Hannah whispered. ''Dear God. How awful

for you. Why did she do that? Was she so in love with this
man that she had to punish you?''

He laughed, but it didn't come out right. ''Hell, no. She
did everything for love, all right, but it was me she claimed
to love. Jenny came to see me in jail just before the trial to
tell me she was sorry. And how much she loved me.'' His
lip curled in scorn. ''That was always her excuse—*love*. Oh,
she loved me, all right. Told me she couldn't go on without
me, and that she'd lie on the stand for me if I'd take her
back.''

''But she was already lying!''

He shrugged. ''I'm not sure Jenny knew the difference
between her stories and the truth by then.''

''She tried to blackmail you.''

''In a sense.'' He looked away. For some reason, this was
the part that shamed him. He didn't like to talk about any of
the events of that night, but he'd come to terms with the rest
of it pretty well—with his mistakes on that one night, and
with the long folly of his marriage. But he'd never told anyone this part. ''She was frantic when I refused to take her
back. She said she would kill herself if I didn't.''

''Oh, Nate. Did she—try?''

''I don't know.'' He met Hannah's eyes. The coldness inside him was both pain and comfort. ''It wasn't the first time
she'd said that, you see. I didn't really think she'd do it, but
I didn't know for sure. I sent word to her brother so he could
watch her, and all through my trial I waited to see if she
would kill herself. If she did make the attempt, I never heard
about it.''

Hannah looked at him in silence for a moment, then she
came forward. She stood next to him and leaned her forearms
on the shelf of rock once more. ''I thought you hated her.
When you spoke about her, you sounded so angry.''

It had been a long time since Nate had tried to put words
to what he felt about Jenny. ''Maybe I'm angry, but I don't
hate Jenny. She's too pathetic. She got trapped in the great
myth of love back when we were teenagers, and never found

her way out. She wanted love to be everything, the entire world, for both of us. I guess it was, for her.''

"She wanted an excuse not to be responsible for her actions,'' Hannah said tartly. ''That's not love.''

"That's all love is. An excuse.''

She frowned at him in such obvious disapproval that he had to smile. "I can see everything you think, everything you feel, right here.'' He stroked two fingers along the curve of her cheek. Such a simple touch, he thought. But not innocent. It was impossible to touch this woman innocently. "Are you still going to let me touch you, now that you know the truth?''

She shook her head, dislodging his hand. "I wasn't going to let you touch me before.''

His smile deepened. "My mistake.'' He drifted his fingertips down the smooth line of her throat. "I thought you liked it.''

She shivered. He was almost certain that it was from hunger rather than fear. "I like raspberries, but I don't eat them. They give me hives.''

He grinned. "Hannah,'' he said, and took her shoulders in his hands to turn her toward him. "You delight me.'' He threaded his hands into her hair to tilt her face up, stroking his thumbs along the vulnerable underside of her jaw.

Her pulse was jumping beneath his thumbs. Her eyes were smoky with desire; her voice, firm with resolve. "I am not going to kiss you.''

"Now, there's a problem. I guess I'll have to kiss you, instead.'' He was still smiling when he covered her mouth with his.

She was stiff, unmoving. He coaxed her with his tongue, and she tasted good, so good. Even better than he remembered. Kissing Hannah was like swallowing sunshine—a sensation so rich and curious he wanted to spend the next hour getting acquainted with her mouth. Just her mouth.

But sunshine is both light and heat. Even as the light sang in his head, making him dizzy, the heat poured into his body, and his body reacted. He moaned and pulled her closer.

Chapter 10

Hannah would have been all right if Nate hadn't moaned.

She held herself rigid, not pushing him away, maybe, but not cooperating. That was an incredible accomplishment when thrills chased each other over her skin and desire coiled, serpent-like, in her belly. She dug her nails into the palms of her hands so she wouldn't reach for him. She shivered, but didn't open her mouth to that sweetly questing tongue. She closed her eyes as fire licked through her veins, but she didn't move.

In a second—just one more second—she was going to stop him. It wasn't fair to let him continue, not fair at all. And she would put her hands out and push him away just as soon as she could be sure she would be pushing, not pulling. In another second or two, she would do that.

Until he made that sound. Until she knew that he needed, just as she did.

He needed *her*.

Logic shut down. Her hands reached for him even as he pulled her closer, and she fit herself up against him. And, oh,

Lord, but he felt good. Right. His body felt as natural up against hers as breathing, and as new and exciting as a birthday morning with presents waiting.

Her mouth opened to his. His hands slid under her bulky parka, and that was better. Much better. She could feel the heat of his palms on her back, and she wanted to feel him, too. She managed to get her hands up beneath his jacket so she could savor the taut muscles of his back, where he was firm and warm.

Hannah was a tall woman. She wasn't used to feeling small, or to tipping her head back so far to meet a man's mouth. She wasn't used to having a man wrap himself around her the way Nate was, as if she were his entire world. Dimly she remembered that she hadn't intended to kiss Nate, but she couldn't remember why. This felt right. *He* felt right.

When he pulled his mouth away from hers to trace kisses across her face and down her throat, she tilted her head to give him better access. When his hands tightened on her waist and his thigh slid between hers, pressing against her, she moaned and pressed against him.

Then he muttered something—maybe a curse—and pulled his head back. His breath came harsh and fast. "Hannah. Look at me."

Slowly she opened her eyes.

His face was taut with hunger. "There's nothing here but rock. We could find a way to do what we want even here, but we don't have to—not if we stop now, anyway."

"Nate—"

He released her waist to cup her face in his big hands, his fingers threading into her hair. "I want to lay you down, Hannah. I want you on your back somewhere soft, especially this first time, so I can look at your face when I push inside you." He pressed one more kiss to her mouth. "Come home with me. Come to my room."

"I can't—I can't just—Abe will still be there!"

"Tonight, then." He stroked his hands down her hair. "Come to me tonight."

She couldn't do that. Hannah rested her forehead on his shoulder, trying to get her breath and her heart back under control. This is all my fault, she thought, stricken. She'd led him on. There was no way a practical woman like her could take a chance on a man like Nate.

"Hannah?"

She raised her head, looked right into his midnight eyes and said, "Yes."

It would be all right, Hannah told herself on their ride back. They hadn't spoken much after climbing down from the rocky ridge, and the tension winding itself tighter and tighter inside her wasn't purely sexual. But she could handle that. She was a grown woman, after all. She could have an affair with a man without—

"I shouldn't have let you talk me into such a long ride," Nate said.

"What?" She blinked in confusion.

"You're hurting, aren't you?"

Not yet, she thought, and shook her head—more in rejection of her fears than in answer to Nate. "I'm okay."

"Sure you are. You've been scooting around in that saddle like you had fleas for the last ten minutes."

Ever since they got back on the horses, actually. But she wasn't doing it because her thighs hurt. "I'm a little sore, but I...it's been a long time," she said, and she wasn't talking about riding.

He didn't answer. Instead, he kneed Kami, bringing her up so close to Ajax that the gelding automatically tried to shift away. Hannah held the horse in place, looking at Nate curiously.

He held out his hand to her.

She hesitated only a second before reaching out to take it. As soon as he touched her, the coils of fear eased, even as those cast by desire tightened. Tears startled Hannah by suddenly sheening her vision, so that she had to blink rapidly to keep them from escaping.

Something was happening inside her. Something large and important and frightening. Something other than lust.

Nate's hand was warm and rough and comforting, but holding hands with him gave her no answers.

But then, she hadn't dared ask any questions.

They rode in silence for several minutes, the sun bright overhead and the wind chilly around them, holding hands. Hannah found herself thinking about her word for the day: *chimera—a mythological monster with a lion's head, a goat's body and a serpent's tail; an unreal creature of the imagination.*

Hannah's imagination had conjured plenty of monsters when she was a child. She'd lain awake on far too many nights, staring into the darkness of an unfamiliar bedroom in a new house, afraid to move. Oh, she'd known there wasn't really a monster under her bed, waiting to grab any stray body part she was careless enough to let stick out over the edge of the mattress. Her big sister had told her that often enough. Then and now, Leslie had had an irritating habit of being right about most things.

That hadn't kept Hannah from tucking all the covers up under the mattress before she went to bed. After every move, especially, she'd had to make sure none of the covers hung down to the floor where the monster could get on them and climb up and get her. Because however imaginary the monster might have been, the fear had been all too real.

When a stand of mesquite made Nate drop her hand so their horses could make their separate ways around the thorny growth, Hannah shivered. The feelings fluttering to life inside her were as unlikely as any chimera. And all too real.

The hand who'd drawn Sunday duty this week was waiting by the barn when they returned. At eighteen, he was the youngest of Nate's employees, but he seemed steady and as sensible as anyone ever is at that age. So when he told Nate that he needed to come have a look at King Lear, Nate set aside his intention of going up to the house with Hannah.

It was just as well, he decided as he swung down from his horse. He needed time to get his body back under control.

Hannah had agreed to come to him. Tonight.

Triumph sang sweetly in his blood. He went to her as she dismounted, wanting an excuse to touch her again. But because Felix waited nearby, Nate did no more than lay his hand on her shoulder. Soon, he thought. Soon he would have the right to do a great deal more. "I'll be along later."

She smiled, but he saw the doubts crowded up behind her eyes. "Does that mean you're actually going to join Mark and me for supper tonight?"

"You're not thinking of cooking, are you? Today's your day off." And just this once he didn't want to share her with his brother. "I'll fix something and take it to Mark."

"I don't mind cooking."

She was having second thoughts. He knew it, and frustration bit hard. He pulled his hand back before giving in to the impulse to clamp down harder, to hold on so tightly she'd quit trying wiggle free. "We'll talk later."

Felix was obviously eaten up with curiosity as he walked with Nate to the barn, but he didn't ask any questions.

Nate did. "What happened?"

"A mouse got in his stall."

Nate sighed. King Lear hated mice. The bull's reaction would have been funny if it didn't cause so much trouble. "You said he didn't do himself too much damage."

"Scraped up one of his hocks some, that's all. But he nearly kicked one side of his stall into splinters."

Nate looked over the damage, both to King Lear—placid now that no tiny rodents were darting under his feet—and to his stall. He checked the weather report, and decided to let the repairs wait until tomorrow. It wouldn't hurt the bull to stay out in the paddock a couple of days.

Then he went to the house.

It was five-thirty and he needed to come up with something to fix for supper. He wondered if there was enough roast left for a second round of sandwiches, or whether he'd have to fall back on opening some cans of chili. As soon as he opened the door, though, he smelled chicken.

Nate shook his head when he walked into the kitchen. Hannah sat at the big table, reading a magazine. "You don't listen worth a damn, do you?"

"What?" She looked up from the magazine—an old issue of *Farm and Ranch*. He felt a touch of guilt. She'd never made it to the library that day they went to town. After the encounter with Mario and his friends, he'd taken her back to Jenks's, loaded up the groceries and headed straight home. "Oh, you mean the chicken? I just cut one up and put it on to boil with a little bay leaf. You can figure out what to do with it now that you're back."

He gave the pot a dubious glance. Chicken sandwiches, maybe? "Do you like to read?" he asked.

"Love it," she said promptly. "I usually don't travel without a book or two, but I didn't have time to pick any up before I came here."

Didn't have the time, or didn't have the money? "I've got some old paperbacks in my office—thrillers, mostly. I don't know if they'd be your type, but I'd be glad to dig a couple out if you like."

"What, no Louis L'Amour or Elmer Kelton?" She grinned. "I don't think my dad has ever read any book cover-to-cover except for Louis L'Amour's westerns."

"My father used to read Louis L'Amour." The scene came back to him suddenly—his father sitting in the big, green recliner with his sock-clad feet on the footrest, one of his western novels in his lap and his reading glasses sliding down his nose. As far back as Nate could remember, Garwood Jones had only owned one pair of reading glasses and they had never fit right. There had been three cone-shaped lights on the floor lamp beside the recliner. One had always been turned off; another always pointed at the recliner for Nate's father to read by; the third had been directed at the pale blue armchair where Nate's mother had sat, working on one of her endless needlepoint projects.

After her death, Garwood never sat in the recliner again. "Back when I was growing up, he read a lot in the evenings. All sorts of books—everything from Louis L'Amour to Steinbeck. I don't think I ever saw him read any kind of fiction after my mother died."

"You said that her death took a lot out of him."

"That's one way to put it." His gaze focused on her and the present once more. "He missed her to his dying day, and he never understood why. I don't think he understood anything except ownership. As far as he was concerned, he owned the ranch, his wife and his sons, along with a good part of the county and the people in it."

"He…wasn't as well-liked as your mother was, I take it."

"A lot of people couldn't stand him." He met her eyes steadily. "And a lot of people will tell you I'm just like him."

"Nonsense. You don't think you own people."

"I've got his temper and his selfishness."

"Well, I have noticed some traces of a temper—though for my money, Mark has you beat there—but you aren't selfish."

"Don't fool yourself. I'm determined to have you in my bed, and my motives are entirely selfish."

Her throat moved when she swallowed. For a moment she looked at him, her eyes large and uncertain, and he wondered what kind of an idiot he was for giving her another reason to change her mind.

Then she pushed her chair back and stood. "Listen, do you know how to make dumplings?"

"What?"

"I'm craving dumplings," she explained, heading for the pantry. "If you don't know how to make them, I'd be glad to show you. It's easy. We'll put some vegetables in, too. When I mentioned chicken and dumplings to Mark, he really—oh, darn, I nearly forgot to tell you. Mark wanted you to stop by his room when you got back."

* * *

Nate strode down the hall, wondering what had made Mark ask for him. Not once since his brother came home from the hospital had he asked Nate to come see him. He didn't seem to mind when Nate stopped by to visit, though, so Nate kept coming around. Sooner or later, he figured, Mark would realize he could depend on him. Sooner or later the failures and constraints of the past would fade.

But Mark wasn't waiting for his brother when Nate reached the door of his room. He was asleep.

Nate stood in the doorway and looked at his little brother, and some unknown feeling took him by the throat and squeezed. Feelings hit him like that sometimes, quickly and desperately. When they did, he could no more name them than he could smell music or sort the wind.

Like the first time he'd seen Mark after the accident. His brother had lain there naked and broken beneath a white sheet in that bed in CCU, hooked up to beeping machines, with tubes at his nose, his arm and his groin. Nate's throat had gotten so tight he'd thought he was going to pass out.

What kind of name did you put on a feeling like that?

Mark's color was better now, thank God, the lines of pain smoothed away. One of his arms was outflung. The other, the one in the cast, was cradled protectively close, and the sheet and blanket were drawn up over his chest.

He still slept the way he had when he was little.

When Mark had first come to them all those years ago, Nate's mother had still been alive. Every night at bedtime she'd tucked Mark in just the way he was tucked in now, with the covers drawn up to his chest and his arms free. He'd been a scrawny little kid, all wary eyes and tangled hair. And dirty. Nate didn't know much about Mark's life before he came to them, but what he did know wasn't good.

Three years after Mark joined their family, Nate's mother died. Her death hit them all hard, but Mark had been really lost. Their father hadn't been much help, since he was convinced sentiment softened a boy, so Nate had started tucking

Mark in at night. He'd done that until Mark decided he was too old for that sort of thing.

Nate stood in the doorway and watched his brother sleeping. He thought about waking Mark up to see what he'd wanted, but in the end he turned around and let him sleep.

Hannah was delighted when she found out that Nate planned to eat with her and Mark. The brothers needed to spend some time together, or how would they work out whatever troubled their relationship?

Her rosy attitude didn't last long.

Nate kept touching her. The whole time they were setting up trays and bringing the supper things into Mark's room, he found excuses to put his hands on her. He caressed her arm when they came into the room together. He stood too close, his hand resting on her shoulder, while she set out plates. He touched the back of her hand when he spoke. It confused her. Shouldn't she enjoy being touched by the man she'd agreed to go to bed with? But she didn't like it. Oh, he stirred her, she couldn't deny that—her body responded with a yearning that was far less subtle than his light touches. But he was making her uncomfortable, too.

She didn't understand why until they sat down to eat.

The meal didn't start out too badly. When Mark found out that Nate had cooked the chicken and dumplings, he teased his brother about it. Nate took the teasing well enough, then mentioned someone named Earl who was giving a party next Friday.

Mark looked interested. "The Navarretes are having a party?"

"That's right. Everyone's invited, of course—you know Earl. He claimed the party is for Susie, but I don't know if that's true."

"Why wouldn't it be?" Hannah asked, confused. "And who's Susie?"

"His wife. You'll like her. Hannah, I want you to go with me."

She shook her head. "I don't think that's a good idea."

"You aren't worried about what people would think, are you?"

"Of course I am. It could be very awkward if everyone thought—well, you know how people are. You're my boss. It would look odd for me to go as your date."

"Hey, what about me?" Mark said quickly. "Aren't I invited, too?"

"Of course you are," Nate said irritably.

"Well, then." Mark smiled at both of them. "Why don't we all go together? No food for the gossips in that."

Nate didn't look as if he appreciated Mark's suggestion. "Since when have you worried about what the gossips said?"

Mark shrugged and broke a roll in half. "Just because you and I are used to that sort of thing doesn't mean Hannah should have to put up with it if it bothers her." He looked at her, a speculative gleam in his eyes. "So, Hannah, did you enjoy your ride this afternoon?"

"I loved it. Of course, I may give you a different answer tomorrow," she said ruefully, "when some of the muscles I abused today start reporting in."

"I wouldn't be surprised. You were gone a long time for someone who hasn't been on a horse in a while."

"We weren't riding the whole time," Nate said blandly.

Surely he didn't mean that as suggestively as it sounded. Hannah gave him a quick frown and said to Mark, "We rode out to a large outcropping of rock. Nate showed me the way to the top. The view was gorgeous."

"Lookout Rock?" Mark raised his eyebrows. "That's kind of a long ride for someone who's not used to it."

"Hannah held up just fine." Nate met Mark's curious look straight on. "She was on the right mount. That can make all the difference to a woman."

This time Hannah couldn't mistake his meaning. She stared at him, and all at once she understood why Nate's touches had bothered her. He hadn't been touching her because he wanted to. No, it had all been for his brother's benefit. Nate was staking some sort of sexual claim on her, showing Mark that he had the *right* to touch her. Like she was some kind of sexual trophy.

Suddenly Hannah wasn't hungry anymore.

"That wasn't necessary," Mark said, tight-lipped.

Nate shrugged and reached for his glass. "I don't agree."

"That's clear enough. Once a bastard, always a bastard, right?"

"Dammit, Mark, I've never thought of you that way, and you know it!"

Hannah looked from one angry face to the other. This was getting unpleasant, fast. She pushed her tray away, thinking it was time for her to leave.

Mark's lip lifted in a sneer. "Don't rush off before you find out what we're talking about. I'm the bastard in the room, not Nate. In both senses of the word."

"That's enough, Mark," Nate said warningly.

"Don't you think Hannah should know? Everyone else sure does. The whole town knew about it the entire time our father was carrying on with my mother, right up until she got sick of the scene and dumped me on his doorstep. Isn't that part of the reason you've had your hands all over Hannah tonight? You wanted to make sure I'm not following in the old man's footsteps and grabbing at anything in skirts?"

Nate stood. In complete silence, he left the room.

Hannah sat there, shaken and miserable. Gradually, the certainty grew in her that what she'd heard, unpleasant as it had been, had skirted around the underlying problem between the brothers rather than uncovering it. Nate didn't hate his brother for having been illegitimate. And Mark knew that.

She was beginning to have a sick suspicion about what that problem might be.

Finally Mark stirred slightly, glancing at her, then away. "I'm sorry."

She stood. "You want to tell me what that was all about?"

He was silent for a long moment. "No. I don't think I do."

Chapter 11

Hannah was glad to get out of that room. She was glad, too, that the kitchen was empty. She didn't know where Nate had gone, but she was sure she wasn't ready to see him. Not yet. Not until she had some idea of what it was she was feeling, other than confused.

After the way he'd acted in there, she ought to be furious. Why wasn't she?

A frown lingered on Hannah's face as she scraped the leftovers from their plates into a big bowl for Trixie, but the expression arose from thought tinged by sadness, not anger. Nate had behaved badly, yes, but his behavior had been aimed at Mark, not her. She didn't want to jump to conclusions. She was trying not to do that, but it was hard not to assume that the trouble between the brothers, which had flared up so suddenly tonight over her, must have begun in a situation involving another woman.

Jenny.

She squirted dish soap into the sink, turned on the faucet and told herself not to speculate when she had so little to go on. She picked up the pot that the chicken and dumplings had cooked in. There was enough left for lunch tomorrow, so she went hunting for a container.

Maybe Mark had had a crush on his brother's wife. It wouldn't be the first time such a thing happened. And if Nate had known about it—no, that alone wouldn't make him act the way he had tonight. Mark had been very young when Nate married—fifteen or so. Surely Nate wouldn't bear a grudge all these years over an adolescent crush. There was more to it.

She shut off the water. It wasn't any of her business. Maybe her instincts were shouting at her that an important key to understanding Nate and his attitude toward her lay hidden in the scene with Mark tonight. It didn't matter, because she couldn't still be considering going to him—not after the way he'd behaved.

Could she?

Hannah emptied what was left of the chicken and dumplings into the container she'd found. Nate was a man scarred by his past. A woman like herself—a practical woman, who knew how easily she could be hurt—shouldn't want to have anything to do with a man like that.

But she did.

She scowled and soothed herself by scrubbing the pot. For Hannah, the need for clean dishes and decent meals was a reassuring constant. When all else in her life was chaos, she knew she could take care of the basics.

She made a lot of decisions impulsively. Nine times out of ten, that worked out fine. The way she saw it, decisions always resulted in some sort of problems, anyway, no matter how fast or slow you made up your mind. So why drag things out? Tonight, though, she was deep-down, heart-and-soul undecided. She could see all too many reasons to change her mind about going to Nate tonight, and only one to follow through.

She wanted him. Oh, how she did want him.

It would be nice, she thought wistfully, if she could empty

herself of feelings as readily as she'd emptied and cleaned out the cooking pot. If that were so, she wouldn't hesitate about going to bed with Nate. Wanting was easy.

But she didn't just *want* Nate. She was a hairsbreadth away from falling in love with him. And, dammit, she didn't want to be in love with a man who looked her in the eye and told her love was a myth. An *excuse*. Scowling, she finished wiping down the counter and slapped the dishrag back in the sink. She didn't want to be in love at all. It was sure to interfere with her goals.

She picked up Trixie's bowl and headed for the side door. She'd started feeding the dog a few scraps every night, and Trixie had quickly figured out what time she needed to show up at the house for her treat. When Hannah opened the door, the big Lab was waiting, her tail wagging a mile a minute.

Hannah stepped outside. The crescent moon hung low in a sky as dark and unrevealing as Nate's eyes, and the temperature had dropped along with the wind.

She set the bowl down and stood there hugging herself for warmth, unwilling to go back in yet. Nate was devoted to Trixie, and unwilling—or unable—to admit it. What chance did a woman have with a man who trusted his heart so little he couldn't even admit he loved his dog?

Hannah was contemplating that unhappy question when Trixie lifted her head and turned to face the darkness, growling.

"What is it, girl?" She remembered how Trixie had acted on the night the sheriff came and she moved away from the house, looking for headlights.

Trixie let out one belly-deep *woof* and took off running across the yard toward the barn. Hannah hesitated, unable to decide if she should go after Trixie or go get Nate.

The flat *crack* of a rifle split the silence, followed by the enraged bellow of a bull. Hannah quit thinking, and acted.

She ran after the dog.

Trixie was barking as she vanished around the corner of the barn. Hannah ran after her, but slowed when she reached

the barn. Impulse had brought her this far, but the light set
high on the outside of the barn didn't reach the paddocks or
the rough area beyond.

What should she do next?

The door to the bunkhouse, which lay some fifty yards on
the other side of the house from the cow barn, flew open.
Someone called out a question.

Trixie's barking grew more insistent even as it faded
slightly with distance.

A second gunshot smacked the night.

Instinct nearly sent Hannah around the corner, but common sense prevailed.

She flung open the small door to the barn. A forty-watt
bulb gave enough light for her to grab the flashlight that sat
on a shelf near the entrance, and the hammer someone had
left sitting out after working on King Lear's stall.

She spun around—and swallowed a scream.

Nate stood in the shadowed doorway. He grabbed her
shoulders. "You little fool, what do you think you're doing,
running around out here when someone's shooting?"

"The same thing as you!"

He grabbed the flashlight out of her hand. "Stay here."

Of course she followed him out the door.

He turned back around. "Dammit, Hannah!"

"You don't have a weapon," she said, and held out the
hammer.

He took it from her, shook his head and moved quickly
off into the darkness.

Hannah waited several seconds so he would get far enough
ahead that he wouldn't try to stop her. As she rounded the
corner of the barn, she heard an engine in the distance. The
sound came from the other side of the row of elms that lined
the mile-long driveway leading to the house.

The light from Nate's flashlight moved across the rough
ground beyond the paddocks. She hurried after it, and prayed.

Headlights came on, shining through the skeletal limbs of
the trees lining the drive. Hannah left the yard behind for the

scrubby grass and weeds in the strip of land between the paddocks and the driveway. It was dark and the ground was rough, and her heart was trying to pound its way right out of her chest.

Nate's flashlight beckoned her, but it would give the shooter a target, too.

The motor of the vehicle revved. The headlights took off down the driveway, heading for the main road. Thank God, she thought. They're leaving. She tripped over a rock in the darkness and moved faster.

Nate's low-voiced curses reached her seconds before she caught up with him. She jerked to a stop. The flashlight lay on the ground beside him, its beam throwing light and shadows across Nate where he knelt in the dirt next to Trixie's motionless body.

Almost everything in the vet's waiting room was some shade of brown. The walls were beige, the wooden counter was stained a dark brown, and brown tiles covered the floor. Behind that counter, high on the beige wall, was a white-faced clock just like the one at the bus station. It read 8:05. Three drops of blood on the brown floor pointed toward the door to the rear of the facility, where the vet and his assistant worked to save Trixie.

Hannah sat on one of the battered brown benches that matched the counter, and watched Nate pace.

He'd hardly spoken since they arrived twenty minutes ago. He'd sit for a minute or two, then get up and pace, then sit again. Then pace. He'd been pacing for five minutes now, and would undoubtedly try sitting again soon.

Hannah couldn't stand it. "Trixie will be all right, Nate. I really believe that. The bleeding had stopped by the time we got here."

He stopped and stared at her as if she'd said something unbelievably foolish. "She'd lost too much blood already. You said yourself, it looked like the bullet hit a vein."

"A vein, not an artery." She'd told him that twice already—once when she first reached him, and again when they loaded Trixie in the back of his truck for the ride into town. "The blood wasn't spurting. And you kept pressure on it all the way in." Hannah had driven them here because Nate wouldn't let her ride in the back of the pickup with Trixie. He'd done that himself.

"She lost enough blood to go into shock."

"That's why we wrapped her in a blanket before we left the house."

Nate looked at the door that led to the interior of the clinic. He'd carried Trixie in her bloody blanket down the short hall on the other side of that door. The three drops of blood had come from the blanket. He'd wanted to stay back there with her, but Hannah had persuaded him to come out to the waiting room with her. The treatment room was small, and the vet had wanted them out of his way.

Nate's hands clenched at his sides, then opened again. "What's taking him so long? What are they doing in there?"

"Dr. Axell said he was going to get an I.V. started to plump out her veins. Shock constricts them, you know. That's why it's dangerous. But he's taking care of that now. It just takes a while."

"How long?"

She had no answer for him, and shook her head.

"Maybe he's operating." Nate's hands opened and closed, opened and closed.

"I don't think they do that right away."

"But he'll have to do something. Her leg is a mess. The bullet tore it up, broke the bone—he'll have to fix it." He turned blind eyes on Hannah. "Trixie has to be able to run. It just wouldn't be right if she couldn't run anymore."

She couldn't stand it. She stood and went to him and put her arms around him. He didn't move. "She'll be able to run," she promised softly. "Even if it's on three legs, she'll run again."

"No, he has to fix her leg." Nate stood there stiffly as if

he were unsure how to go about accepting comfort. "Do you think we got her here in time?"

Hannah blinked back the tears that were trying to fill her eyes. She wished he would go ahead and cry. Maybe then *she* wouldn't have to. "I think so."

"It's my fault," he said.

"What?"

"They were trying to shoot my bull, and they shot my dog."

"How does that make it your fault? And anyway, we don't know what they were after. José said it didn't look like King Lear was hurt."

"There's not much on that side of the barn for them to shoot at. Just the paddock where King Lear spends his days—and where he was spending the night this one time."

She leaned back, holding his arms. "Well, that proves one thing. You have to call the sheriff."

He shook his head. "He can't do anything." His eyes turned hard and cold. "I can."

Her heart stumbled. "Nate, let the law handle this."

"The law concerns itself with evidence, not justice."

She was *not* scared, Hannah told herself, because Nate had too much sense to do something stupid that would end up with him behind bars again. "You're not going to go beat anyone up," she told him firmly. "You don't even know who did it."

"I can guess." He pulled away and started to pace again.

"Sheriff Thompson is already looking for whoever has been shooting the cattle around here."

"It may not be the same person. All the other cattle were shot from the highway. Tonight, someone went way out of their way to shoot, not just a cow, but a bull worth thousands of dollars."

"But you just said they couldn't have known the bull would be out in the paddock where they could get to it."

"Maybe they didn't care what they shot, as long as it was something that would hurt me."

Because that seemed possible, she was silenced for a moment. She watched him start his blasted pacing again. "So who do you think did it?"

"I'm not sure. If I knew for sure…" His fists clenched again. "It might have been Ben Rydell. He hates my guts, and he's convinced I'm the one who shot *his* cows. He might have decided to even the score on his own. The only thing is…"

It did sound plausible. "What?"

"Rydell keeps three or four dogs around his place all the time. Hell, the man rescues strays. It's hard to imagine him shooting Trixie."

How could anyone shoot a dog? Especially someone who loved animals. "Then it couldn't be him."

"If Trixie was coming at him like she meant business, he could have panicked. He might not have thought he had any choice but to shoot. Then there's Bustamante."

"Who?"

He looked impatient. "Mario Bustamante. The creep who keeps hassling you. He didn't like the way I took him down in front of his buddies the other day, and he's the sort who wouldn't mind killing an innocent animal to get back at someone who had humiliated him."

"And how do you plan to find out which of them it was— *if* it was one of them?" She moved closer to him. "Nate, call the sheriff and let him do his job."

"Dammit, he can't *do* anything! If they'd shot my bull, then, yeah—King Lear is worth enough to put someone behind bars. But a dog?" He shook his head. "Thompson isn't going to be able to do a damn thing."

"He might!" Anger, frustration and fear made a sick lump in the pit of her stomach, because Nate was right. The law didn't punish a person for killing a beloved pet—just for destroying property. "Look, I don't blame you for wanting to make someone pay, but I don't want you going to jail."

"I'm not going to go to jail."

"Oh, so you're not going to do anything about this?"

He didn't answer.

That was answer enough. She walked over to the counter. Behind it, on the desktop, sat an old-fashioned black rotary phone. She moved the phone so she could open the thin phone book that rested beneath it.

"What the hell do you think you're doing?"

"Looking up the number for the sheriff." She found it and picked up the receiver.

"Hang up."

Hannah looked at the raw anger in his face. She didn't hang up, but she didn't start dialing, either. "What is it you're thinking? That as long as you don't talk to the sheriff, you can go beat up whoever did this and he won't know you did it?" She shook her head. "You're not usually an idiot, Nate."

For another instant he glared at her. Then, all at once, the fury drained out of him. He rubbed his hand over his face like the tired, worried man that he was. "You're right. Thompson will hear about this whether I talk to him or not. I'm not thinking. I just..." His gaze drifted once more to the door to the treatment room. "They've been back there a long time. If things were going well, it wouldn't take this long, would it?"

"It might. The vet said it would take a while to stabilize her. And as long as they're back there, still working on Trixie, we know she's alive."

He didn't turn around. "I guess I might as well talk to the sheriff while I'm waiting."

She started dialing.

Sheriff Thompson was a slender man, a couple of inches shorter than Hannah. He had dark hair, a tidy mustache and knife-edged creases in his khaki-colored slacks. He took Nate's statement first, and by the time he'd finished, he obviously shared Hannah's opinion of Nate's intentions. He closed his notebook and fixed Nate with a warning stare.

"You stay away from Rydell, Jones. Keep away from young Bustamante, too. I'll check them out."

Nate's expression was stony. "Just be sure you do your job."

If the sheriff was intimidated by the fact that Nate was nearly a foot taller and fifty pounds heavier, it didn't show. "I always do. I'll talk to Rydell tonight. In the morning, when it's light, I'll send a deputy out to your ranch. You think it was a .22 he used?"

"Yeah. I heard the second shot clearly."

"We'll try to recover the bullet or bullets, then. We've had ballistics run on the bullets we've recovered from the cattle that have been shot, so we'll be able to find out if this was done by the same person. If so, he'll probably be charged with shooting the cattle rather than with shooting your dog— unless we can get him for shooting at your bull, even though he missed. I'll have to run the possibility by the DA."

"*If* you get him."

"Oh, I'll get him, sooner or later. And if it's the same shooter, you'll at least have the satisfaction of knowing he's locked up. Did the bullet lodge in your animal?"

"No. It hit her hind leg, breaking the bone." For about the fourteenth time since the sheriff arrived, he glanced at the closed door to the treatment room.

The sheriff turned to Hannah. "You didn't see the vehicle the shooter drove?"

She shook her head. "It was too dark, and the driveway is too far from the barn. But I don't think it was a truck. The headlights were too low, more where a car's lights would be."

"Mr. Jones said that when he responded to the first shot fired, he saw you go into the barn. Why were you out there?"

"Because of Trixie. I'd stepped outside to feed her some scraps. She must have heard something, because…" Without warning, Hannah's eyes filled. She could *see* that half-eaten bowl of scraps waiting back at the house. Her voice broke. "She didn't get to finish her treat."

At that moment, the door Nate had been watching for so long opened. A fiftyish man in jeans, a beard, a ponytail and a green scrub top came into the waiting area. He looked pleased. "You folks can go on home."

Nate took one quick step toward the vet. "Is she—?"

"She's out of danger. Her color's good—the mucous membranes in the mouth, you know, turn pale when a dog is shocky. Her blood pressure is up where it should be and holding steady. I'll keep her here, of course. She needs to be stable for twenty-four hours before I can operate on that leg."

Hannah saw the strain and relief on Nate's face, and read love there, helpless and mute. Because he couldn't find his voice, she spoke for him. "What about her leg?"

"The bullet fractured the femur in mid-shaft, which means I can't cast it. I'll have to use plates and pins."

"But will she run? Once she heals, I mean. Will Trixie be able to run?"

Dr. Axell smiled at them through his salt-and-pepper beard. "She's young. She'll heal fast. If I do my job right, she'll be running all over the place in six weeks."

Relief didn't exactly transform Nate's expression. For a second, he closed his eyes. She thought she saw his lips move, and his chest rose and fell in a single deep breath. Hannah had no idea how she could tell, from those small signs, that the relief sweeping through him was as vast and very nearly as desperate as his worry had been. She just knew.

She knew something else, too. Soft as a whisper, sure as a sunrise, the truth drifted into her mind. That "funny feeling" wasn't just in her stomach. It was in every part of her—blood and bone, muscle and sinew. And heart. And it was too late to worry about falling in love with this man. Much too late.

The sheriff agreed that his deputy could ask Hannah any further questions when he came out the next day, and Nate and Hannah were free to leave.

It was only a quarter past nine, but she felt as if it were after midnight by the time she climbed into the truck and pulled the door closed. Nate already sat behind the wheel. "Whew," she said, pushing her hair out of her face. "I don't know about you, but I'm wiped out. That was as nerve-racking as any visit I've ever paid to an emergency room."

"You have a kind heart."

His words startled her. She looked over at him. He sat in the darkness with his arms crossed over the steering wheel. He hadn't started the truck. She put her hand on his arm. "Are you okay?"

He didn't look at her. "It's stupid to get this worked up over a dog."

"Why?" Her fingers curled around his arm.

"They don't live long. You can't afford to get attached. That's what my father always..." Suddenly he sat back, releasing the steering wheel and pulling away from her touch. "God, I didn't think I'd hung on to much of anything from him, but I guess I did." He shook his head. "The old man wouldn't let me have a dog. He thought a rancher who got sentimental about animals was a fool. After he was gone—I was married by then, and Jenny didn't want pets. She said it was because we were planning to have kids right away, and the pets would be neglected when we had babies to take care of."

"You don't think that was the reason?"

"Hell, no. She didn't want children." He leaned forward and started the truck. The air that blew from the vents was cold. "Oh, she said she did. For a year after we got married, I thought we were trying to have a baby—right up until the day I found the birth control pills she'd hidden. She'd been taking them all along. I was worrying that maybe one of us was infertile, while she—" He put the truck in gear. "As it turned out, she was right. We were much better off not having children."

She was quiet as he pulled out of the parking lot.

The veterinary clinic was situated just north of Bitter

Creek. A few houses dribbled out from town along the narrow blacktop road, but those lights were few and scattered. Hannah looked out the window beside her, and saw little but darkness.

Nate might say that it was better he and Jenny hadn't had children. He might even believe that, but she thought part of him grieved for the children he didn't have. Just as part of her grieved for the boy who hadn't been allowed to love a pet. "Is Trixie the first dog you ever owned?"

"Yes."

"She's going to be all right, you know."

Nate was silent until he'd turned off the quiet blacktop road onto the highway that led to the ranch. "I got her as a pup. She was a real handful at first, but she's turned into a good dog."

"She sure has. She saved your bull."

"Dammit, I didn't want her to do that! I didn't get her so she could go get herself shot. I didn't want that."

"I know." She wanted to reassure him, and didn't know how. "How did you decide on her, anyway?"

"When I decided to get a dog, I read up about the different breeds."

"Labradors are often used as hunting dogs, aren't they? Did you train her to—"

"I don't hunt."

That's right. He couldn't own a gun. So...Nate had carefully researched the breeds before buying his first dog and he'd chosen a Labrador, but not because he intended to hunt. It must have been some of the breed's other characteristics he'd been attracted to—like intelligence, playfulness, loyalty, a loving nature.

Labs weren't loners.

Hannah rubbed her chest. He was making her heart hurt. "It's okay for you to love your dog."

"I don't...I'm used to her, that's all. Attached."

He couldn't admit to the word, but he was more than capable of the feeling. "How old is Trixie?" How long had it been after his unloving father and his crazy wife were out of his life before Nate took a chance on caring for something again?

"Only two. That's why I wanted the vet to fix her leg. She's young. She needs to be able to run."

Only two. A band tightened around her heart. That meant it had taken Nate four years to take the risk of caring about a dog. How much longer would it be before he was ready to gamble on a woman?

And was she sure she wanted him to?

Dammit, she hadn't planned on this. She had *goals.* Hadn't she spent seven years digging herself out of the hole she'd fallen into the *first* time she'd been in love? But what she felt now was so different from the jumble of cravings and dreams she'd bestowed on her nineteen-year-old bridegroom all those years ago. And Nate was nothing like Barry.

She looked over at him. The light from the dash cast a greenish glow on his face. He drove with both hands on the wheel, his eyes straight ahead, and his mind, from what she could tell, a thousand miles away.

He was a straightforward kind of man. She liked that. There were so many things she liked…the strength that had carried him through the last six years and the integrity that had made him tell her about the night he caused a man's death.

Then there was his body.

Hannah had to smile at the way her pulse picked up when she thought about Nate's body. No doubt it was shockingly superficial of her, but she couldn't deny it—she was fascinated with the man's body. But love? How could she love a man she'd known such a short time?

Yet how could she not love him? She remembered the day he'd saved her from Mario and the others when she'd tried to walk to the library. Even on the night they'd met, when he'd thought the worst of her, he'd moved quickly and surely to protect her from the creeps at the bus station. He was a man whose honor went bone-deep.

She thought about the way he was with Trixie, and the way he had leaped at the chance to do something for his brother. Nate was also a man with so much love to give it kept him knotted up inside...even if he didn't know it. Even if he couldn't say the word ''love'' without his mouth twisting in derision.

What was she going to do?

What was the right thing to do?

Chapter 12

Hannah had hardly spoken since they left the vet's. Nate hoped she was just tired, but he couldn't help wondering, as he parked the truck beside the house, if he'd managed to screw things up earlier. He sensed that she was considering changing her mind about him and her decision to come to him. And he wanted her. Tonight. He ached for her.

Maybe he should apologize.

Women put a lot of stock in words—pretty words, words of explanation and declaration. Nate didn't understand that. Actions didn't lie the way words could. Women wanted sweet words tied up in promises, and he had none to give. He had thought Hannah might be different, that maybe she could see behind the words he lacked to what he *did* have. He'd hoped...but Nate didn't approve of hope.

He frowned, hardening himself against that frail and futile enemy. He turned the engine off. "I'll get Mark ready for bed."

"Hmm? Oh, yes." She opened the door without looking at him.

He shouldn't have said anything about Jenny. He'd talked about his ex-wife twice today, and maybe the first discussion had been necessary so Hannah would know the truth, but the second time… What had possessed him to mention her again? Women didn't want a man to think about anyone or anything but them. Nate slammed the truck door behind him. "I don't think about her very often anymore."

She wrinkled her nose in puzzlement as she rounded the truck's hood. "What?"

Great. She hadn't even been thinking about Jenny, and now he'd brought her up again. "Never mind." He went to the side door and unlocked it. He could have sworn he felt Hannah standing behind him on the stoop, only that didn't make sense. He didn't feel the warmth from her body, not with both of them in jackets. She wasn't wearing any scent. And she wasn't moving, so he didn't hear her.

But he felt her.

The kitchen light was still on. Nate started for the hall. Then he stopped, turned around and frowned at her. "We'll talk after I get Mark settled." He didn't know what the hell they were supposed to talk about, but she could damn well tell him.

She had her head tilted to one side as if she were curious about him, her hands in the pockets of her parka. "Okay. I guess I'd better finish the dishes."

"It's your day off."

"I don't want them staring at me from the sink when I get up in the morning." She slipped off her jacket and draped it over the back of one of the kitchen chairs.

"Hannah…"

"Yes?"

He knew he should say something. But what? The things that came to mind—*I want you, take off your clothes, don't change your mind about me*— weren't likely to fix whatever he'd done wrong. "Never mind." Frustrated, he started for his brother's room.

Abe was there. Nate told both of them about Trixie's condition so Abe could pass the news on to the hands, and Abe reported on King Lear, who hadn't suffered so much as a scratch. Nate shook his head. "I can't decide if the shooter was lucky but basically a lousy shot, or unlucky but a great shot. He hit a dark brown dog on a moonless night, and missed a thousand pounds of bull."

"King Lear doesn't show up too good in the darkness," Abe pointed out. "Besides, I figure Trixie startled him, running at him the way she did and barking her fool head off. She made him miss his shot."

"Maybe."

"He had a lot more range when he was shootin' at the bull, too. I took the light out there and looked around. Think I know where he was standing. He didn't get very close. Probably wanted to stay near enough to his vehicle so's he could make his getaway."

"Guess he had that part figured pretty well, then. He did get away." Nate shifted restlessly. He wanted to be with Hannah.

"Thompson's no dummy. He'll find out who did it."

Nate gave Abe a skeptical look.

Mark spoke. "Thompson was just a deputy six years ago, Nate. No point in blaming him for what the fat fool who held office before him did."

Nate met his brother's eyes. He understood that Mark wanted to put their argument behind them, and he was willing to do that. "Same glory-hunting DA, though. He's not going to put much energy into prosecuting a case like this. He can't get much press from convicting someone for shooting cows."

"Thompson will do his job," Abe insisted.

Nate didn't want to argue. "It's time for Mark to get some sleep."

Mark grinned. "Tell Hannah I'm ready for my sponge bath."

"Heh! Heh!" Abe stood and picked up his hat. "Makes

you all eager to get tucked in, does it, when Hannah's doing the tucking? Can't say I blame you."

"Hannah's off duty," Nate said flatly. "I'll take care of you."

"You are *not* giving me a sponge bath."

The expression on his brother's face reassured Nate that the two of them were back to normal. "Damn right I'm not."

Abe left, his dry *heh-heh-heh* trailing down the hall after him.

Mark was wearing a pair of the cutoffs Hannah had altered for him. Nate frowned. "How do those things come off?"

Mark tugged them apart, one-handed. "Why don't you have Hannah come show you? She won't mind. She likes my *gluteus maximus*."

His butt, in other words. Nate scowled at his brother.

Mark grinned.

Nate stabbed the button that made the bed flatten itself. He didn't like the idea that Hannah knew Mark's body a lot better than she knew his. There wasn't much he could do about it, though—except introduce her to his own body. As soon as possible. "She's a medical professional," he told Mark. "You should treat her with respect." He put one hand on Mark's back, well above the rib area, and one on his thigh, then rolled him gently onto his side so he could pull the cutoffs out of the way.

Mark had a cocky, amused look on his face that made his brother want to belt him. "You don't have to worry, you know. The woman empties my bedpan. That makes for an intimate relationship, but it sure as hell isn't romantic."

Nate felt foolish. He handed Mark his toothbrush and toothpaste. "Here."

"Am I supposed to brush dry and spit on the floor, or—"

"Just stick something in your mouth long enough to shut it up." He went to get the water, basin, washcloth and towel.

With mixed feelings Mark watched his brother go. He never had brought up the subject with Nate that he'd meant to discuss earlier that day. He'd intended to ask Nate what his intentions were toward Hannah.

Feeling protective about a woman was new to Mark. He wasn't sure what to do about it. He didn't think he was jealous of what was happening between Hannah and his brother—or not exactly. Oh, there was a twinge or two of envy, maybe. Hannah was smart and funny and sexy as hell. Any man would want her. But he'd gotten to know her pretty well the last few days, well enough that he would have kept his hands to himself even if his big brother hadn't decided to hang Keep Off signs all over her.

Hannah was a woman hungry for promises and permanence. Not his type at all. The problem was, he liked her, and he didn't think his big brother had any happily-ever-afters in mind for her, either. No, Nate's intentions were obvious. He meant to have Hannah.

Mark pushed the button that raised the head of the bed so he could sit up. Yet his brother was too honest to deceive Hannah about his intentions. And surely Hannah was too smart to think she was going to change Nate, and too sensible to get herself hurt by settling for less than she deserved. He had been thinking that it was time Nate came back to life, and there was nothing like a case of unrequited lust to wake a man up. The more Hannah turned Nate down, the more he would want her; the more he wanted, the more he would focus on the present, not the past. It sounded like a win-win situation to Mark.

Of course, if Hannah ever gave in, she'd quickly cease to be important.

No, he wasn't going to warn his brother off, but he really ought to have a talk with Hannah, just to be sure she understood the way things were with Nate. He'd do that, he decided. In the morning.

The wind was in a hurry tonight.

Hannah stood out on the long front porch, her arms hugged around her for warmth, since she hadn't zipped her jacket.

Usually the wind died down toward sunset, but maybe there was some kind of weather moving in, because instead of easing off, the wind had picked up. It was kicking dust and winter air along at a pretty good pace now.

Her back was to the front door when it opened, then closed. A second later, she heard Nate's voice. It sent chills over her faster than the wind had.

His words were less attractive than his voice. "What the hell are you doing out here?"

She shrugged and didn't turn around. "This is a great porch. You don't use it much, do you?"

"Not in the winter. Not with the wind blowing like this."

"The wind might be cold, but look how it scrubbed the clouds out of the sky. Isn't that odd? You'd expect a front to bring clouds with it, not hurry them away. And the stars…" Slowly she turned, facing him. "The stars are really something tonight."

Nate hadn't moved away from the door. Behind him, the darkness paled slightly, washed by light leaking from a crack in the living room drapes. But where he stood was in complete shadow, making him the darkest shape in front of her. "Why didn't you tell me you were coming out here?" he said. "I couldn't find you. You weren't in the kitchen or the living room or your room." His voice dropped. "You weren't in my room, either."

Her heartbeat skittered. "I didn't say I would be."

"I said we'd talk." He started toward her. "I'm not going to jump on you. You didn't have to come out here to get away from me."

"That isn't—I just had a need to see the sky. Do you ever feel that way? Like you just have to look at the sky?"

"Yeah." He stopped in front of her. "Sometimes I do. I don't see how people can stand living where city lights and pollution keep them from the stars." He rested his hands on her shoulders, his voice low. "What did you want to talk about, Hannah? I know something is wrong. You were too quiet on the ride home."

Home? The word tugged at places inside that she didn't want touched. Not now. Not when she felt so desperately vulnerable. "This afternoon you were determined to tell me your secret. You thought that was the right thing to do, because—because you wanted me."

He squeezed her shoulders gently. "I do."

"I've got a secret, too. It's something you should know before we go any further."

"All right." He didn't seem worried. In fact, he moved even closer. With her parka unzipped, she could feel the heat from his big body now, where before she'd been chilled by the wind. Her breath caught. Hannah believed in getting over the hard ground fast. This ground was rough enough to make her heart pound with fear, so she spoke quickly before she could lose her nerve. "I'm in love with you."

His head jerked back. "The hell you say." His hands fell away. "What the hell is that supposed to mean?"

She sighed. "Just what I said. I know you aren't looking for that sort of thing—"

"Damn right I'm not."

His anger hurt. She hadn't expected anything different, but it still hurt. "Well, I wasn't, either. I sure didn't want to fall in love right now, but it happened, and I figured I'd better tell you." That's what she'd realized in the car. And given how she knew Nate felt about love, she had to be honest with him about her own feelings.

"Did you think it would make me back off?" He grabbed her shoulders again, but this time he wasn't gentle. "Maybe it should. I hadn't thought you were the kind of woman who needed a crutch like *love*. I hadn't thought you would try to manipulate a man that way. If that's what you hoped to do—" his hands slid up to coil around her throat "—you're in for a disappointment." He bent and took her mouth with his.

She forgot how to move.

Hannah had thought she was ready for all sorts of reactions from Nate. She'd been afraid that he would back off, yes.

That fear had sent her outside tonight, seeking the stars, reaching for the strength to do what she had to do. So she hadn't expected the quick claiming of his kiss—or the flash-fire of her response. Surprise held her still for three long seconds.

Still, but not frozen.

Heat snarled through her, a swift-footed monster—stronger, faster, fiercer than ever before. She knew instinctively that this beast would eat her alive, gobbling her up from the inside out. And she wanted that. Craved it. She grabbed his shoulders, opened her mouth to him and hung on, overwhelmed.

Frightened.

Eager.

His tongue swept inside, and the taste of him made her hunger, made her need. How could she have expected this? Until this second, she'd never kissed him knowing that she loved him. This time, the sensations that shivered through her weren't sweet or curious. This time, desire had claws.

Nate pulled his head back to mutter, "You *will* give to me." His hands streaked down, sliding under her jacket to cup her breasts. "You said you would come to me. And you will."

Hannah arched her back, pressing herself into his greedy hands. She reached up and threaded her hands in his short hair. "Damn right," she said. She took a deep, strangled breath. "And you're going to give to me, too." She pulled his mouth back to hers.

Her hands raced over his body, testing, seeking flesh. His clothes frustrated her. The hunger growing in her was too new—a vast, unsteady beast whose hot-as-sin breath was building a furnace in her belly. Hannah had no idea what to do with such a rich excess of feeling, except to act on it. Quickly.

Her hands went to his belt buckle, and she tugged. She'd forgotten that it was winter, and the porch's wooden floor

was hard. He could have her here. Now. She didn't care. I
was dark enough for privacy.

Or maybe she was the one who needed to have him. Here
Now. In the dark.

But Nate clamped his hand over hers, stopping her. "No,'
he said, though his breath came as raggedly as hers. He
leaned his forehead against the top of her head. His voice
dropped so low that she barely heard him over the pounding
of her heart. "In my bed, Hannah. I want you in my bed.'
He smoothed his hand along the length of her hair.

That simply, he gentled the beast. Oh, hunger still growled
in her. Need still swelled. But one gentle stroke of his hand
had awakened other needs—needs that weren't simple
enough to be satisfied by a hurried coupling in the dark.
Though she'd wanted them to be. She closed her eyes.

Damn. He wasn't going to make any of this easy, was he'

Nate walked with Hannah to his room, his arm circling her
waist possessively. He didn't speak. What was there to say
He didn't stop to kiss or reassure her. He had no reassurance
to offer, no promises or pretty words. And if he stopped to
kiss her again, he'd have her clothes off, her legs spread and
her back against the wall before they took another step.

And he wanted her in his room. In his bed. He didn't know
why that mattered, but it did. It mattered enough that he'd
stopped her when she was fumbling with his belt buckle
even though he'd been so hard he'd come closer to embar
rassing himself than he had since he was fourteen.

At the door to his room, he let go of her hand. Automat
ically, he waited for her to precede him through the doorway

She glanced up at him. Her eyes brimmed with humor and
something perilously close to tenderness when she reached
up to stroke his cheek. "You do have such lovely manners.'
Then she dropped her hand and walked into his bedroom
stopping next to the king-size bed.

Earlier, when Nate had hunted through the house for her
feeling panicked and foolish because she was missing, he'

left the lamp by his bed on—and two small, foil-wrapped packets on the table beside it. The lamp's soft incandescent glow lay on her skin now, smoothing gentle shadows beneath the curves of her cheeks and jaw, tucking one into the hollow of her throat.

She looked right, standing there in his room next to his bed. She would look even better when she was in his bed, naked and reaching for him.

Nate went to her and grasped her waist with his hands. "This is better, isn't it? This way I can see you." He eased her up against him. "I want to see you, Hannah. Every bit of you."

When her lips parted, he bent and caught her tiny gasp with his lips.

Nate intended to go slowly. Now that he had her where he'd planned and plotted and seduced her into coming, he meant to take it slowly, to savor her kiss by kiss until they were both crazy with waiting.

Hannah had other ideas. And insanity was a lot closer than he'd ever dreamed.

First there was the taste of her, a quick punch to his system. Then there was the feel of her beneath his hands, live and supple and warm. And there were her hands—the way they slid up his chest, petting him, then tugging at the buttons on his shirt. He liked that so much that he had to show her by crushing her up against him. She felt good there. Held snugly against him that way, Hannah felt better to him than anything ever had in his life.

Better than anything?

He frowned at the thought.

"Nate," she gasped, breaking the kiss. "I could use a little help here. If you'd stop—ahh," she said when he moved her, turning her so that her breasts rubbed against him. "I can't— get this shirt of yours—off—when you're doing that."

Good idea. He could savor her much better when he had her naked.

Nate wanted her clothes off. She was equally determined

about his. Their hands tangled, bumped and shoved even as their pulses jumped and sped. He had her shirt and bra off; she'd just tossed his shirt aside and was working on his belt, but she kept getting in his way. "Dammit, Hannah," he said, and pushed her hands aside, reaching for the button to her jeans.

"Dammit, Nate," she said, and shoved his hands aside. She was reaching for the snap to his jeans when she looked up, catching his eye as he pushed her hands away again so he could reach for her jeans again. She started to laugh. "Maybe we could negotiate? Draw straws to see who goes first?"

Her face, glowing with laughter and desire, was the most beautiful thing he'd ever seen. "How about a race. Whoever strips first—"

"Wins."

Hannah couldn't stop laughing. She pulled her jeans and panties down, but she hadn't taken her boots off. She stopped to get them, but the denim and lace now bunched up at her knees threw her off balance and she toppled backward onto the bed. That sent her into fresh *whoops,* which further interfered with her efforts.

Nate, who had already yanked his boots off, took quick advantage of her distress. He shucked out of his own jeans in record time. Hannah had only managed to get one boot off when Nate tossed the last of his clothes aside and came down on top of her, full-length.

Her eyes got big. Her laughter faded.

"So," he said, stroking his hand down her throat, raising himself up enough that he could cup one of her breasts. "What do I win?"

"Me," she whispered, and twined her arms around his neck.

He smiled, and bent his head.

She had beautiful breasts, ripe and round and full, and he told her so, murmuring his praise between lavings of his tongue across first one hard nipple, then the other. He told himself to slow down, but even as he thought that, his hand was sliding across the smooth skin of her belly. How could he take this woman slowly? Her voice was already breaking when she said his name, her body already hot and slick and wildly responsive.

And his. Every movement she made said so. She was *his*.

The sheen of sweat on her skin was nowhere near as damp as the welcome he found when his hand moved between her legs. She bucked when he touched her there. He stroked and fondled and petted her while he sucked at her breasts, and the pleasure sounds she made fed his hunger until he couldn't stand it. He had to be in her.

He put two of his fingers up inside her. It wasn't enough. He raised his head and started to pull his fingers out, but her inner muscles clamped around them and her hips followed his hand. Her eyes were big, her breathing quick and shallow, and he knew she was right on the edge, knew he could tease her and play with her and make her climax while he watched.

He wanted that, suddenly, more than he'd ever wanted anything in his life.

More than anything?

Again the thought slid through his mind, one thin thread of fear quickly lost in a wealth of hunger and sensation.

He propped himself up higher on his elbow so he could see her face, and ran his thumb slowly up that wet cleft to the sensitive nubbin. She moaned. He pulled his fingers out and she protested; he slid them back in and she gasped. He teased her and toyed with her until she grabbed his hand with both of hers. "Now!"

"Not yet." He took her hands, pulled them above her head and held them there, both of her hands pinned by one of his. And he kept teasing her, circling his thumb around and around, up and down, until she was all but sobbing. His own breath rasped in his throat as if he'd been running for miles when he finally let go of her hands so she could grab hold of him. He parted her with one of his hands so he could see what he did, so he could be sure he didn't hurt her. Then he pushed his fingers up inside her. "Now!" He pressed his thumb down firmly.

She screamed. Her body bucked hard against his hand.

She was still trembling in the aftershocks when he pulled her remaining boot off and jerked her jeans and panties down. He grabbed one foil-wrapped packet from the table, ripped it open and rolled the condom on in feverish haste. Then he moved between her legs, pushed them wide, put two hands beneath her bottom to lift and position her, and he thrust inside.

She climaxed again immediately.

A few hard, desperate thrusts later, the world came to an end in a flash of sensual oblivion so bright it left him blind in brain, body and spirit, left him sliding off into a cozy darkness even as he slid off her limp body, rolling to his side and gathering her automatically into his arms.

Minutes or eons later, before the world had finished re-forming itself around him, Hannah called him back by slipping out of his arms. He blinked, frowned and reached for her, but she sat beside him, smiling like Eve, naked like Eve, and every bit as full of mystery.

She pushed him over onto his back. "My turn," she said softly.

Then she showed him what she meant.

An hour later, Hannah lay with her head pillowed on Nate's upper arm. His left arm was draped over her waist. One of her legs lay atop one of his. His chest heaved with the same need for air hers did. His skin was damp like hers. When she inhaled, she breathed in musk and sweat and Nate.

She wondered if she could stay just like this for the next thousand years or so. "Mmm," she said, and, mustering all her energy, managed to slide her leg a couple of inches along his, so she could enjoy the slight abrasion from his hair.

His fingers twitched, toying with the ends of her hair. "Your hair looks like fire," he murmured. "But it's just the tip of the flame, isn't it?"

She wanted to tell him that she'd never responded like that before. Only with him. She wanted to point out that she belonged right where she was, at his side—and that he belonged where he was, at her side.

She wanted to say she loved him.

But those words would send him deep inside himself again, all his defenses up. The words that should be the sweetest thing one lover can hear from another would make him think she was his enemy. Hannah had heard his disgust when she said she loved him earlier, but it had been dark. She hadn't had to see those feelings on his face.

She didn't want to see them now, either. She settled for stroking his flank. Eventually he would understand, she assured herself. He'd see that what she felt was nothing like the destructive emotion his ex-wife had burdened him with. This was one of those things she had to be patient about.

She could do that. "Have I mentioned that I'm crazy about your body?"

"I don't think so." He shifted onto his back, pulling her on top of him. He was smiling. "You gave a pretty convincing demonstration, though."

He looked so happy. Love hit her in a rush, bringing tears to her eyes. She blinked rapidly.

"Hey, what is it?" His hand was tender on her cheek.

"Nothing." She smiled brightly because she couldn't say the words. She couldn't expect to hear them from him, either—not any time soon. Maybe not ever. But she knew he was capable of the feeling, and that was what counted, wasn't it? "I'm just feeling mushy," she said, running her hand up his chest. "And tired." She sighed. "I guess I'd better get back to my room."

He frowned. "Stay here."

"But Mark—"

"I'll get the intercom." He took her shoulders in his hands and shifted her off him as easily as if she'd been a kitten curled up on his stomach—all five feet ten inches of her. Oh, my, she thought. She did like the way he did that.

"You stay here," he repeated, swinging his feet over the edge of the bed.

"Down, girl," she murmured, amused. "Sit. Stay."

He grinned. "Be a good girl and I'll bring you back a treat."

She eyed his body—his fabulously naked body—and smiled. "You do that. I'll be waiting patiently." Her smile widened. More or less patiently, anyway.

Chapter 13

Hannah hummed as she prepared Mark's breakfast tray the next morning. She felt pretty darn good for a woman who'd gotten so little sleep the night before. But what was there not to feel good about? The day was sunny and cool, Trixie was going to be all right, and Nate had woken her with a hungry kiss and asked her to move her things into his bedroom.

Well, actually he'd *told* her to do that, but when she'd pointed out the problem with his attitude, he'd grinned and corrected himself.

It was a start, she told herself as she carried the tray down the hall. He hadn't wanted just a one-night stand with her. He wanted her beside him at night, all night. Surely that all meant something, with a man as intensely private as Nate.

She nudged Mark's door with her hip. It swung open and she stepped into his room, smiling brightly. "Good morning."

Mark glared at her. "You're sleeping with him."

She stopped dead. How did he know? And why was he angry about it? "Why do you ask?" she said cautiously.

"I'm not asking. I know." He reached out and tapped the intercom. "No reason for this to be turned on if you're in your own bed, is there? Though even if I hadn't noticed the intercom, the way you're glowing gives you away." He shook his head, looking disgusted. "I thought you had better sense."

She squared her shoulders, stepped forward and set the tray on his bedside table. "I fixed muffins this morning."

"I was going to talk to you today, but now it's too late."

"There's marmalade for the muffins," she said, sliding the table in front of him.

"Hannah, he's not going to marry you."

She swallowed. "Try the bacon. It's some of that part-turkey stuff. Less fat."

"Never mind the damn bacon! I know Nate. He didn't make you any promises, did he?"

"That's really none of your business," she said, stiff with hurt. She'd thought they had gotten past Mark's initial distrust. Apparently not. Apparently he still thought she was after Nate's money.

He studied her face. "Oh, hell." He leaned back against the raised head of the bed. "You're in love with him, aren't you?"

"I don't think I care to talk about this with you." Her hand wasn't entirely steady when she poured his coffee from the carafe. "And I don't know why you're so bent out of shape about it," she added, setting the carafe down with a thump. "And I really think you might try to be a little happy that your brother has someone who cares about him, instead of looking all upset and—and *dismal*." Her hands were free now, so she fisted them on her hips. "And I am *not* after Nate's money."

"Whoa!" Mark held up one hand. "I didn't think you were after his money. I quit worrying about that days ago."

She kept her hands on her hips. "Then what's your problem?"

"I'm worried about you."

"About...oh." She smiled, back in charity with Mark and the world. "That's sweet."

He winced. "I am not sweet."

She patted his hand. "I won't tell anyone. Mark..." She wasn't at all sure this was the right time or the right way to bring this up. But when would it be right to ask such a thing? "If you want to help me, you can."

He looked wary and reached for his coffee. "What did you have in mind?"

"I need to know what was really going on last night when Nate sort of—flaunted me at you. And you got so angry."

For a moment, when his face closed down and his voice turned cold, he reminded her strongly of his brother. "I don't think that's any of your business."

"I think it is, though. Because—because you're right. Nate hasn't made me any promises. He isn't thinking of marriage, and I..." Her chest ached. She had to pause for a moment, but she was determined not to give in to a hurt that hadn't happened yet. "I need those promises."

His voice turned gentle. "I know, but I don't see how I can help you with that, Hannah."

"I have to know what I'm up against, where his scars come from. I have to know...about Jenny. And I think you can tell me."

He looked away. "She was unfaithful to him."

"Yes, he told me that much. It was her lover who died that night."

For a long minute he stared out the window without speaking. The early morning sunshine turned his skin to copper and washed his striking features with a gentle light that left him looking hard and strained and, somehow, painfully young. Finally he said roughly, "Ramos wasn't her only lover."

She waited. When he didn't continue, she asked softly, "How old were you when you were her lover?"

His head jerked. "How did you—did Nate—?"

"No, he hasn't said anything about it." She moved closer

to the bed. "But you have, though you didn't mean to. It wasn't Nate who called you a bastard last night. It was you. And you weren't talking about your birth, were you? I knew you had to be carrying a big load of guilt about something. How old were you?"

"Sixteen," he said, and his voice was tired now, sad and tired. "Old enough to know better, but too damn young to—though I did manage, just barely, not to do everything Jenny wanted me to do." The smile that touched his mouth was thin and bitter. "The difference between what actually happened between Jenny and me and what Nate thinks happened is pretty technical, but I did manage not to screw my brother's wife. Barely."

Her heart seemed to be stuck in her throat. She swallowed. "Then you weren't lovers?"

He shrugged one shoulder impatiently. "Like I said, the distinction is purely technical."

"But Nate thinks you were."

"Oh, he has reason. Don't doubt that. He walked in on the two of us one day while we were tonsil-to-tonsil. And she told him her version—very tearful, very sincere, I've no doubt, though I wasn't there to see it." His mouth twisted. "Jenny was fond of confessing."

Instinctively she reached out, laying her hand over his. "Nate believed her instead of you?"

He pulled his hand away. "Why wouldn't he? She planned it that way. She wanted to be caught." He stopped. He was white around the mouth from some strong emotion, but his voice was flat when he continued. "I was packing when he came to see me that night. Jenny had already done her tearful confession number, telling him how lonely she'd been with him working so hard, and how I'd just kept after her and kept after her. She begged him to forgive me, damn her. That was a good touch. Made it hard for me to convince him that she'd been the one after me instead of the other way around."

She ached for the boy he'd been, but she knew better than to let him see that. "Were you in love with her?"

His glance held scorn—but not, she thought, for her. "Oh, I was halfway infatuated back when they got married. Hell, half the males in the county were stuck on Jenny. But she pretty much left me alone that first year. By the time she decided to get Nate's attention by seducing me, I knew too much about her. I didn't even like her much."

And he'd liked himself far less, for responding to her seduction. "What did Nate do?"

"Nothing. That's the worst of it. I've always wished he'd gone ahead and hit me, yelled at me—instead, he just shut down. It was like we weren't in the same room anymore. He saw that I was packing, and asked me what I had in mind. I told him I thought I'd see if a cousin of ours who lives in El Paso would like some company. He just nodded and said that was a good idea, and he'd arrange it. And he left."

Hannah hardly knew what to say in the face of such guilt and love. "Are you sure he blamed you?" she asked tentatively.

"Oh, he knew she was at fault, too. I don't doubt that. But he let me leave. He *wanted* me to leave." Mark's eyes were bleak. "Of course, I should have left long before I did."

"You were only sixteen!"

He shrugged one shoulder. "Leaving would have been better than letting her get to me. But once I was gone, once I was away from her, I realized she'd won. That she'd gotten what she really wanted."

"What do you mean?"

"Jenny pretended she wanted me, but what she really wanted was to get rid of me. That was her goal all along. Oh, she'd tell me how much she needed me, how much—" He made an impatient gesture. "Never mind. She was good at making people believe her. But the fact is, she wanted me gone because she didn't want to share Nate with anyone or anything."

"But that's sick."

He just looked at her.

She didn't understand. What Jenny had called love was a selfishness so complete Hannah couldn't grasp it. The woman hadn't wanted to share her husband with his own brother. What did that have to do with love? She shook her head. "Yet people believed her," she said, baffled. "When she told them Nate intended to kill that man, people believed her instead of Nate."

"Everyone always liked Jenny, and she'd been telling folks for months how jealous Nate was, and how frightened she was of him. And she put on a great performance on the witness stand." He sighed. "Jenny was one hell of a good liar."

A lot of what Mark had told Hannah she didn't understand, but one thing was clear. "You and your brother have to talk about all this."

"Oh, no." He shook his head. "We do okay the way things are. Talking about the past would just get everything stirred up again." He ran a hand over his bristly chin, and frowned. "Don't go getting it into your head to meddle."

"Of course not." She wasn't going to meddle. She was going to help. There was a big difference.

"I don't know why the hell I told you all that."

Hannah had a pretty good idea. He'd *needed* to tell someone, and she'd been there, not only willing to listen, but insisting on it. "You wanted to help me."

"I wish I'd kept my damn mouth shut. I don't know how any of this will help you."

"Nate isn't an idiot," she said, and reached out absently for Mark's coffee. "He must know Jenny was…disturbed. I'm sure he doesn't think everyone is like her." She sipped at his cooling coffee. "You should eat your muffins."

"Never mind the muffins."

"I could pop them in the microwave and warm them up."

"I'll eat the blasted muffins later. But about Nate and you—"

"Know what I think? I think Nate doesn't know which

parts of the craziness were Jenny, and which were him. That's how it is in a marriage, even a bad one. You wind up with pieces of each other tangled up together, and you can't always tell which pieces are them and which are you. Even after the marriage is over, it can take a long time to sort things out.'' She thought about how many years it had taken her to unknot all the pieces of Barry and his family that had gotten tangled up in her opinion of herself. And they'd been married less than a year. "How long were Nate and Jenny together?'' She pushed the plate of muffins at him.

"They were married four years.'' He picked up one of the muffins. "But they were sweethearts in high school, too.''

High school sweethearts. She made a face and sipped at the coffee. Nate and Jenny had quite a history, all right, but it was time for Nate to start coming back from whatever lonely place he'd locked himself away in. She knew now why he'd gotten so good at keeping all his feelings inside. He'd had to, in order to survive. Jenny's lies would have gotten tangled around any part of him that he left vulnerable.

"You want to share that coffee?'' Mark asked drily.

"Sure,'' she said absently, and took another sip. Responsible people tended to blame themselves when things fell apart, and Nate was nothing if not responsible. It must have been horrible for him, learning that the woman he'd loved and married was such a troubled soul, and being unable to help her or himself. Then, when the marriage came apart in such a grisly and public way, the power of the law stepped in. And the law, along with public opinion, had sided with Jenny, and punished Nate. He'd been told in court that he was guilty of murder.

Nate had said that Tony Ramos's death was an accident. Hannah believed that. But did *he?* Had he felt guilty about so much else that part of him accepted the verdict of the jury?

She set the empty coffee mug down with a click. "What we have to do,'' she said firmly, "is to exonerate Nate.''

Mark stared at her. "What are you talking about?''

"He should never have been convicted. How would we go about getting a six-year-old verdict of murder overturned?"

"Forget it. He had a good lawyer, but the best deal the lawyer could get for him was probation."

"That's not good enough."

"Nate isn't going to like it if you go digging around in this," Mark warned.

"He won't know about it. Not right away, anyway." Hannah's mind was made up. Nate said he hadn't spent much time in jail, but she didn't think he had been free, either. Not for years and years. She was going to find a way to clear some of the shadows from his past, and once the law and his friends and neighbors realized he was innocent, he might believe it, too.

Maybe if he started believing in himself again, he could begin to believe in her, too—and in the future she desperately wanted them to have.

The place to start, she decided, was the library.

Hannah had an opportunity to practice her patience, because she couldn't get to the library for several days.

They went into town that same afternoon, but that was for Trixie's surgery. Hannah thought it was hopelessly sweet that Nate wanted to be there while his dog was operated on, even though he wouldn't be able to take the animal home until Tuesday or Wednesday. It apparently didn't occur to him that he didn't have to make the thirty-minute drive into town so he could sit in the waiting room throughout the two-and-a-half-hour surgery. She suspected that, deep down, he intended to be close enough to *will* Trixie to be all right. It was totally irrational, of course.

Of course she had to be there with him, so she could add her prayers to his.

She hadn't expected him to take her hand there in the waiting room, but he did—just before one of the gossips from church, Ona Biggs, came in with a flatulent pug that looked remarkably like his mistress. The woman stared at the two of them as if they were performing an indecent act in public. Hannah wanted to stick her tongue out, but settled for staring right back at her.

This time, he wanted to take her in the dark.

When Nate came out of the bathroom after his shower, naked and halfway aroused, Hannah was waiting for him in his bed. All day, he'd looked forward to this moment. Whatever he had done—feeding cattle, checking on his bull, talking to Abe, waiting through Trixie's surgery—at the back of his mind he'd known that tonight he would have Hannah in his bed again. The thought had filled him with satisfaction, anticipation…and uneasiness.

He didn't *want* to want her this much. Nate was a highly physical man, but sex had never been this important to him before. He didn't like it. And when he saw Hannah now, sitting up in his bed with her silly, prim, oversize flannel nightgown covering up everything but her face, glowing with pleasure at the sight of him, desire hit him so hard that he stopped in the doorway.

He reached out and turned off the light.

"Nate? Are you sleepy?"

Maybe in the darkness he could forget who he was with. Maybe it wouldn't matter so much. "No." He started across the room, knowing the room well enough that he didn't need sight to make his way to his bed.

She chuckled. "Want to tell ghost stories, then?"

"I had another game in mind." He put his knee on the bed. When he reached for her, she was there—her body warm and generous, her mouth opening easily beneath his. She tasted of hunger and life. *Hannah.* The darkness was no help in his effort to fool himself.

She pulled her head back, her fingers threading themselves through his hair. "Ah, that is nice. There's something I wanted to talk about, though."

"Not now," he said, and bent to find her throat with his mouth.

"It's about your brother."

"Hannah, I don't want to talk about my brother when we're in bed together." He cupped her breast, rubbing the material over her nipple. "Why do you insist on wearing this flannel sack?"

"It's about your brother and Jenny."

He went still.

"You need to talk to him, Nate."

"*No.* I don't know what you think you know, and I don't care," he said harshly. "What happened is in the past, and that's where it will stay."

She didn't sound impressed. "Oh, sure it will. The way the two of you act around each other—"

"Hannah." He cupped her face in his two hands, but he could see nothing of her in the blackness. "I cannot stand to have my failures poked at." And he'd failed Mark, failed him miserably. He'd been blind to what was happening when his sick wife decided to seduce his sixteen-year-old brother, and then, when it was too late, he'd sent his brother away instead of his wife. He would never forgive himself for that.

"Nate—?" Her hands soothed their way up his back. Her touch gentled one kind of tension in him, even as it built another.

"I don't want to talk," he said, and covered her mouth with his.

Tuesday morning the vet called and said that Trixie had bounced back from the surgery beautifully and could go home. Nate didn't ask Hannah to go into town with him. When she said that she might as well, so she could get a few groceries, he told her he really couldn't spare one of the hands to stay with Mark, and offered to get what she needed. Hurt, but determined to be reasonable, she gave him a list.

He returned at lunchtime. She held the side door open for him when he reached it, carrying eighty pounds of excited

Labrador retriever. Trixie was alternately licking his face and panting happily. For once there was no pretense about the dog staying outside. Nate carried her into the kitchen, where he'd fixed her a bed with an old blanket and pillow.

"What did the vet say?" Hannah asked, following. "What are we supposed to do for her? Oh, look at the poor thing's leg." It was shaved, of course, and slashed and stitched, and the pins he'd used to piece the bone back together stuck out. Hannah knelt to pet Trixie, whose head rested wearily on Nate's foot while her tail thumped happily.

"She has to take antibiotics. He said to let her pretty much do whatever feels right. She can stand on three legs already, but she gets tired." He glanced at Hannah, his eyes unreadable. "Maybe you could bring the groceries in."

Her eyebrows went up. "Well—okay." She went back outside to get the two sacks of groceries from the truck—and saw the bouquet laid carefully on top of the eggs, bread and milk. Waxy yellow petals beamed up at her like a slice of sunshine peeping out from the green florist's paper.

Daffodils. He'd wanted to surprise her. Her heart stuttered happily. "How did you know?" she said when she'd set the bags on the table. "I love daffodils. They're like a promise. You bury the bulbs in winter, and then in the spring you have beautiful yellow flowers."

He stood. "They're because of Trixie. I didn't hire you to take care of—"

"Nate," she said warningly.

"I wanted to thank you. That's all. I thought the flowers were pretty." He tugged his hat down and headed for the door as if he were late for an appointment with a cow.

She frowned at his back. "Lunch is ready."

"I'll eat later." The door closed behind him.

What was that all about? she wondered, shaking her head. First Nate surprised her with flowers, then he hurried out the door as if he were afraid she might attack him right there in the kitchen. She grinned at the thought, but her grin faded quickly.

Maybe the flowers had been meant strictly as a thank-you, and he'd left because he realized she'd taken them as a romantic gesture. Nate didn't exactly need to court her. He already had her in his bed, and he'd never indicated that he wanted more from her than sex.

Oh, but she didn't believe that. She *wouldn't* believe it. He needed her, even if he was too pigheaded to admit it.

That afternoon, Hannah carried her suitcase from her old bedroom to Nate's. Little by little, she'd been moving her things in. So far he hadn't commented. She didn't know if he liked seeing her clothes hanging in his closet next to his things, or if he was annoyed at the way she was invading his space.

If so, that's just tough, she thought as she heaved the big old suitcase up on the bed. Whether Nate realized it or not, Hannah was staking her claim. For now, she'd settle for claiming his room by moving the last of her things in. She was sleeping here. This was *her* room, now, too.

It was possible he wasn't going to like the idea.

When she unlatched the suitcase, her fingers trembled slightly. All her life she'd heard how foolish a woman was if she gave herself too easily to a man. She could almost hear her father now, drawling out his customary warning in his raspy voice: "Remember, girl. A man never buys the cow if he can get the milk for free." Hannah smiled in spite of her nerves as she carried her jeans over to the big dresser. Some of Patrick McBride's ideas would have fit in comfortably a century ago.

She wasn't letting Nate have everything his way, she told herself as she moved some of his jeans into another drawer, making room for her own. That's why she was doing this.

But she knew she had been easy for Nate. She'd fallen quick and hard into his arms and his bed. He had everything from her now that a lot of men wanted from a woman—good meals, a clean house and a willing bedmate—and he hadn't had to give up much of himself in return. He'd made it clear he hated the idea of marriage almost as much as he hated the idea of love.

She was not going to be a convenience for him, she promised herself as she put away the last of her things. She just had to be patient and show him how good they could be together. But Hannah hadn't given any man very much of herself since her disastrous teenage marriage. However firm her resolve to woo and win Nate's trust, sometimes her confidence was no more than a thin and shaky film over the fear that churned below.

There. She closed the bureau drawer and straightened, glancing around to make sure she'd tidied everything.

Nate had built himself a big, comfortable nest in his bedroom, with a television against one wall and his books filling the shelves near the bed. The furniture was oversize, built along masculine lines, and, now that Hannah was here, it was polished to a fine gloss.

There was nothing here from the years he'd spent with Jenny.

Mark had told her what had happened to Jenny's things. Hannah thought about that as she lugged her suitcase over to the big walk-in closet. Nate had been in jail for murder when Jenny and her brother came to get her things, but Jenny hadn't taken everything. She'd left quite a bit behind, and Hannah couldn't help thinking the woman had meant to claim a place at the house and in Nate's life that way, much as Hannah was doing today by moving her things in.

But Nate hadn't accepted Jenny's claim. The day after he was released on bail, he'd made a huge bonfire from everything of Jenny's that remained.

Hannah shivered. She was sleeping here, she told herself as she looked for a place in the closet to store her suitcase. He wasn't going to toss her things out in the yard. But if he thought she was pushing him, pressing for more than he wanted to give… Never mind, she told herself firmly. She didn't need to worry about that now. Now, she just needed to put her suitcase away.

There was room on one of the built-in shelves along the back wall, she decided, if she moved things around a bit. She'd barely begun when she found a large metal box. The latch had been broken at some point, and when she tried to pick it up, the lid came open.

Inside were photographs. Among other things.

She told herself she had no right to go through anything as personal as this without permission. But the voice of Hannah's conscience was drowned out by her need to learn everything she could about the man she loved. After staring at it, frozen, for a few seconds, she sank to the floor of the closet and pulled the box up beside her.

Beneath the top layer of photos she found memories. Memories of grade school, junior high, high school. Carefully she removed football trophies, swimming trophies, yearbooks, clippings. She looked at each of them, and she learned. And what she learned made her ache, deep inside.

Nate had been the quarterback for his high school team. Newspaper clippings described his skill on the football field, articles that glowed with the pride his hometown had taken in him. He had sung in the choir of the church that he would no longer set foot in. He'd been on the student council in high school, and in his senior year he'd been voted homecoming king.

Jenny had been his queen.

She stared at the picture in the yearbook of the homecoming king and queen. It was the only picture of Jenny she'd found, and it wasn't very clear. Hannah couldn't see the resemblance everyone else claimed existed between her and Nate's ex-wife, but it was obvious that Jenny had been a very pretty girl, with long, shiny hair and elfin features. She was smiling at Nate as if he were her entire world.

It was the pictures of Nate that got to Hannah the worst. He'd been serious even then, but he'd had so much hope for the future. She could see it shining in the captured image of his young eyes. Her own eyes were damp as she put away the photo box. She was sliding her suitcase onto the newly-cleared shelf when she heard Nate's voice.

"Hannah? Are you in there?"

Her heart jolted. He'd almost caught her looking through his things. "I'm in here, Nate," she said, leaving the closet as quickly as any criminal ever left the scene of the crime. "What are you doing back at the house so early?"

He stood in the center of the bedroom. His eyes were hooded, his mouth tight. "Do I need a reason?" His hand went to the buttons on his shirt.

"No, but you never..." Fascinated, she watched as he unbuttoned his shirt. The sight of his bare chest made her forget what she'd been about to say. "Did you come back to change clothes?"

"I'm not changing clothes." He tossed the shirt to the floor. His eyes held hers—eyes as hot and dark as the nights that they'd lain together.

Hannah bit her lip. She ought to object, shouldn't she? He was taking a lot for granted, walking in and stripping, acting as if she were available to him any time he held out his hand. But...oh, my, she thought as he tossed his shirt on the floor and the first slick twists of desire spiraled through her. He did have a beautiful chest.

His hands paused at the snap of his jeans. His lip curled sardonically. "Enjoying yourself?"

She licked her lips. "Nice view. You planning to take a bath?"

"You know damn well why I'm here. I started thinking about you. I couldn't stop." He sounded furious about it as he jerked his zipper down. "I was fixing that blasted windmill in the south field, but all I could think about was how you feel beneath me. The way your eyes get all hazy when I push inside you." He kicked his pants and underwear aside. "I want to be inside you, Hannah."

She swallowed. "You didn't close the bedroom door."

"Mark's at the other end of the house, and no one else is

here.'' He stood beside the bed, naked and magnificent and held out his hand.

And, dammit, that was all he had to do—reach out for her. She went to him. Her heart was pounding, the pulse of it thrumming down low as her body responded to his urgency.

He wasn't patient. His mouth was hard and his hands were demanding as he tumbled her to the bed. He kissed her like a man already at the edge, shoving her clothes aside so he could taste and touch. She matched him need for need, hurrying her hands over him, kissing whatever part of him she could reach. They rolled together. She ended up on top, exhilarated, breathless. She wriggled against him, sending delicious thrills throughout her body.

''Not today,'' he said, and grabbed her hips, stopping her. ''I can't take any teasing this time. I need...''

''What?'' she whispered, her heart stumbling.

His hands went to her face. His own face was fierce and troubled. ''Why do I need you so much?'' he asked harshly. ''I don't like it, Hannah. I don't want to need you.''

Hope and hurt crashed inside her, and desire won. ''Tough,'' she said, and slid down over the length of him. ''You need me, and I—''

He pulled her head down and kissed her into silence and right out of her mind.

Chapter 14

On Thursday Hannah ran out of patience.

Mark had his checkup that afternoon. The specialist who was monitoring the way his bones knit was in Amarillo, so Mark and Nate would be going there for the eleven o'clock appointment. But Bitter Creek was on the way.

Hannah was no good at lying, even by omission. Her palms were clammy when she asked Nate if he would drop her at the library in Bitter Creek on his way to the doctor so she could get a couple of books.

"I'd forgotten all about your wanting something to read. Of course you can go to the library. We can meet for lunch, if you like—assuming Mark gets the okay to spend some time in a wheelchair. He'll be ready to celebrate."

She almost confessed her real motives then and there.

Three hours later, Hannah was on her way to Green's Drugstore, four blocks from the library. She had a paperback book and two hardcover novels in her backpack—and a sheaf of copies she'd made from some of the texts she'd looked up.

She hadn't ever dipped into law books before. They were a mess. It had taken her forever to figure out how to look up the information she needed, since she hadn't wanted to ask the librarian for help, and she wasn't sure she'd understood everything. In fact, she was pretty sure she hadn't, which was why she'd copied a lot of it to study later.

From what she could tell, though, there were two basic ways to exonerate Nate: obtain a retrial, or a pardon from the governor. There was something called an "expunction order" that erased all records of a conviction, but if she understood that part right, Nate would have to get a pardon from the governor first, then apply to have his record expunged. It was all terribly complicated, and it would all take much longer than seven weeks. And seven weeks was all she could be sure she had left with Nate.

He hadn't said anything about her staying with him once he didn't need her to take care of Mark anymore. And if he did ask…if he did, what then? If he wanted her to continue to live with him without marriage, what would she say?

She had seven weeks, Hannah reminded herself as she reached the old-fashioned drugstore. All sorts of things might happen in seven weeks.

Nate had thought he and Mark might be able to meet her here about twelve-thirty, but it was nearly that now and she didn't see the big black Lincoln he was driving today instead of his pickup. The car had been his father's, bought new in the year of his death, and Nate had kept it around for those rare times when he didn't want to use his truck. Mark and his broken leg wouldn't fit in the cab of the pickup, but he could spread out comfortably in the back seat of the old Lincoln.

Hannah pushed the door to the drugstore open, making the bell above it jingle. Her spirits lifted slightly as she stepped inside. The mustiness of old floorboards blended with the faint, floral scent of the colognes at the front of the store, overlaid by the smell of hot grease from the lunch counter at the rear of the store.

Hannah loved old drugstores. She liked the clutter, the bargains and the surprises. Maybe it was just as well that Nate wasn't back yet. Poking around in here might perk her up. She'd cashed her first week's paycheck, and the check from her sister would be here any day now, so she could afford to buy herself a cheer-me-up present while she waited. And if Nate ran really late, she would go ahead and eat—and study the pages she'd copied.

There were several other customers, but most of them were eating lunch at the rear, so she almost had the store to herself as she wandered around. She picked up some panty hose and found two greeting cards she couldn't resist, then headed for the cosmetics section.

The aisle that held various powders, lotions, spritzes and splashes dead-ended at a counter with a display of costume jewelry. Three teenaged girls had their heads together over the necklaces and bracelets. Hannah had noticed some other teens at the lunch counter. Apparently the drugstore was close enough to the high school to be a hangout.

Hannah stopped to sniff some lavender-scented lotion. One of the girls looked over at her, giggled and said something to the other two, who started whispering and darting glances at her. Then they all giggled.

Well, Hannah thought, it's obvious who their topic of conversation is. She refused to take it personally. Girls that age ought to have better manners, but rarely did. And she should have expected the gossip about her and Nate to be flying. Good grief, they'd been holding hands in the vet's waiting room when Ona Biggs saw them. Of course people were talking.

A heavyset woman with battleship-gray hair sailed past the girls. Their giggles hushed as if her passage had laid down a wake of silence. She came to a stop in front of Hannah. "May I help you, ma'am?"

The clerk looked like her fourth grade teacher. Mrs. Marvel had been telepathic, and she'd hated children; Hannah was convinced of both facts. "I don't think so," she said

cautiously. "I was just browsing a bit while I wait for..."
My friends? My employer and my patient? My lover and his
brother? "...before I eat lunch."

"I will be glad to assist you." She folded her hands in
front of her. "Are you interested in some cologne to go with
that lotion?"

Irritation was edging out intimidation. "No, thank you."

"Allow me to introduce myself. I am Mrs. Andrew
Green."

Hannah caught a glimpse of the girls. One of them was
making a face at Mrs. Green's back. Hannah had to bite her
lip to keep from laughing. "I'm pleased to meet you, Mrs.
Green. My name is Hannah McBride."

She inclined her head once. "I am aware of that, of course.
I hope you will excuse my making your acquaintance in this
fashion. I believe you visited St. Luke's last Sunday?"

The girls were giggling again. Someone else moved into
view, coming from the back of the store. Someone Hannah
knew. She stared over Mrs. Green's shoulder. "Uh—yes.
Lovely church."

It was the youth from the bus station. Not Mario, nor any
of the ones that had scared her the day she tried to walk from
the grocery store to the library. This was the scrawny one
with the pale, stringy hair and empty eyes. He was talking
to the girls.

"I understand from Irene Robbins that you do not have a
church home."

"That's right. My job keeps me on the move."

"I wish to extend an invitation to you to visit the Faith
Temple Church on Broadway while you're here. We have a
wonderful pastor."

Hannah relaxed. Apparently the woman's pushiness was
inspired by congregational rivalry, not suspicion of an out-
sider. "I'll be glad to." She kept part of her attention on the
scruffy youth while she chatted with Mrs. Green—or, rather,
while Mrs. Green issued pronouncements with which Hannah
was allowed to agree.

The girls giggled and acted silly in the way of young females who think they're being daring, but the boy seemed to be behaving himself. Hannah wasn't sure about the girls, though. One of them, a dark-haired charmer of fifteen or so, was up to something, judging by the furtive glances. Hannah couldn't tell what. There was rather too much of Mrs. Green blocking her view.

Just as the girls moved away, heading for the back of the store, the bell tinkled over the entry. Hannah looked over that way, hoping for Nate.

A short, dark-haired man wearing a fancy western-style shirt walked in. Beside him was a woman Hannah had never seen before—a pale, skinny woman with haunted eyes and long, strawberry blond hair...and an oddly familiar face. A narrow face with delicate features.

Hannah stared. *Jenny?* Could this sad-faced woman actually be Nate's ex-wife?

The pale woman clutched the arm of the man with her, and stared back.

Did Hannah herself really look like that? She frowned. Surely not.

The man said something to the woman, who shook her head and started for Hannah.

"Oh, my," Mrs. Green said.

Hannah suspected that was something of an understatement. She braced herself, unsure what to expect.

Jenny was one of those rare people who walk with such grace that people compare their movement to floating. The effect was heightened by the ankle-length skirt of her dress, a very feminine creation in a dainty floral print with a white Peter Pan collar and wide cuffs. She wore a dark blue crocheted sweater-vest over the dress, and her long, shiny hair spilled halfway down her back.

She looked sweet...and either ill or anorexic. The pretty dress hung on her as if she'd recently lost a great deal of weight.

Jenny stopped in front of Hannah and smiled uncertainly.

"Hello," she said in a soft voice. She was three or four inches shorter than Hannah. "I hope you don't mind my speaking to you like this. I thought...there are things you should know."

The man who'd come in with her came up behind her and rested his hands on her shoulders. "Honey, you don't have to do this if it upsets you."

"Oh, but I do. I need to be sure she understands. Nate can be so..." Her lower lip quivered, but she continued bravely. "He can be terribly compelling. She needs to know the truth before it's too late. I have to warn her so she won't be hurt."

"From what I've heard," he said contemptuously, "it's already too late. She's made her bed. With *him*. Now let her sleep in it."

Hannah thought that was about enough. "I hate to intrude on this conversation the two of you are having about me, but I think we should introduce ourselves. My name is Hannah McBride. I haven't the foggiest idea who you are, mister, but the young woman who wants to warn me about something must be Jenny." She held out her hand. "How do you do? Nate has told me so much about you."

Someone gasped.

Hannah glanced around. Mrs. Green had been tactful enough to move away, though she hadn't gone far. She was meticulously straightening the jewelry that the girls had been trying on earlier. The gasp had come from the personal hygiene section one aisle over. Several people who had been eating a few minutes ago had developed a sudden need for deodorant or a toothbrush.

She looked back at the woman in front of her.

Slowly, as if she expected Hannah to strike her instead of shaking hands, Jenny held out her hand. Her palm was dry and rather bony. She had long, narrow fingers, a tiny wrist and a weak clasp. Hannah could see a pulse fluttering in the woman's throat, and she was reminded of a bird.

"What did he say about me?" Jenny whispered.

Hannah hadn't expected to ever meet this woman. Now

that she had, she waited to have some sense of evil, some recognition of the monumental selfishness that had destroyed lives. But all she saw was a frightened child. She shook her head and dropped Jenny's hand. "Never mind."

"I want to know. I need to know."

Hannah tried to steer the conversation into safer channels. "Are you in town for a visit? I understood you were living in California."

She shook her head, making all that red-gold hair shimmer around her face. "I'm going to move back home. It's time. I'd been wondering if it might be, and then I heard about you from my aunt, and I had to be sure you understood. He's just using you, you know."

"I beg your pardon?"

"I don't want you to be hurt. What Nate and I have is sacred. We're soul mates. That's why I need to know what he said about me. I was hoping—" She swallowed. "It doesn't matter. Just tell me what he said."

Hannah couldn't think of anything at all to say.

The man standing behind Jenny closed his eyes as if he were in pain. "Oh, honey," he said, helplessly. "Oh, Jenny, honey."

The bell over the door chimed again. Everyone looked that way.

Mark's leg came through the door first, sticking straight out in its white plaster cast. He was riding in a wheelchair, his broken leg on the extended leg rest. For once he was fully dressed in a shirt and a pair of jeans she'd altered for this occasion.

But Hannah didn't waste much time looking at Mark, because Nate was pushing him. And Nate wasn't surprised. That was the first thing she noticed: he wasn't at all surprised to see Jenny. Someone must have warned him who was here, and he had himself locked up as tight and hard as she'd ever seen him.

"There you are," Hannah said with all the cheeriness she

could muster. She started toward him, but Jenny stood in the way. "Excuse me," she said politely.

The other woman had turned to face Nate. She glanced back at Hannah, her eyes wide and blind with feelings Hannah didn't want to witness. "This time," Jenny said very softly. "Just this one time." And she moved aside.

"Nice wheels, Mark." Hannah hurried forward, thinking they might still manage to brush through this without a direct—and painful—confrontation between Nate and Jenny. "Can I take you for a spin?"

"Spinning I can do on my own." Mark grinned, ready to help her slick a little normalcy on these troubled waters. He indicated his casted arm, currently held in front of him in a stylish blue sling. "When I try to get this rig rolling one-handed, I end up going in circles."

"Ready for lunch?" Nate asked abruptly.

She met his eyes and her stomach jittered. "Sure. You going to let me drive Mark's new wheels?"

His answer was slow in coming. "All right," he said, letting go of the grips and looking straight into her eyes. "I trust you."

Did he mean that the way her heart hoped he did?

The commotion from the jewelry counter was as unwelcome as it was loud. Hannah glanced that way and saw that Mrs. Green had hold of the scrawny youth's arm. She shook it. "For shame, Sammie! Give them back right now, you hear?"

His answer was clearly audible. "I don't have anything of yours, bitch."

"How dare you!"

"Hey!" The man in the pretty western shirt moved closer to the other two. "You don't talk to a lady that way, boy. You want me to take him out back and teach him some manners, Mrs. Green?"

"Who *is* that man?" Hannah muttered.

"Ben Rydell," Nate said, his voice flat as a ruler. "Jenny's brother."

Oh. Hannah grimaced.

Mrs. Green was informing the boy of the penalties for shoplifters and instructing someone to call the sheriff. Hannah bit her lip. She hadn't had her eye on the youth the whole time. And he was an odd one. He might have taken something.

And yet…

Jenny drifted their way. Mark grabbed the wheel of his chair with his one good hand and gave it an abrupt twist, turning so he blocked her before she could drift all the way up to Nate.

Hannah wasn't sure Jenny really noticed Mark, or anything except Nate. She did stop, though. She stood there and looked at him, her blue eyes huge with longing, and held out both hands. "Oh, Nate," she said, "haven't you punished me enough?"

Out of the corner of her eye, Hannah saw three teenage girls making their way to the front door—very quietly. No giggling now.

She sighed. Much as she wanted to give her entire attention to Nate and the sad, beautiful leech he had once been married to, she had to take care of something else right now. "Mrs. Green?" she called, raising her voice enough to be heard over Jenny, Jenny's brother—who still wanted to hit someone—and two of the customers. "If you're looking for a shoplifter, I think you should check out the young lady who's edging toward the door right now with two of her friends."

Forty minutes later, Hannah stood next to the Lincoln's open trunk. It took Nate's size and strength to get Mark and his casts disposed of comfortably in the back seat of the Lincoln, so Hannah was taking care of the wheelchair while Nate took care of Mark, and Mark was grumbling about the indignity of being toted around like an infant. Hannah suspected his complaints came from pain as much as indignity. Being lifted and moved hurt those healing ribs.

The dark-haired teenager who had pocketed several pieces of costume jewelry was home now with her parents, who had persuaded Mrs. Green not to press charges. The scrawny youth—Sammie, Mrs. Green had called him—had fled the moment the woman let go of his arm.

Jenny and her brother were gone, too, but they probably hadn't gone as far as Hannah might have wished.

Hannah had just folded the wheelchair flat and fitted it into the trunk when she glimpsed movement out of the corner of her eye. Startled, she turned her head and saw Sammie coming out of a nearby alley, heading for them.

Nate muttered something and shut the car door. Hannah closed the trunk and turned just as Sammie stopped a few feet away. He pushed a strand of his long, dirty hair out of his eyes. Those eyes still gave her the shivers. "Hello," she said, trying to sound friendly.

Nate came to stand beside her. He put one hand on her shoulder.

Sammie's unblinking gaze never left her face. "I didn't want to go to jail. You spoke up for me. You told Mrs. Green I didn't steal anything."

"I was pretty sure that little brunette had done it. I knew she'd been up to something."

"Bethany wanted me to say I did it. She said she'd be nice to me if I said I did it, but she isn't nice. She's pretty and I'd like to touch her, but she isn't nice."

"No, well, Bethany shouldn't have said that."

"You're pretty, too, but you helped me. I'll remember you. I remember it when people help me."

"Hannah," Nate said, "this is Sammie Reddington. Sammie, this is Hannah."

She glanced at Nate. His voice had been surprisingly gentle, considering his protective stance beside her. "I'm glad to meet you, Sammie."

For the first time, Sammie's gaze shifted to Nate. "Mr. Jones," he said. "I remember you. You don't hit people who are littler than you are."

"That's right."

"Mario doesn't like you."

"I don't like him, either."

Sammie's gaze darted between Nate and Hannah. "I heard about your dog. That made me mad. People shouldn't shoot dogs. It's bad."

Hannah's compassion was stirring. It almost drowned out the uneasiness. "Yes, it's bad to hurt a dog."

"Cows are different. People eat cows."

"Sammie," Nate said, "do you know who's been shooting cows?"

"Cows are different," he repeated, and stepped back one step, then another. His gaze stayed fixed on Hannah's face with unnerving intensity. "But he shouldn't have shot your dog. I'll take care of it." He turned and ran.

"Good grief," Hannah said. "He's...odd."

"Yeah," Nate said, "he is."

"He's mildly retarded, isn't he?"

Nate glanced at her. "Don't let your sympathy interfere with your good sense. I feel sorry for Sammie, too, but he's got more problems than being a little slow."

"He's dirty," she retorted. "If he were in a home where he was cared for properly—"

"He's been in at least five homes. Sammie likes to start fires. Among other things."

She thought about that, and about what Sammie had said about Nate not hitting people smaller than him. "He was abused, wasn't he? How did you meet him?"

He started for the driver's side of the car. "Four or five years ago, some of the older kids were picking on him down at the park—holding him down, rubbing his face in the dirt. I saw it, and made them stop. He wanted me to hit them, and I told him I didn't hit people smaller than me." He opened the door. "The concept seemed to stick with him. Every time he sees me, if he speaks at all he mentions that."

She was silent as she got into the car.

It wasn't up to her to fix everyone's problems, she reminded herself as she buckled up. She was going to have her hands full figuring out a way to exonerate Nate. And yet... "Didn't you say you were shorthanded?" she asked Nate when he slid in behind the wheel.

"Not so shorthanded that I'm going to hire an underage pyro who shoots cattle."

Put that way, it did sound a little unreasonable. "We don't know that *he* shot the cows. He just didn't see anything morally objectionable in it."

Unexpectedly, he smiled. "Hannah," he said, and leaned over and kissed her firmly on the mouth, "you are a wonder to me." He straightened and started the car.

His kiss left a pleasant buzz in her system. She didn't listen to what Mark was saying as they pulled away from the curb, her mind busy with her own thoughts. They'd stopped at one of the town's three traffic lights when Hannah spoke one of those thoughts aloud. "She has blue eyes."

"What?"

"I don't know why people said Jenny and I look alike. Her hair is nothing like mine, and she's shorter and a lot skinnier, and her feet are too small. She looks like a Barbie doll. I don't look like that, do I?"

"I don't want to talk about Jenny."

"I was talking about *me*. I don't think I look like her."

Mark spoke up from the back seat. "You don't. Not a bit. And Nate, unless you're dumber than I give you credit for being, I'm sure you'll agree with me."

The light changed. Instead of moving the big car forward, Nate slid the transmission into park, unsnapped his seat belt, and scooted over. He cupped Hannah's shoulder with one hand and her chin with the other, tilting her head so that her startled eyes met his dark ones. "You are nothing like her," he said fiercely. "Not in looks. Not in mind or body or soul. Understand?" And for the second time since they got in the car, he kissed her.

He took his time about it, too.

Hope sang a happy song in her heart the rest of the way back to the ranch.

Hannah didn't think she was anxious about the party that night—the one Nate had insisted she was going to with him. The one where all his friends and neighbors would meet her as his date, not his employee. But maybe she was a teensy bit self-conscious. If only she could find the right thing to wear, she'd feel better, but she hadn't brought any party clothes with her.

Of course, she didn't really own any party clothes. All she had done for years was work and go to school, and when she did socialize, it usually involved pizza or a movie. Nothing fancy. So tonight she was going to a party, and she had nothing to wear.

No wonder she had no appetite for the lunch she'd just fixed.

She poked at a macaroni with her fork. Maybe her black sweater—? No, her black sweater had a hole at the hem. She could fix that, but the sweater itself was shabby.

She used her fork to escort a couple of noodles back into the macaroni mountain she'd built in the center of the plate, but then three others slithered back down.

What about her green church dress?

Stupid, she thought, stabbing a helpless noodle with her fork. The party tonight was a barbecue. No one wears a church dress to a barbecue.

She would have asked Nate what to wear, but she hadn't seen him today. When she'd woken up that morning, his side of the bed had already been cold. But then, she'd known it would be, because he had left it hours before dawn. Hannah had woken the moment he left her side, but she'd said nothing. She'd lain awake for what had seemed like forever, waiting for him to come back.

He hadn't.

"What's wrong?" Mark asked. He sat in his wheelchair, enjoying his first meal at the table since the accident. Nate had helped Mark into that wheelchair early that morning while Hannah still slept.

"Nothing," she said, and smiled brightly to prove it to both of them. "I'm not very hungry today." She'd fixed macaroni and cheese at his request. Nate would be home shortly to eat and then get Mark back in bed, since the doctor had insisted he had to spend the afternoon horizontal if he wanted to go to the party tonight.

"Right," he said drily.

She set her fork down. "Do you think I should cut my hair?"

"Why?"

"Just a trim, to get rid of the dead ends." She lifted a handful of hair and studied it. Yes, some of the ends were splitting. Damn. She should have thought of this earlier and made an appointment. "Do you know how to cut hair? I never can trim mine and get it straight."

"No way am I going to touch your hair, Hannah. I'm not crazy. If I cut off an eighth of an inch too much, you'd take the scissors to me."

She grinned. "I'm pretty nonviolent. I'd probably just hit you over the head a few times." She tilted her head to one side. "How did a man without any sisters learn so much about women and their hair, anyway?"

"Gosh," Mark said innocently, "I guess I'm just observant."

Hannah rolled her eyes. "It's the face, I suppose." It was funny, but now that she was used to Mark's face, he just looked like Mark to her. She shook her head sadly. "Women can be so shallow."

"Hey, I'm not just a pretty face," he protested. "Don't forget the incredible body that goes with it."

Nate heard Hannah's laughter the minute he opened the side door. The sound stopped him as if it were a hand pressed on his chest. He stood there in the doorway looking at the neatly folded clothes stacked on top of the dryer while the sound of her laughter pressed against him. Then, suddenly, it wasn't pushing on him anymore. Somehow it slipped in, slid right past his clothing and skin and up inside him. It filtered through him like smoke, and his heartbeat picked up. Laughter was a good sound, but his heartbeat was racing with fear, not pleasure. He didn't understand. He didn't know what was happening to him lately.

Trixie found him standing there, unmoving, about the same time Mark called out something. The spell was broken. He took a moment to rub the dog behind her ears and compliment her on how well she was getting around on three legs. Then he raised his voice as he moved on into the kitchen. He was relieved by how normal he sounded. "What are the two of you laughing about?"

They sat together at the table, Hannah and Mark. His brother and his lover. The sight of them affected him, too, but not the way her laughter had. This felt right. He liked walking in the kitchen and finding these two people here, waiting for him.

Hannah's face was alive with happy mischief when she answered him. "Male pulchritude," she said.

"Male what?"

"I'll bet it's one of her vocabulary words," Mark said.

Nate took his jacket off and hung it on the hook just inside the laundry room. "Is that your word for today?" He'd never seen anyone as determined to improve themselves—and as little in need of it—as Hannah. Someone, sometime must have done a real number on her, because she didn't seem to have any idea how smart she was. He wished he knew how to make her believe that. This was one of those times that words wouldn't work, though. Telling her she was smart wouldn't get the belief down inside her where she needed it.

"Whose pulchritude were you laughing about?" he asked as he came over to the table.

"Mark's, of course. Doesn't he just ooze it?" She grinned as she stood. "There's some roast chicken left from last night to go with that macaroni. I'll get you some."

"I'll get it. You sit down and finish eating." He took his

plate over to the stove so he could dish himself out some of the macaroni and cheese.

"Oh, she's not going to eat. Hannah doesn't have any appetite today," Mark said.

"What's wrong?"

"Nothing," she said much too cheerfully.

He turned around. She had the refrigerator open and was digging around in it, giving him a distracting view of her backside. "Hannah, you lie as poorly as anyone I've ever known."

"There's nothing really wrong," she insisted. She took out a foil-wrapped package and used her hip to swing the refrigerator door closed. "It's stupid for me to be bothered by something so trivial. And I'm not upset about it. Maybe a little uncomfortable, but it's entirely too unimportant to talk about. You want white meat or dark?"

"I want you to tell me what's wrong."

"It really isn't important."

"Hannah."

"All right!" She flung one hand out. "I don't have anything to wear."

Nate set his plate down and tried to see what was wrong. She had on a perfectly good pair of jeans. Her blue-and-green flannel shirt was a little worn, but he liked the way the soft, well-washed material draped over her breasts. He shook his head, confused. "Are you talking about uniforms? I noticed you stopped wearing them after the first few days, but I like the way you look in jeans. I'd rather you didn't wear a uniform, but if you think you should—"

"Nate," Mark said, "I think she's talking about the party."

Oh, damn, he'd forgotten about the party. He hadn't wanted to remember. But he had asked her to go with him, so now he was going to have to go, wasn't he? Scowling, he dug into his back pocket. "I can stay with Mark a couple of hours," he said, pulling out his wallet. "Take the truck into town and get what you—"

"Don't."

He looked up. She stood in the middle of the floor clutching that foil-wrapped package of chicken, her face white. "I don't want you to give me money, Nate."

Hell. She thought he was trying to pay her again, the way he'd once offered to do. "I just—I didn't think. I didn't mean it that way."

She turned and set the shiny foil package on the counter carefully as if it held eggs instead of leftovers. "I don't need your money."

"I know." He felt helpless and angry. "I didn't mean it the way you're thinking. I'd like to buy you something. A present. That's all."

"You know what a lot of people are going to think, don't you?" she said, her voice low and intense. "When I go to the party tonight, I mean. I work for you and—and we're involved, and they'll think that means I'm bought and paid for. I guess that seems petty to you. You've had people thinking a lot worse things about you. But it bothers me. I can't go to that party wearing something you paid for."

How could anyone think badly of Hannah? He crossed to her. "I'd like you to go to the party with me because I'd enjoy showing you off. But if the thought of what some idiots might think makes you uncomfortable, we can skip it."

"Oh, no." She shook her head. "I want to go."

"Even though you don't have anything to wear?"

She shrugged. "I'll come up with something. I don't want you buying me clothes, Nate."

"Okay." He didn't like it, but he'd agree to it. For now. Because it had been hours since he'd touched her, he put his hands on her shoulders. "I won't buy you anything. But you could, couldn't you?"

"Well…"

"Go on into town and pick up something. There's not a lot of selection, but the little dress store on Main used to have some pretty things."

"But you didn't hire me to go shopping."

She was grinning so impudently that he really wanted to kiss her. "I'll get Mark settled, and I need to work on the books anyway, so I can stay in the office this afternoon while you're in town. You can afford to buy yourself something, can't you?"

"Well…" A smile tugged at her mouth. "I was going to buy myself a present yesterday, before—before everything happened."

Before Jenny showed up, he thought grimly. "You could do me a favor while you're in town."

"What's that?"

"I've noticed lately that the place is getting kind of shabby. Like the carpet. It's pretty worn. And here in the kitchen, you did something to the cabinets that made them look really good again."

She flushed with pleasure. "I just applied a little elbow grease and lemon oil. The wood is beautiful."

"Well, that beautiful wood makes the floor look bad. I thought you might stop by the hardware store and look at some of those sample books—see if there's anything you think would work in here. If not, we'll head in to Amarillo, but I give the local merchants my business when I can."

She blinked. "You want me to pick out new flooring for the kitchen? What kind? I mean, there's vinyl, like you have now." Her voice picked up speed as enthusiasm lit her face. "But wooden floors would be gorgeous in here, too, if you wanted to spend that much—though they might be a pain to keep up. And there are all kinds of ceramics. They're expensive, but they last forever. I saw some that looked like slate once, and that was gorgeous, but I don't know what you want to spend or what you like."

"Blue," he said. "I like blue." He looked down, bemused, at her glowing face. Yes, he was going to have to kiss her.

"What shade of blue? Turquoise or navy or powder blue or cerulean? And do you want solid, or a pattern? A white background with a blue design? Do you like traditional stuff, or something a bit bolder? And you didn't say if you want vinyl or tiles or what. You could get—''

He bent and covered her mouth with his. She made a muffled noise, then looped her hands around his neck. Her mouth was soft and warm and welcoming, and he wanted her, suddenly, more than he wanted his next breath. The very strength of that need made him pull his head back, his heart pounding, his muscles tight with hunger—and terror. He wanted to push her away. He wanted to push inside her.

He couldn't move.

She tilted her head to one side and grinned. ''I think you're trying to change the subject. And you're embarrassing Mark.''

''I'm all blushes,'' Mark agreed from over at the table.

Nate was thankful for the moment to compose himself, but he was still badly unsettled. ''I don't think it's Mark who's embarrassed.''

Something in his face or his voice must have given him away. Hannah's smile slipped. She searched his eyes, her own gaze troubled.

''I guess I'm ready for bed,'' Mark said.

Startled, Nate turned to look at him. He looked fine, but for Mark to actually suggest going back to his hospital bed told Nate that something was very wrong. Nate let go of Hannah and started toward his brother. ''What is it? What's wrong?''

Mark grimaced.

Behind him, Hannah said, ''He's being gallant, Nate.''

Nate reached Mark's chair in time to hear him mutter, ''Better 'gallant' than 'sweet,' I guess.''

Chapter 15

Mark was not looking forward to making the transfer back to his bed. He wasn't about to admit it, but spending the morning sitting in the wheelchair had left him pretty sore. His arm wasn't too bad, but his ribs ached and his leg—well, the damn leg hurt. Shifting to the bed wasn't going to feel good.

But at least he'd have Nate alone for a minute. And then his stupid brother would have a little time alone with Hannah.

"Ready?" Nate said from behind him.

Mark nodded. His brother slid his hand under Mark's armpits and lifted, while Mark got his good leg under him and pushed. He balanced on one leg with the casted leg supported by the chair's leg rest at an awkward slant that made the leg throb. Nate came around and lifted Mark's cast, while Mark turned himself and sat on the bed.

There. His forehead was damp and he hurt everywhere but his toes—but he'd done it. Nate helped him get the broken leg up on the bed with him, which raised a little more sweat, but that was okay. Soon he was leaning back against the raised head of the bed, and Nate was offering him a couple of ibuprofen tablets and some water.

Mark grimaced. He still hated taking anything, but he'd decided it was better to take these and wean himself from the prescription pills. "So," he said, accepting the tablets and the glass, "you do realize what you just did in there, don't you?"

"I kissed Hannah," Nate said drily. "It doesn't take a powerful understanding to figure that out."

"You asked her to fix up your home, for God's sake! Hannah's hungry for a home. What do you expect her to think when you start talking about her picking out tile and carpet?"

Nate was silent a long moment. "Maybe I'm thinking the same thing. Maybe I'd like her to stay."

Mark almost choked. "You're going to marry her?"

Nate's face tightened and closed down even more. "Hell, no. I haven't promised her anything, and I'm not going to. I just…I might like it if she stayed."

"She's hoping for marriage."

"Then she's a fool."

Mark sighed. "Someone here sure is."

Hannah reheated the macaroni and sliced some of the roast chicken for Nate. She kept her hands busy, but her mind stayed curiously blank. She was balanced between hope and hurt, and it was a precarious place to be. A single wrong thought could turn a wobble into a fall.

Like letting herself wonder where he'd been last night after he left their bed. Or whether talking about tile and carpet meant that he was beginning to think of his future, and if he wanted her in it.

Cowboy boots on vinyl weren't very loud, but she knew the sound of his footsteps by now. "Ready to eat?"

"I guess. You heading into town now?"

"In a minute." She started to dish up his macaroni, then stopped with a sigh and leaned on the counter. She just wasn't any damn good at balance. She said, low-voiced, "I missed you this morning when I woke up."

"I couldn't sleep."

She turned around. His face had that closed-down look she hated.

"So where did you go?"

"I went out to the stable and messed with the tack for a while."

"You were restless because you saw Jenny yesterday."

"Yes."

She swallowed. Ask a stupid question...well, while she was at it, she might as well ask another one. "Do you still—"

He interrupted quickly, his voice hard. "I don't love her."

"I was going to ask if you still *hated* her."

He didn't answer, but something cracked open behind those dark eyes. She saw inside, and what she saw made her heart hurt. The only people, she thought, who need such big, high walls are the ones with so much to give that they hurt themselves in the giving.

"I'm not used to talking about her," he said at last. "Hell, I'm not used to thinking about her, not anymore. I didn't think I felt anything for her one way or another. But I hadn't seen her since right after the trial; and then all of a sudden, there she was."

"I guess that was confusing."

"Yeah." He ran a hand through his hair. "We have a lot of shared history, Jenny and me, and she's all tangled up in my mind with some of the things I used to think, the kind of life I expected to have, once upon a time. And when I saw her yesterday... She's in pretty bad shape, isn't she?"

"Yes," she said, her heart aching for herself, for him...for all of them.

"I wish she hadn't come back."

So do I, she thought, turning around to dish out his food. *So do I.*

He came up behind her and ran his hands down her arms,

then back up them, letting his hands rest on her shoulders. "I don't hate her," he said, his voice low. "It took me hours to figure that out. That's why I couldn't sleep. It was strange to find out that I wasn't angry anymore, after everything she's done."

She turned in his arms. "Strange, and maybe a little scary?" Anger made a great fence—strong, hard and barbed. Had that wall come down because he didn't need it anymore? Or because the sight of Jenny had stirred his compassion— or other, more powerful feelings?

"It doesn't matter. She's my past, not my present."

Hannah badly wanted to ask where *she* fit—in his present, yes, he wanted her in his bed right now. But what about the future? She didn't know if it was fear or good sense that kept her from pressing him for an answer. Instead, she managed to say lightly, "So, are you going to give me any guidelines at all about the floor?"

"I told you. I like blue." He smiled and rubbed his hands over her arms again. "And you'd probably better be going if you're going to find something special for the party. There's bad weather on the way. I'd rather you were back before it hits."

"Bad weather?" she said, surprised. She'd listened to the radio all morning. "Isn't it too early in the year for the spring storms? The weather report did say something about a thirty-percent chance of rain tomorrow, but it's supposed to be clear tonight."

"I could be wrong, but the horses are jittery, Abe swears his rheumatism is acting up, and the air has the feel of a storm on the way."

Earl and Susie Navarette lived in a huge, two-story adobe home about thirty minutes away. Cars and trucks were parked all over the place when Nate, Hannah and Mark arrived—in the curving drive in front of the house, along part of the access road and in the flat, weedy area that lay between the house and the rest of the ranch buildings.

They were running a little late. Abe and the hands were already here. Hannah had vanished into the bathroom about six o'clock, and she'd stayed in there so long, Nate had wondered if he would have to drag her out. When she finally did come out, though, the results had been well worth the wait.

Earl had told Nate that he would save a parking space for them, and so he had. A makeshift sign on a metal barrel announced that one of the spots in the drive in front of the four-car garage was Reserved for Guests with Broken Legs. If You Don't Have One When You Park Here, You Will When You Leave.

Nate was smiling as he got out of the car.

"Your friend has a sense of humor," Hannah said, getting out on her side. "At least, I hope he's joking. Here, let me have the keys and I'll get the wheelchair while you get Mark."

"Earl's a subtle man in some ways, but his sense of humor isn't one of them." Nate tossed her the keys, and she went around to the trunk.

The sun was setting, and making a fuss about the business, too. Clouds piled up halfway across the sky, dark and gravid with rain, and painted by the setting sun in lurid shades of purple, orange, yellow and a deep, brooding crimson. The wind wasn't blowing strongly, but it had a bite to it that convinced him he'd been right about the storm headed their way.

Hannah unloaded the wheelchair, dropping the keys in her jacket pocket. Nate unloaded Mark, lowering his brother into the wheelchair. Mark sat down with a grunt, and Nate turned to say something to Hannah about the keys. And forgot how to speak.

Silhouetted against the setting sun, bathed in the long shadows of dusk and the last fiery light of the day, she took his breath away. She had made an effort to subdue her hair, pulling it back in some kind of fancy braid. But a few strands had already worked loose. They frisked in the wind now, outlining her face like unruly question marks.

"I really didn't need this jacket, Nate," she said, hugging it around her. "I don't know why you insisted I wear it. Here, let me get Mark's chair."

"I've got it." Nate started pushing Mark along the paved drive toward the house. He knew why she hadn't wanted to wear the jacket. It was old and worn and it hid her newly purchased finery. He wished he could have bought her something pretty to wear instead of that parka. "You can take the jacket off as soon as we're inside. When's your birthday?" She wouldn't refuse a gift if it was for her birthday.

"What?" She laughed as she fell into step beside him. "Are you wanting to know my sun sign? I'm a Taurus. We're not exactly known as party people."

"Are you worrying about the party?" Mark asked, turning his head to aim a leer up at her. "You can hold my hand if you're nervous."

"I'm not nervous. I never was. I just needed something new to…" Her voice drifted off as she looked at another set of new arrivals, who were approaching the front door from the opposite direction. There were five of them—three women and two men—and they all wore jeans beneath various sorts of dressy jackets and coats. "I'm overdressed, aren't I?" she asked starkly.

"No," Nate said without pausing. "You're beautiful."

She turned a startled face towards him—and promptly tripped over something. "Oh, I am not! Especially not if you're looking above the neck. But thanks."

He stopped. Surely he'd told her. Or had he only said it while he was making love to her? Did she think only her body was beautiful to him? "Mark," he said, "set the brake on your rig, would you?" And he turned and took Hannah's face in his hands. "You are beautiful," he said firmly. "Everyone but you is aware of this, Hannah. I don't want to hear any arguments from you on the subject." To prove his point, he kissed her.

Mark disappeared into the crowd almost the moment they crossed the threshold, his wheelchair and his attention claimed by several women eager to fuss over his injuries. Hannah kept an eye out for him, but he seemed to be having a great time.

So was she. The food was fantastic, the people were friendly, and even after Hannah's head had stopped spinning from that kiss, she was prepared to believe she was wonderful, too. And not overdressed at all, she thought with a smile as she followed her hostess to the kitchen two hours later.

Hannah had paid far too much money that afternoon for a tawny-colored dress she'd found on sale. The soft, sueded fabric reminded her of buckskin. The western-style yoke of the fitted bodice was trimmed in fringe and turquoise beading, and the skirt was full, tiered and deeply fringed along the hem. She felt like a combination of Annie Oakley and Pocahontas in the dress, and she loved it.

So did her hostess—as Hannah had realized the moment they came face to face for the first time at the front door. The older woman had been wearing an identical dress, only in aqua instead of fawn.

Susie had been the first one to laugh. Hannah had joined her a second later.

Susie Navarette was a small, well-padded woman of about sixty with very short, very white hair, a square face and round glasses. She'd come to claim Hannah's help a minute ago, saying she could use a hand in the kitchen. It was an excuse, of course, and a flimsy one. Hannah followed her out of curiosity as much as courtesy. She held the three glass dessert plates and single highball glass that Susie had handed her. Her hostess had three glasses in her hands—and two maids in her home, who circulated constantly through the parts of the house thrown open for the party, offering drinks and picking up used glasses and plates. Susie's need for "help in the kitchen" was as transparent a ruse as any Hannah had seen.

But it worked.

Hannah figured she was in for some sort of interrogation, but she didn't mind. For one thing, Susie had greeted Nate at the door with a hug when they first arrived—and Nate had hugged her back. For another, when Susie came to steal Hannah away, Nate had let her go, after sticking by her side all evening like a large, brooding watchdog.

Hannah was glad Nate had a friend who cared enough to want to check her out.

The kitchen was large and modern, and presided over by an enormous woman with a mustache and a long, graying braid hanging down her back. The cook sat on a stool at a work island, preparing a bowl of punch. "Here you go, Juana," Susie said, setting her three glasses down near one of the sinks.

The cook muttered something in Spanish.

Susie patted the woman's arm and turned to Hannah, smiling. "I suppose you're wondering why I dragged you away from the party."

"It was neatly done, though I did feel a bit like a cow being maneuvered by a champion cutting horse."

Susie giggled. "I like that comparison. The thing is, dear, we couldn't talk out there in front of everyone. And I'm dying to talk. I thought Nate would never—" Abruptly, the woman's eyes filled with tears. "Oh, how foolish. No, ignore me, my dear. I cry at weddings, movies, christenings—even commercials, sometimes. There." She dabbed at her eyes with one finger. "All done. I'm just so happy that Nate has found someone."

"I think—I mean—you may be jumping to conclusions," Hannah said weakly.

"I've embarrassed you. I didn't mean to. It's just that I was afraid he would never let anyone in again. And it couldn't have happened at a better time." She leaned forward and said in a low voice. "I heard about the scene in the drugstore yesterday. You handled that well."

Over by the punch bowl, Juana set a lemon on a cutting board, muttered something unintelligible and slammed a knife through the fruit, halving it neatly.

"Oh, don't be silly, Juana. Hannah is nothing like Jenny. Anyone can see that."

Hannah couldn't resist asking, "Did you know Jenny well, then? And Nate—you've known him a long time."

"Since he was a boy. DanaRae was a dear, dear friend." She sighed and turned on the tap. "Bring some of those plates over here, will you?" Absently she unbuttoned the cuffs on her sleeves and rolled them up. "Such a sad, serious boy he was after his mother died. That's one reason Jenny seemed good for him, at first. She made him laugh. Did he tell you I taught him English his junior year?" She squirted dish soap into the sink and turned the water on.

Hannah handed her hostess a stack of plates. "Nate hasn't told me much about his past," she admitted. "Um—is the dishwasher broken?"

"Juana doesn't like it." Susie lowered the plates into the sudsy water. "I've tried and tried to convince her that the dishwasher does a better job of sanitizing things than we can, but she doesn't believe me."

Juana mumbled something and whacked another lemon.

"There are some cup towels in that top drawer, if you want to dry for me," Susie said.

Hannah pulled out a towel. "So you taught Nate in high school," she prompted. "And you were friends with his parents."

"I don't know if anyone was truly friends with Garwood Jones. He was a difficult man. I suppose I'm prejudiced because of my friendship with DanaRae. He wasn't a good husband to her, not to my way of thinking, but she loved him. Garwood was a hard man. Honorable, in his fashion, but hard."

"I...heard about Mark." Hannah took the plate Susie handed her and started drying.

"That's the sort of thing I mean. Garwood did wrong by DanaRae in having an affair, but then he did what he considered the right thing by Mark when the little boy's mother abandoned him. He took him in and provided for him. And

DanaRae, bless her, was too tenderhearted to do anything but love the poor little boy. But Garwood never treated Mark as a son. Of course, he didn't really treat Nate as a son, either. Mostly Garwood piled obligations and expectations on that boy until it was a wonder Nate didn't explode.''

"I wonder," Hannah said, taking another plate from her, "if maybe Nate grew up a little confused about how to show affection, since his father was so distant. I mean, he's obviously devoted to Mark, in spite of—of some problems they've had. But he sure has trouble showing it."

"I knew I was going to like you!" Susie beamed. "That's very perceptive. I've always felt that in one important way, Nate was more his mother's son than his father's. You hear folks talk about how much he's like old Garwood, but people can be dense at times. Oh, if you don't know Nate well, you might not realize that his resemblance to his father is mostly physical. He does hide his emotions behind that stony mask of his, but Nate has his mother's loving heart, not his father's cold need for control. Only the poor boy has never known what to do with all that love. That's his father's training, I'm afraid."

"He…" Hannah swallowed, and got it said. "He loved Jenny, I think." What she'd done wouldn't have hurt him so badly if he hadn't cared.

"Very much, at one time." Susie sighed and rested her hands on the counter. "I thought, when they first started dating, that it would work out. She seemed very fresh, very natural—childlike, even, in some ways, and he needed that. His father had tried to make an adult of him much too young. But…have you ever known someone with a thin soul?"

Susie's phrase startled Hannah. "A thin soul? You mean—someone who's shallow?"

"More like there simply isn't enough of them. I said Jenny was childlike, but the truth is, she *was* a child, emotionally. She couldn't seem to grow up. She needed so much attention…it began to seem unhealthy, the way she clung to Nate. She was dreadfully jealous. Then Garwood Jones died." She sighed, handed Hannah the last plate and reached for a towel to dry her hands.

"That had an effect on his marriage?"

She nodded. "It was the ranch, you see. Garwood had taken on too much debt—that's so easy for a rancher to do, though who would have thought it would happen to Garwood? But it had, and Nate had the devil's own time bringing everything about. But that was what pushed Jenny rather round the bend, I'm afraid."

"I don't understand."

Juana chose that moment to heave herself to her feet. She gripped the enormous punch bowl in her thick, muscular arms, grunted something at Susie and waddled toward the door.

"I suppose you're right," Susie said, smoothing her sleeves back down. "I'd better get back to the party. Would you mind buttoning this cuff for me, dear?"

Hannah reached out obediently. "Why did you say Nate's financial problems pushed Jenny around the bend? Was she worried about money?"

"I don't think so," Susie said thoughtfully. "No, I've always thought that she just didn't want to share him with anyone or anything, not even the ranch. He had to work very long hours to keep from losing it, you see, and she couldn't stand that." She gave a last look around the kitchen. "Now, if you would help me carry some of these plates back out to the buffet? Then it will look as if we were busy with something in here other than a good gossip."

Hannah grinned and picked up a small stack of the glass plates. "Do you think anyone will believe that?"

"Of course not. You'd better tell me something about yourself, so I'll have something interesting to mention when they start prying."

"I'm twenty-four," she said promptly. "My father is a cowboy, has been all his life. He's up in Wyoming right now. I have one sister, Leslie, who's the brain in the family. She's got a degree, but no direction. I've got direction, but no degree. I'm working on that, though it will take me a while. But I can be patient when I have to be.''

Susie laughed and patted her hand. ''You forgot to mention your excellent taste in dresses. Did I tell you how much I love the one you're wearing? I am glad to hear you can be patient, though, because I think you'll have to be, if you want to make things work with Nate. Betrayal is never easy to forget, is it?''

''No. It isn't.'' Jenny had taught Nate far too much about betrayal, and Hannah reminded herself now that Susie was right. Hannah couldn't expect Nate to unlearn those lessons all at once.

Susie picked up another small stack of plates and started for the hall, adding almost casually as she pushed open the swinging door, ''I've always thought that they put the wrong person in jail that night.''

''What do you mean?''

''When Nate killed that man. The one who was really responsible was his wife, of course. He did exactly what she wanted him to do, as did the unfortunate man she'd taken as a lover to make Nate jealous.''

''No,'' Hannah said. ''I'm sorry, but you're wrong. It was an accident.''

''Perhaps it was, on Nate's part. I rather think it was exactly what Jenny intended, however. She was the center of attention for the entire town for months. In fact, Jenny got almost everything she wanted as a result of what happened that night. Everything except Nate.''

Susie paused before going through the door to the dining room, where the barbecue had been served, buffet-style, earlier. An assortment of desserts now covered the big dining table. She looked over her shoulder at Hannah, utterly serious. ''I do hope you'll be careful, dear. In a manner of speaking, Jenny has already killed once for him.''

Hannah stayed by Nate's side after that and tried to forget Susie's last, melodramatic words. At eleven o'clock, Susie decided that no party was complete without dancing. Earl and Nate and several of the other men moved furniture, clearing most of the huge, tiled living area, while she programmed the stereo. Then she turned down the lights and turned up the volume.

Nate came to stand in front of Hannah and held out his hand. He didn't speak, but he was smiling with his eyes. He looked happy.

Her heart turned over. She'd already been glad they'd come to the party, but at that moment, she wanted to sing out her own happiness. Instead, she put her hand in his, and let him lead her out onto the makeshift dance floor.

The first song was a fast-moving, boot-stomping Cajun number that got everyone's blood pumping. Nate was as smooth a partner as Hannah had ever had, and she was breathless and laughing when the song finished. After a brief pause while the CD player hunted up the next song programmed into it, George Strait started singing about Texas ladies, and she went into Nate's arms. They danced slowly, her head on his shoulder, the music filling her head while love flowed around and through her. She felt light and whole and perfect.

When the song ended, she stayed in Nate's arms. Maybe everyone felt as dreamy as she did, because no one spoke in the brief silence between songs.

Then the doorbell chimed. And chimed again. And again.

The urgency of that repeated summons had Hannah lifting her head from Nate's shoulder. Others were turning to look, too. Whoever was out there just kept ringing that bell, spreading alarm through the crowd. Hannah and Nate were at the end of the living room nearest the entry hall, and she saw Earl hurrying to answer his door.

The next song came on, but only for a second. Someone promptly turned the stereo off. In the renewed hush she heard the muted howl of the wind, and she realized that the threatened storm had hit.

Maybe, she thought, the weather explained the impatience

of the person outside. Maybe he had been ringing the bell for some time, unheard over the music, and he was tired of getting wet. Maybe there was nothing really wrong.

A moment later, Earl came back into the living room, his expression grim. There was a man with him—a man Hannah had met before. His beige Stetson was wrapped in plastic to protect it from the weather. Raindrops glistened on the clear covering, and on the black slicker he wore over his khaki uniform. Sheriff Royce Thompson stopped a couple of steps into the living room. His gaze flicked rapidly over the crowd and came to rest on Nate. "Mr. Jones," he said with a small nod of greeting, "I need to ask you a few questions."

Nate was still and taut. "What's this about, Sheriff?"

"Someone beat Mario Bustamante badly early this morning. He's been in the hospital over in Amarillo since Ignacio Torres found him in the field out behind his house. He came to about an hour ago." Thompson paused. "He says you did it."

Nate's arm dropped. He moved an infinitesimal distance away from her. Just enough so that he stood alone. "Of course, Sheriff," he said with a courtesy so smooth his very civility was mocking. "Shall we talk in one of the rooms here, or did you plan to arrest me immediately?"

Thompson's face was impassive. "Bustamante admits he's the one who's been shooting cattle around here. He says he shot your dog to get back at you. You suspected as much, didn't you?"

Hannah's heart thudded in her chest. Her mouth was dry, so dry she had to lick her lips to summon enough moisture to speak. "When, Sheriff?" she asked, her voice hoarse. "How early this morning did this happen?"

Thompson looked at her thoughtfully. "Why do you ask?"

"If it was before dawn, I can swear Nate didn't do it. Because he was with me. All night."

Chapter 16

The past had bled into the present, staining the night with nightmare. Nate felt disoriented, swamped with a sense of unreality as one of his deepest, most secret fears slipped out of his unconscious and took shape before him in the person of the quiet sheriff—the fear of being locked up again, cut off from the land and the sky. Imprisoned.

In the midst of that waking nightmare, he heard Hannah's words with a deepening sense of disbelief...and fury.

She was lying. She hadn't been with him all night. He'd gone to the stable, and she'd woken up and found him gone. Hadn't she told him that a few hours ago? Hadn't she probed and pried to find out where he'd gone, and why?

So why was she lying now?

He didn't challenge her, though. Not in front of the sheriff and all the whispering party guests. With the brutal control he'd learned over the years, he forced those feelings down out of sight. "No," he said calmly in response to a question from Thompson. "I haven't seen Mario since the day he and a gang of his buddies accosted Hannah. He slapped her."

Remembered anger heated Nate's blood and chilled his voice. "I left him sprawled in the dirt that time."

"Are you aware that he's been bragging about how he was going to pay you back for that?"

"No, but it doesn't surprise me."

"Do you blame him for shooting your dog?"

"Yes, but I didn't beat him up for it."

"Where were you this morning at five a.m.?"

"Like Hannah says, I was at home. I didn't leave the ranch all day today until I came here." Nate managed to answer Thompson's question without mentioning that he'd woken up about four that morning and gone to the stable. That he felt forced to back up her lie added to his rage. Never again had he wanted to be at the mercy of a woman's lies. But Hannah had slid hers around his neck like a noose—and he had let her, dammit. That fact baffled him as much as it frightened him.

Now she was in control. She could tighten that noose whenever she liked, couldn't she? All she had to do was threaten to tell the sheriff that she'd lied about Nate's whereabouts. She could always say that she'd been afraid to tell the truth, afraid he would hurt her. That would do the trick. Hadn't he learned how easily people believed that particular lie?

Thompson asked a few more questions, directing some of them to the room at large. He left without arresting Nate, though. No doubt he felt he didn't have a solid case. Because of Hannah's lie.

When Earl escorted the sheriff to the door, conversation broke out around the big room in a babble of startlement and speculation. Hannah turned to Nate. "Thank God," she said, and rested her hand on his arm. "Mario must really hate you, if he was willing to lie about who beat him in order to pay you back. Do you think Sammie did it? He said he was going to do something about Trixie being shot."

"Probably." Anger grew, first matching, then overtaking the fear.

She shivered. "I didn't think Thompson would believe that, though. I was so afraid he was going to arrest you."

"You saw to it that he didn't, though, didn't you?" He grabbed her arm. "Come on. We need to talk."

There was an alcove just off the entry hall opposite the entrance to the living area. Nate headed for it now, his hand clamped around Hannah's wrist. They passed Earl in the entry hall. Nate's friend gave the two of them a quick, assessing glance, but he went on into the living room without speaking.

Nate pulled Hannah into the darkened alcove.

"What is it?" she said. "You act like you're angry, but that doesn't make sense."

"Doesn't it?" There was a single window in the alcove. When lightning flashed outside, the livid glare played across Hannah's face. "Why did you lie?"

She stared at him. "Isn't it obvious? I didn't want you to go to jail! And—and it isn't really a lie. I know you didn't put Mario in the hospital. Do you think that Sammie did it?"

"So what changed your mind? You were worried about what I might do to someone when we were at the vet's the night Trixie was shot."

She shook her head. "That was different. You were in the grip of a rage and I thought you might do something you would regret later, but I never thought you'd cold-bloodedly beat someone badly enough to put him in the hospital."

"So you think I'm only dangerous when I'm angry." He grabbed her shoulders and pulled her close to him, staring down into her face. "Then you should be frightened now. Because I'm very, very angry."

"Dammit, Nate!" She shoved against him, but of course he didn't move. "What's wrong with you? The way you're acting, you'd think I'd just lied because I wanted to get you put *into* jail, the way Jenny did, instead of lying to keep you out!" She blinked rapidly several times. "I'm not Jenny. You told me you knew that."

His fingers tightened on her shoulders. "But you've put me in almost the same position she did. All you have to do now to get what you want from me is to threaten to change your story. Just like all she had to do was keep telling her lies. She wanted me to take her back. I wouldn't. So don't think—''

She yanked on her arm so suddenly that she managed to wrench it free from his grasp. And then she slapped him. Hard. She drew her arm back to slap him again, but he caught her wrist. ''Don't.'' His voice was cold. His cheek was hot and stinging from her blow.

''Don't you ever tell me I'm like that. Like her. Don't you dare!''

''Why not?'' he said, his voice low and ugly. ''You say you love me. Just like she did.'' How many times had he heard those words? Spoken sadly. Spoken in anger, or through tears, or in that needy voice he'd grown to hate. Spoken so often as an accusation, because she'd been certain he hadn't loved her back. Not enough. Never enough. Nothing he'd said or done had ever been enough, and toward the end of their marriage, she'd been right. He hadn't loved her. He dropped Hannah's wrist. ''Tell me you haven't been thinking about marriage. Tell me you haven't been hoping I would end up marrying you. *Tell me you don't love me.*''

She looked at him, her eyes huge in the dimness. Huge, and shiny because they were wet. One tear leaked out and trickled down, leaving a glistening trail along her cheek. ''I can't,'' she said softly. ''Because I do love you, Nate. Very much.''

The prison walls closed in around him. He pushed her away.

She lifted her chin proudly, but her lip trembled. And she turned and left.

Nate stood in that dark, empty alcove for several long minutes. The emptiness grew and grew inside him. He hadn't meant to push her away. He just didn't want her to love him. He couldn't stand that. He wanted her to stay, but he didn't want those chains wrapped around him ever again.

He ran a hand over his face. "Christ," he said out loud, unsure whether he cursed or prayed.

The squeak of rubber wheels on the tiled entryway roused him slightly. Apparently Mark had figured out a way to propel himself in his chair without help, because he sat in front of Nate now, right in the entrance to the alcove.

"What the hell did you say to Hannah?" he demanded.

"We argued," Nate said wearily.

"You made her cry. Dammit, Nate, if I could get out of this blasted chair I'd show you what I think of a man who—"

But Nate wasn't listening anymore. Behind Mark, Hannah hurried toward the front door. She wore her bulky jacket. Memory and realization flashed through him simultaneously. Hannah hadn't given him back the keys to the Lincoln after she unloaded the wheelchair. They were in the pocket of her parka.

She was leaving.

"Wait!" he said, and tried to get past Mark. "Hannah, wait."

His brother gave the wheel a quick jerk, turning the chair so it blocked him. "Leave her alone."

"Dammit to hell, Mark!"

Hannah didn't even slow down. She flung open the door, letting in the rushing sounds of wind and rain, and ran outside. He heard the slap of her running footsteps an instant before lightning flared again, followed by a clap of thunder.

Nate managed to get his brother's chair out of the way, but it took precious moments because Mark did everything he could to hinder him—including landing a single short jab in Nate's stomach with his one good arm. The second Nate got past the wheelchair, he ran after Hannah.

Too late. He stood in the pouring rain and watched as the big Lincoln pulled out of the short drive and headed off into the storm.

Hannah didn't cry often or easily. When she did give in to tears, it wasn't a pretty sight. She sobbed and gulped and wiped her runny nose, cursing Nate and pounding the steering wheel all the way back to his house. Her tears and the rain forced her to drive slowly and cautiously, but both were letting up by the time she pointed the nose of his car down the long driveway leading to Nate's house. She felt drained and sad, mortified that some of the party-goers had seen her cry, though she'd managed to stifle the worst of her personal storm until she'd reached the privacy of the car.

Fortunately, Mark was one of those who'd seen her. He'd been in the darkened hallway where she'd fled, being entertained by one of the more persistent members of his frequent caller's club. Hannah had dashed into the bedroom that Susie had designated as cloakroom, grabbed her parka from the pile on the bed, and emerged to find him waiting for her, alone.

He'd asked what was wrong. She'd been too upset to be very coherent, but he'd grasped the fact that she wanted to leave, *needed* to leave. After extracting her promise to drive very slowly and carefully, he'd offered to run interference with Nate for her.

Hannah sniffed and thought about where she would sleep that night. Lying in Nate's bed beside him didn't just sound painful, after what he'd said and done; it sounded impossible. She turned into the driveway that led to the detached garage, thinking that she would move back into her own bedroom, just for tonight.

Tomorrow she had some very hard decisions to make. For now, for right this moment, she couldn't stand to think about what she was going to do.

Nate always parked the pickup next to the house, leaving it out in all kinds of weather, but he kept the car in the garage. Fortunately, the remote for the garage door was clipped to the visor. Unfortunately, the garage sat a good twenty yards from the house. Hannah got the car safely tucked away in its nice, dry garage, and then had to go back out into the rain herself. She sighed and left through the side door, the car keys in her left hand.

It was still raining, but the wind had died. There were

puddles on the sidewalk that wound from the garage to the house. The branches of the old oak nearest the house creaked and groaned in the wind, sounding mournful as any ghost. Hannah's feet crunched on the dirt and debris the storm had left on the cement. She was wet and cold and too deep-down miserable to care about the drizzle soaking her uncovered head.

The sudden glare of a light blinded her.

"Hey!" she said, automatically raising a hand to shield her eyes. "Watch it!"

"Sorry," said a soft voice.

The beam of light lowered. Hannah blinked, clearing the dazzle from her eyes, and saw someone standing several feet away on the cement path, holding a metal flashlight.

Jenny.

Hannah scowled. "What are you doing here?"

Jenny's face was a pale oval in the darkness. She wore some sort of dark slacks or jeans and a bulky sweater, but no coat or hat. Her hair clung to her head and shoulders in long, wet clumps. "I'm so glad you're back, Hannah."

"What is it? What's wrong?" Something certainly was. The other woman was soaked and shivering, as if she'd been out in the downpour for some time.

But when Hannah took a step forward, Jenny stepped back.

"Where's Nate?" Jenny asked breathlessly.

"He—uh, he'll be along shortly."

"He didn't come home with you?"

Hannah didn't answer. Alarm prickled along her nerve endings.

"Never mind." Jenny's strained expression eased. "I can see that he didn't. Good. I'd thought of all sorts of ways to get you away from the house later tonight. I still have my keys, you know, so I could have done it. But it would have been tricky." She smiled. "This way is better. Unconsciously, Nate must know what I want. He's helping me."

Hannah's heart pounded out a warning. Her hands tightened into fists, making the keys she still held dig into her palm. "What are you talking about?"

Jenny lowered the hand holding the big silver flashlight, and raised her other hand. It held something metal and shiny, too. A gun. "You'll have to come with me, Hannah. I really can't let you interfere between me and Nate anymore."

Earl was at the back of the white Caddy, stowing Mark's wheelchair. Susie stood by the driver's window, leaning down to give Nate entirely unwanted advice. Mark was in the back seat, and Nate was behind the wheel. The garage door was already open, letting some of the rain in. "I won't scratch the paint," Nate told her, trying to stifle his impatience. "Thanks for letting me borrow your car."

"Oh, just get going," Susie said, straightening. "And *try* not to be an idiot when you get home! Skip the explanations and the justifications and go straight to groveling. You don't want to lose that woman, Nate."

No. He didn't. Nate pushed a button and the window slid closed. The moment Earl slammed the trunk closed, he pulled out of the garage. Once out of the driveway, he accelerated smoothly and strongly.

Though rain drummed down outside, it was too quiet in the car. Mark didn't speak. Nate wanted him to. He wanted his brother to say something—to condemn Nate, or explain himself. He wanted Mark to argue or yell, anything to prevent the two of them riding along, trapped together in grim silence. It was too empty, and entirely too familiar, that silence. It had lasted six years.

But Nate didn't know how to break it, or how to bridge it.

The storm was easing. Rain still came down, but more gently, and the Caddy was a big, heavy car with excellent tires. Nate could keep the speed up in spite of the wet roads. He told himself as he took the second curve that the Lincoln was just as large and heavy.

But Hannah had been crying when she took this curve.

Between them, Nate and Mark had sent her out into the night in tears. All of a sudden he couldn't stand it. "Dammit to hell!" he exploded. "Why did you help her get away from me? She was crying. She shouldn't be on the road when she's crying."

"Hannah's not stupid. Not about most things, anyway. She'll take it easy heading home."

"Why did you help her?"

"Why did you hurt her?"

Nate couldn't answer at first. He tried. His knuckles were white on the steering wheel, but it was so hard to get the words out. "I didn't mean to. I didn't want to. Everything got tangled up for a while." The past with the present. Old fears with new ones.

"Yeah, well, that's not good enough, Nate. Hannah tried to tell me what happened, but she kept stopping and gulping back tears, and she wasn't making much sense. I thought she said something about you hating her because she didn't want you to go to jail, but surely that was wrong."

"I lost it," Nate said bleakly. "That's what happened. For a few minutes I thought I was going to be locked up again, and then…Hannah lied. I couldn't handle that. She told the sheriff she was with me all night. She wasn't."

"But dammit, Nate! She did that to *help* you! What's the matter with you? Are you too proud to accept help from anyone?"

Proud? Nate shook his head. "Pride has nothing to do with it. As soon as she lied—as soon as she had everyone believing her lie—she had control. Just like Jenny. Maybe I overreacted, but…" His voice dropped. "For God's sake, Mark, you were *there*. You lived there with us. More than anyone else, you should know what it was like for me with Jenny."

"I'm not sure I do, though," Mark said softly. "Yeah, I was there, but I was fifteen when you married her. I saw everything through a haze of hormones and stupidity. Since then, I've figured some things out, but at the time—hell. Like I said, I was stupid."

"You weren't stupid," Nate said as he slowed for the turn onto the last stretch of highway before reaching home. The rain had let up considerably, and for the first time he saw another vehicle on the road. It was a Bronco or Explorer, though, heading in toward town. Thank God, he thought. Nate was terrified of seeing the crumpled wreck of a Lincoln on the way home. "You were only fifteen when we got married. I was twenty-two, and I obviously didn't know better."

"She's one hell of a liar."

"Oh, Jenny's a world-class liar. She always has been. I knew that. Even back when we were dating, I knew she made things up, but I thought it was just about little things—'the dog ate my homework' sort of lie. I didn't realize…" Maybe he hadn't wanted to realize how serious her problems were. "But I was pretty young, too, when we went together in high school. I didn't take time to really get to know her again when I came home from college before we got married."

"I always wondered about that. You two did get hitched pretty quick."

Nate shrugged. "She said she'd waited for me. She was devoted to me, and, God help me, I thought that was just great. And I…" Nate couldn't finish that sentence. He'd loved her, too. Once. "Lying was Jenny's way of staying in control. I didn't understand that until it was too late. She lied easily and well. People always believed her."

"I did," Mark said. "At first. Right after Dad's death, when she came crying to me about how you were neglecting her, I felt sorry for her. At first. That's one reason…"

"You don't have to talk about it."

"No. Hannah said I should make you listen. Maybe she's right. I never slept with Jenny, Nate. In spite of what you saw that day, I was never with her."

"Hell, I know that."

There was a thud from the back seat, followed by a string of curses.

"What? What is it?"

"My stupid leg fell on the floor when I tried to lean forward."

"What? Why would you do that in a moving car?"

"Because I'm almost as big an idiot as you are."

"Are you all right?"

They were nearly home. Mark didn't answer his question. Instead he asked him one. "Nate," Mark said, "why were you so damn eager to get me out of the house if you didn't think I'd been screwing your wife?"

Nate was shaken. "Dammit, Mark, you can't have thought I believed her!" The silence from the back seat told him that was exactly what Mark had thought. "I *never* believed Jenny. I thought you knew. How could you have thought I did? Didn't you think I would have been a hell of a lot more angry if I'd believed her?"

Mark's voice was soft. "I thought you didn't trust yourself—that you didn't want to lose control."

Nate shook his head. "I was afraid you had started to care about her. She was good at that, and I didn't want her sinking her hooks into you any deeper than they already were. But I didn't know what to do, what to say. She was still my wife. I couldn't make myself talk about her that way."

"Like Mom never let us say anything bad about Dad."

Nate hadn't thought of it that way, but Mark was right. That's just how it had been. The silence that fell between them lasted the length of the driveway, but it felt different. This time it wasn't empty.

Nate parked Susie's white Cadillac behind his pickup. He turned the car, but then he just sat there, absorbed by what he'd learned. "All this time, I thought you knew. I thought you couldn't forgive me for letting you leave instead of sending Jenny away. And for not protecting you." God knows he'd been angry with himself for failing Mark that way.

Mark sounded stunned. "You thought I was mad because you didn't protect me?"

"You were sixteen. Underage. What she did to you wasn't right."

Mark cleared his throat. "I—uh, let's get inside so you can make up with Hannah." He hesitated. "You do want that, right? I mean, you want *her.*"

"Wanting her may not be enough. I don't know if she'll forgive me."

"She loves you."

"I don't want her to love me," he said, tensing. "I don't want that, ever again."

"That's about the stupidest thing I ever heard you say."

"Love is a trick. A weapon."

"Hannah isn't like that."

"This isn't about Hannah. It's about *love.* I didn't just learn this from Jenny, though God knows she taught me more than I ever wanted to know on the subject. Don't you remember Mom? How sad she was because of the way Dad treated her? But she *loved* him."

"That's not—"

"And Dad. I think he loved her, too, in his way. It pretty much wrecked him when she died." Nate shook his head. "Love is a sickness."

"Nate, if you would just shut up for—"

"Love makes people into victims. I don't want any part of it."

"You stupid, pigheaded son of a bitch! I love you, too! So which one of us is the victim here?"

Nate opened his mouth. There was something he was going to say. Something important he was supposed to say. But his mind was blank. Entirely blank.

After a moment, Mark cleared his throat. "Of course, I just meant that I, uh—you know. Care. You're my brother. That's what I meant."

"Sure." Slowly, one by one, thoughts sifted back into Nate's mind. They weren't quite the same thoughts he'd had before. They didn't fall into quite the same shapes. "That kind of—feeling—is different, though. Between brothers, I mean. I mean, I care, too. But that isn't what it's like between a man and a woman."

Mark apparently recovered faster than Nate, because he sounded amused. "I sure as hell hope not. But maybe it's not completely different. Maybe you've got the wrong idea about what love means."

Slowly, Nate reached over and opened the door. The thoughts taking shape in his mind were beginning to make sense. "Maybe I do," he said. "Come on. Let's get in the house."

He needed to find Hannah. Quick. He had a feeling she could help him understand.

Chapter 17

The portion of the storm over the ranch might have slackened, but the part of it that squatted down over Bitter Creek was still going all out. The windshield wipers on the little Bronco barely kept the windshield clear enough for Hannah to see the stop sign her headlights picked out straight ahead.

Good, she thought. She could stall the blasted vehicle out again when she downshifted.

The barrel of the gun pressed against her was warm now. It had been icy cold when Jenny climbed in the back seat back at Nate's house and pushed it against Hannah's neck. "Keep it running this time," Jenny said.

"I'll try, but I told you, I'm not used to driving a standard." Delay. It was the only weapon Hannah had. Nate's ex-wife might be nuts, she might be shaking with cold and whatever brand of mental breakdown she was having, but she wasn't stupid. She'd kept that shiny gun trained on Hannah constantly.

They were in Jenny's brother's vehicle. She'd borrowed it without his knowledge, along with his gun, which she'd used

to force Hannah to drive into town. Hannah had stalled the
Bronco three times getting it backed out, but Jenny had gotten dangerously close to hysteria, so she'd had to quit pre-
tending she couldn't use the clutch at all. She'd driven as
slowly as she'd dared, praying to see a cop car or at least a
passing motorist.

The only vehicle they'd passed had been Susie's Cadillac,
heading the other way.

Nate would look for her. Hannah knew that, clung to it.
She'd dropped those keys on the sidewalk so he would know
something was wrong—if he found them. No, *when* he found
them. He would come looking for her. But he wouldn't know
where to look unless someone saw them creeping along the
rain-washed road in the Bronco. It might be up to her to
rescue herself, since, unfortunately, the storm seemed to be
keeping everyone inside.

Everyone but maniacs. "Do it right this time." Jenny's
voice was hoarse.

"I'll do my best." She downshifted, clutching awkwardly
enough to make the car buck a bit. The gun dug into her
neck. Her stomach lurched sickeningly.

"Don't!" Jenny's voice was shrill. "No more tricks."

Hannah breathed in, slowly, carefully, hanging onto her
control. Control was the one thing she had that Jenny lacked.
"Sure," she said, clutching more smoothly as she braked.
"There. That was better, wasn't it?"

"Keep going."

"Just give me a minute. I don't want to do this wrong."
Hannah eased away from the stop sign as slowly as any little
old lady. "I really think you should move that gun back from
my neck a little. If it were to go off accidentally—"

"You'd be dead." She actually giggled. "That isn't a
problem for me."

Hannah licked her lips. "But you'd have trouble explaining all the blood in here, wouldn't you? Isn't that why you're
taking me…wherever it is you're taking me?" She wasn't
sure where they were now, but they seemed to have skirted

the edge of town. House lights shone dimly through the downpour along the right side of the road. On the other side—nothing. "You don't want to have a lot of explaining to do."

"I'll think of something if I have to. I'm good at that. Besides, Nate would never let me be arrested."

Hannah had already discovered that when Jenny grew fearful she invoked her "soul mate." She tried another approach. "Have you ever seen someone who's been shot, Jenny?"

"I'm not squeamish." But she sounded less certain.

"I've worked in hospitals." Nowhere near the emergency room, but never mind that for now. "A bullet makes a real mess. Do you know what brains look like?"

"I'm pointing this at your neck, not your head." But the gun didn't press against Hannah's neck quite so firmly.

"But it's a pretty big gun. I'll bet the bullet would go right through my spinal cord. Then my brains would leak out—along with all that blood. There would be a lot of blood."

"Brains don't…leak."

"They do if you sever the spinal cord. It's all attached, you know." Desperation lent a real flourish to Hannah's creative version of human anatomy. "And then there's the spinal fluid, which gets mixed in with the brains. It's yellow, kind of a mustardy color, and it's runny, and it smells—"

"Stop it. Stop talking. Pull over right here. This is far enough."

Hannah swallowed and slowed the car. "We're apt to get stuck if I pull off the road."

"Just stop, then." Jenny's voice rose. "I can't think of everything. There's so much to keep track of—I can't figure out everything. Just stop."

The Bronco's headlights picked out something Hannah recognized at last, on the right side of the road—a pair of wagon wheels embedded in the ground, standing upright on either side of a dirt driveway. Good God, she thought. They were on Canyon Road. Right there, by that wagon wheel, Mario and his friends had surrounded her. And off to the left, where Jenny wanted her to pull over, was the arroyo with the dry creek bed that gave Bitter Creek its name.

Dry…except when it rained.

This wasn't exactly her lucky spot, was it?

"I said to stop." The gun dug into her neck again, hard. "It doesn't matter what color your spinal fluid is in the dark, does it?"

Hannah swallowed and did as she was told. Her mouth was dry. Her stomach was churning. Fear was a monstrous presence inside her, roiling her gut, making her hands shake. But I'm in control, she told herself. She could wait for her chance. Hadn't she always said that she could be patient when she had to be?

But she would rather have had the gun.

"Get out," Jenny said. "Slowly. Take the flashlight with you. I'll be right behind you."

Hannah prayed for just one second's inattention on Jenny's part when she could grapple for the gun, slam the car door, hit her with the flashlight. She burned to do *something*. But that shiny gun barrel followed her unwaveringly as she stepped out into the cold, soaking rain. She turned to watch Jenny climb out of the two-door vehicle, holding the gun aimed with both hands. It should have been an awkward maneuver. Damn the woman for being so coordinated.

"Turn on the flashlight." Jenny smiled. "We're going for a little walk."

"I told you," Nate said, his knuckles white where he gripped the phone. "She couldn't have left on her own. The car is here. The truck is here. And I found the keys on the sidewalk. She just dropped them there, in the rain." He paused while the sheriff asked another question. "No, nothing seems to be missing." Except Hannah. Everything in the house was just as it should be, only Hannah was gone. And she'd dropped those keys.

Nate had been scared when he didn't find her in the house, but he hadn't really panicked until he found the keys. Hannah was a woman who paid attention to what she was doing. She was a practical woman. She didn't drop keys and leave them out in the rain.

''All right,'' he said heavily. His hand shook slightly as he hung up.

''He's going to look, isn't he?'' Mark demanded. ''He'll get his deputies out looking for her?''

''He's telling his people to watch for her, but he doesn't know where to look.'' No more than Nate did.

''It's my fault. If I hadn't helped her get away—''

''It's the fault of whatever bastard has her.'' Nate felt very close to violence.

When he thought about what someone might be doing to Hannah, he felt ready to explode. But he had no target for the rage swirling in him. It was useless to him, and it would make him useless if he gave in to it. ''I was sure it was Bustamante who was out to get me. I thought he was the one who shot Trixie. But if he's in the hospital, he can't be behind—''

The phone rang. Nate grabbed it. ''Yes?''

''Mr. Jones. This is Sammie.''

Sammie, the strange one. The one who liked to light fires. The one who had probably beaten Mario badly enough to put him in the hospital. Nate's voice was very low when he answered. ''Yes?''

''I thought you should know. It didn't seem right, so I thought I should tell you. I found your name in the phone book.''

Nate forced patience on himself with the brutal control he'd learned six years ago. ''What isn't right, Sammie?''

''That other woman—the one with the shiny hair who was at the drugstore that day—she didn't like Hannah. I could tell. I do, though. Hannah helped me. I told her I would remember.''

''Yes.'' Nate's muscles were rigid. His throat was so tight he could barely get the words out. ''I'm glad you called me, Sammie. Do you know where Hannah is? Because she needs some help now. She needs you to help her, like she helped you."

"She's with that other woman. I like Hannah. She shouldn't be out in the rain like this."

With "that other woman"? With *Jenny?* Nate was suddenly sick. "Where? Where are they?"

"Right across from my house. I was watching the storm, and I saw them. They went down in the big ravine, Mr. Jones. That's not right. When it rains, that ravine isn't safe."

Fifty seconds later, Mark was on the phone, and Nate was turning the key on Susie's Cadillac.

Hannah could not believe how surefooted the madwoman behind her was. She herself had slid, slipped and twice she'd nearly fallen as they made their way slowly along the steep, muddy sides of the arroyo. The route had been roughly diagonal, as if Jenny were looking for something.

Hannah's awkwardness hadn't been entirely faked in order to slow them down, either—but some of it was. She let her foot slide out from under her, grabbing for the scrubby bush beside her, but missing. She wound up on her hands and knees in the mud.

Right where she wanted to be. The slope wasn't too steep here. If she could distract Jenny for just a minute...

"You clumsy cow!" Jenny said behind her. "Get up."

"I think I twisted my ankle." Hannah gathered her feet under her as if she were trying to stand, then she fell over. Now she was partially facing Jenny for the first time since they started down the ravine, and what she saw scared her. The woman's face was white, her eyes huge. She was drenched and freezing. Long shudders ran through her body every so often.

She didn't seem to notice. "Get up," she said, "or I'll shoot you here."

"I can't." She tightened her grip on the flashlight and collected herself. Her heart pounded fiercely.

Jenny's lips moved. She might have been muttering to herself. She might have been praying. She raised the gun, her eyes narrowing as she sighted on Hannah's head, her arms shaking as she extended them in the approved two-handed grip.

Hannah hurled the flashlight at the gun and flung herself to one side. The *crack* of the gun going off was louder than any thunder and she almost wet her pants, but she was unhurt. And then she was moving, pushing to her feet—

Jenny's shouted command to stop came a split second before the second gunshot. Hannah froze, her muscles quivering. *Damn,* she'd missed. Her chance had come and she'd missed and now the madwoman was going to shoot her.

"Looks like you can walk, after all," Jenny said cheerfully. "I think I'll keep the flashlight from now on."

Apparently shooting at people brightened her mood. Hannah straightened.

"Start walking. We don't have far to go now. Lovers' Leap isn't far."

Lovers' Leap? That didn't sound good at all.

It didn't look good, either, when Hannah stumbled to a halt three feet from the place where the ground stopped. From below, far below, she heard water rushing along, invisible in the darkness. From behind, she heard that horribly cheerful voice. "Just keep going."

"You've got to be—" Hannah swallowed. Telling Jenny she was crazy was probably not a good idea. But she was running out of ideas—good, bad or indifferent. She turned around slowly. "No."

"It's best if you jump. They'll think you did it because Nate was going to leave you for me, now that I'm back. Go on." Jenny gestured with the gun. "Maybe you'll just break a leg or something. Wouldn't you rather take that chance than have me shoot you?"

The fact that Jenny wanted her to step out over nothing was reason enough for Hannah to stay where she was. Maybe Jenny was a really bad shot. Maybe if she rushed Jenny she could cover the feet between them before a bullet—

"Put the gun up, ma'am," said another voice from somewhere off to the left in the darkness. "Put it up, and no one has to get hurt."

"Who's there?" Jenny cried. A long tremor shook her and her gun hand trembled badly. Hannah took a quick step toward her. "Back!" she shrieked. "I'll shoot, I will. Both of you stay back. No, wait. I want to see you, whoever you are. Come out where I can see you, or I'll shoot her!"

The gun was pointed at Hannah's head again.

The next voice came from off to the right. "You don't want to do that, Jenny."

Nate! Gladness rushed through Hannah.

"Nate?" Jenny said, her voice high and wobbly.

Nate had never been so scared in his life. The fear was a stomach-clenching monster nipping at him with cold, cold teeth. He'd run into one of Thompson's deputies at the top of the arroyo when he'd screeched to a halt up there, after doing ninety and better all the way into town. The deputy had told him where Thompson was, so Nate had been trying to work his way down from the other direction, hoping to flank the crazy woman who was holding Hannah at gunpoint.

Nate tilted his flashlight up so his ex-wife could see his face. "Sure, Jenny, it's me. See?"

"Nate." She sounded querulous, uncertain. "You aren't supposed to be here. You aren't supposed to—to see."

Nate saw, all right. He saw stark relief on Hannah's face, and she was watching him with complete trust. She didn't look hurt. Muddy and mussed and scared, but not hurt. Nate looked from her to the frightened petulance on the face of the woman he'd once married. The gun in Jenny's hands looked like a .38 or a .357. It had a short barrel—not accurate at any distance, but she was close, all too close, to Hannah.

Words, Nate thought helplessly. He didn't have a gun. He didn't have any weapon at all—nothing but his knowledge of Jenny, and words. He had never been good with words. This time, though, he had to be. This time, he had to lie with all his heart. "I'm glad I got here before you shot her," he said, his voice low and reassuring. He moved closer. "I don't want you going to jail. You'd hate that."

"No—stay back. I don't trust you. You didn't come for me."

"But I have come for you, Jenny." He took another step. The rain was slowing. "I'm here, aren't I? I've come to take you home with me. I'm sorry I was angry so long. That was cruel."

"Yes!" Her lip trembled. "Yes, it was cruel. I waited and waited for you to come for me. Mama said I should forget you, but nothing was right without you. I tried being with other men, Nate. It was never the same. I knew you'd want me back eventually, though. Except then I heard about *her*. You've been living with her, Nate. I couldn't wait any longer when I heard that."

"I'm sorry. I was wrong. Can you forgive me?" Another step, and, slowly, another.

Her lower lip pouted. It looked macabre, that girlish pout on her pale, gaunt face, with her wet hair hanging in strings and her shiny gun still gripped in both hands and pointed at Hannah. "I don't know."

"I wanted you to come to me, but I couldn't admit it. I've always been stubborn, Jenny. You know that. Remember how I made you wait before I asked you to the prom?"

She blinked, then giggled. "Yes, but I taught you a lesson about taking me for granted, didn't I? I went out with Davie Mathews. Then you asked me fast enough."

"You always did know how to handle me, didn't you?" The words made him sick to his stomach, but he kept smiling...and moving forward, one slow step at a time. Nate could see the sheriff, still several yards away but slowly closing the distance. "But you went too far with Tony Ramos, Jenny."

The pout grew more pronounced. And, for the first time, the gun lowered slightly. "I said I was sorry. I said it three times."

What the hell was Hannah doing? Instead of moving away while he had Jenny distracted, she'd edged closer. He tried to catch her eyes. "I was too angry to listen. I didn't like being in jail."

"That was your own fault. You didn't *have* to be in that awful jail. I told you. All you had to do was admit you hadn't meant all those terrible things you said about leaving me. All you had to do was admit you loved me, and I would have told them you never meant to kill poor Tony."

Nate's smile was frozen in place. Visibility was better, and he was only a few feet away now. Hannah was looking at him, steady and trusting. It made his heart hurt. "I'm too stubborn," he said to the woman with the gun. "I wanted you to back down first."

One of Jenny's arms lowered. She still held the gun, but one-handed now. A smile dawned on her pallid face. "You do love me, though, don't you, Nate? Tell me you love me."

"Of course." Just a few steps away now. He held out his hand. "You know I do, Jenny. I always have. Prove to me you love me, too, Jenny. Give me the gun."

Well, Hannah thought, watching tensely, that was certainly the wrong thing to say.

Jenny's smile twitched into a frown. Her hand tensed around the butt of the pistol. "You didn't say it. I love you so much, Nate, and you never say it. You were thinking about *her* when you asked for the gun back, weren't you?"

"No, of course not. I just—"

"I've told you and told you!" Jenny's voice was ragged. "You aren't supposed to let anything come between us. Nothing should come between us. Not the ranch or your stupid brother or—or *her*." Abruptly the barrel of the gun swung back toward Hannah. "I won't let her—"

Hannah didn't wait for the woman's finger to tighten on the trigger. As soon as Jenny lifted the gun, Hannah threw herself forward in a tackle. The gun discharged harmlessly over her head as she collided with the woman's midsection and they tumbled together to the ground. Hannah ended up more or less on top. She reared back, ready to do battle for the gun—but the fight had gone out of Jenny. She lay on her back in the mud, crying softly.

A second later, Nate was there. He yanked the weapon out of Jenny's hand. She didn't move. She didn't seem to notice.

Hannah sat up. That, apparently, wasn't good enough for Nate, because he grabbed her arms and pulled her to her feet. He ran his hands over her. "You're all right. Tell me you're all right," he demanded.

"I'm okay," she said obediently. The angry expression on his face as he continued to run his hands over her, checking for the injuries she didn't have, struck her as funny. Wonderfully, endearingly funny. "Nate," she said, taking his hands in hers. "I *am* all right. Really."

He stopped moving. "You scared me. I've never been so scared in my life."

"I—" *I love you,* she wanted to say. But for the first time, she had some idea of what those words meant to him. So instead, she smiled and cupped his face with her hands. "I was scared, too, but I knew you'd come looking for me. You found the keys, didn't you?"

Thompson spoke before Nate could answer. "What did you do with the gun, Jones?" He'd pulled Jenny to her feet.

"I tossed it under that mesquite."

Jenny leaned against the sheriff. She was still crying. "He never loved me," she said. "I just wanted him to love me. Is that so terrible?"

Thompson looked weary as he pulled her hands behind her and slipped a pair of cuffs on. "You have the right to remain silent…"

For a few minutes, things went on that Hannah was only vaguely aware of. A deputy arrived with a floodlight, and left with Jenny in custody. Nate asked the sheriff to have one of his people call Mark and tell him what had happened, and Thompson agreed.

And Nate held Hannah. He held her and held her, as if he

were unable to get enough of the feel of her wet, muddy body against his.

"How did you find me, anyway?" she asked at last, when she'd absorbed enough reassurance from having his big body pressed up against hers.

"Sammie saw you and Jenny going into the ravine. He called me. Mark called Thompson."

She shivered. "Imagine owing my life to Sammie."

A tremor shook him, and all at once he buried his face in her hair. "I'm sorry. I'm so sorry."

"Nate, it wasn't your fault." She stroked his back soothingly.

"I sent you out into the storm. You were upset because of what I'd said, what I'd done."

"You can apologize for being rotten to me. I think you *should*. But you can't take the blame for what happened with Jenny. Nothing she's done has been your fault, Nate." She suspected he didn't believe that yet, not deep down, and kept stroking his back, gentling the pain in him the only way she knew. "You couldn't help her or heal her, but that wasn't your fault. You couldn't have guessed she'd go nuts and come after me, either. Not your fault, Nate."

He lifted his head. "What I said, back at the party—I don't want you to leave me."

"Okay. I won't."

He sounded as though he nearly choked on a laugh. "Just like that?"

As if she *could* leave him. "Haven't I been telling you I was staying whether you wanted me to or not since the night we met?"

"I meant...I want you to stay with *me*. Not as Mark's nurse."

"Good. That's what I meant, too."

This time the laugh came more easily.

She snuggled up as close as she could get, needing his warmth. "I hope you aren't looking for any big, dramatic speeches, because I'm all out. I've about had it with drama tonight. But just try to get rid of me, Nathan Jones.''

"I don't want to." He began to stroke her hair. "You are a muddy mess, you know that?''

"Jones, we're finished here for now," the sheriff said. He'd retrieved Jenny's gun and was sliding it into a plastic bag. "You coming?''

"In a minute.''

Thompson was a tactful man. He looked at them a moment, then said, "Bring the floodlight with you when you come," and started up the slope.

Nate continued to stroke her sodden hair. "I don't want to make you any big, dramatic speeches, either.''

"That's good. You know, I'm not sure my legs are working. It's going to be hard getting back up to the road with my legs not working.''

"I'll carry you. Hannah—''

"I'm too heavy.''

"Okay, I won't carry you. Hannah, I want you to stay with me for good. For always.''

Her heart gave a crazy leap. She lifted her head to search his face. The light wasn't very good, yet she could see in his eyes what he was feeling. Hope. And fear. Her mouth was dry when she asked, "You mean the kind of 'for always' that goes with 'till death do us part'?''

He nodded.

She closed her eyes. She wanted more than anything to say yes, to grab him while he was scared and vulnerable. Nate would keep his word. Even if he changed his mind, once he'd pledged himself, he would follow through. But—

"I can't. Not without—I'd have to say the words, Nate. If we got married, sooner or later I'd say it. I know now why those words hurt you, but—''

"Hannah," he said tenderly, "shut up." Then he kissed her like a man who had found something he'd been looking for all his life—slowly, with a painstaking care that curled her toes and warmed her from the inside out. When he raised his head, his eyes were smiling. "You can say those words if you want to."

"But—I don't understand."

"I was confused. I didn't understand about the difference between loving and wanting. I think I do now. Wanting is part of loving, but it's only part. Jenny wanted me, she needed me—or at least the screwy ideas she had about me—but she never loved me. Love is that other feeling. The one that makes my throat get tight." Nate swallowed. "It's tight right now."

"Nate?" She stared up at him, hoping, her heart pounding.

He looked at her, and the smile spread, taking over his whole face. "Hannah, I love you."

Epilogue

Two months later

The clock on the vanity said it was ten minutes until midnight.

"Damn," Hannah muttered, trying to tuck a strand of hair back into her chignon. "If he's late, I'll—I'll—"

"Relax," Leslie said. "You know what Dad is like. He's probably still swapping stories with Abe. Here, let me do that. You just knocked your veil crooked."

Hannah tried not to fidget while Leslie fixed her hair. "Everyone else is here, though, right?"

"Everyone from the minister to that silly dog who thinks she's the best man instead of Mark. Quit that," Leslie said, swatting at the hand Hannah raised to her hair. "Every time you touch it, I have to fix something. I'm glad Susie and Earl came early so I got a chance to talk to them before you got all bridal and nervous on me."

Hannah smiled. "Susie and Earl are something, aren't

they?'' She glanced at the mirror in front of her. She'd chosen to dress for her wedding in the room where she'd slept when she first came to the house, and she was seated now at the antique vanity there. She frowned. ''I don't like this shade of lipstick. It's too pale a peach.''

Leslie rolled her eyes. ''You've already changed your lipstick twice, but if it makes you feel better—here. Go for it.'' Leslie held out a tissue.

Hannah and Nate had decided on a very small wedding in a ceremony held there at the house. Nate still wasn't comfortable in the church where he had once sung in the choir. Not yet, anyway, Hannah thought, searching the tubes of lipstick for the right color. Given time, he'd come around.

Besides, Hannah loved the idea of being married here, in her own house.

She picked up the tube of lipstick she'd tried on just before the peach shade, and reapplied it. Yes, she thought, leaning forward to study her reflection. That was better, only— ''I've got too much blush on.''

''Hannah, you're not wearing any blush.''

''Oh.'' If she sat there one more second, she decided, she would go crazy. When she got up and started pacing, the long, lacy skirt of her wedding gown swished around her legs. It was a luscious dress, sinfully expensive, with tons of lace in a pale, pale cream color—the clerk had called it ''winter white.'' Hannah loved the idea of marrying her man with the winter voice in a winter white gown.

''If Dad doesn't get here in five minutes,'' she growled as she paced, ''so help me I'll go downstairs without him.''

''I'll go see what's keeping him.''

Leslie had come up from El Paso, and their dad had come down from Wyoming, and of course Nate had asked Earl and Susie to attend. Other than that, their guests included Abe and the hands, a friend of Hannah's from Lubbock—and the sheriff. Ever since Royce Thompson had written the Pardons and Paroles Board on Nate's behalf, he and Nate had been easing cautiously toward friendship.

Nate's case hadn't come up for review yet, but Hannah was certain the board would recommend that the governor issue a pardon. It would take longer to completely clear his record, but soon Nate would no longer be a felon. Not all the shadows from his past could be erased as completely as the record of his conviction would be, but there were fewer of them.

He smiled more often now. A lot more often.

Nate had wanted to wait until his record was clear before getting married. Hannah, naturally, had vetoed that idea. She was capable of great patience when necessary, but she didn't intend to waste it on such a silly notion.

"Look who I found coming up the stairs," Leslie said.

Patrick McBride was tall and as skinny as a snake, with a graying shock of red hair on his head. He scooped Hannah up in a bone-crushing hug, called her his bonny daughter and knocked her veil off. By the time Leslie had everything pinned in place again, it was three minutes after midnight.

"Damned silly time to get married anyway, if you ask me," her father grumbled as they started down the stairs together.

"I didn't ask you, though, did I?" Darn it, Hannah had wanted to be married at midnight. She and Nate had met just after midnight at the bus station; it had been around midnight when he saved her life and told her he loved her.

Music swelled from the living room when she was halfway down the stairs: Mendelssohn's "Wedding March." Sudden, sentimental tears sprang to her eyes, and her father cleared his throat. Leslie hurried ahead, joining Mark to start the procession. The best man's gait might be uneven when he escorted the maid of honor into the living room, but he was upright and mobile now, with the help of a cane and a walking cast.

Oh, well, she thought as she and her father paused in the hall, giving Leslie and Mark time to reach their places. Hadn't Nate been late for their first meeting because of a cow? Maybe it was fitting that she be a little late for their wedding because of an ornery old cowboy.

The music reached the chord that was their cue. Hannah found it suddenly hard to breathe, yet her feet carried her along beside her father.

She passed into the living room. There were candles everywhere—dozens of tall, white tapers that provided the only light. People she knew and loved sat in rented chairs set so as to leave an aisle open for Hannah to walk down. And at the other end of the room, waiting for her, was Nate, looking tall and magnificent in a black western-style suit.

At his feet sat Trixie, her tongue lolling in a doggy grin.

Nate turned to Hannah and smiled, and she didn't see anything else. A few heartbeats later, she stood at his side. They held hands as the minister spoke, and at a quarter past midnight, Hannah Maria McBride Jones came home for good.

*   *   *   *   *

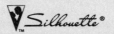

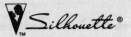

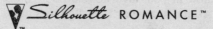

SILHOUETTE® *Desire®* is celebrating the 10th Anniversary of
MAN OF THE MONTH

For ten years Silhouette Desire has been giving readers the ultimate in sexy, irresistible heroes.

So come celebrate with your absolute favorite authors!

JANUARY 1999
BELOVED by Diana Palmer—
SD #1189 Long, Tall Texans

FEBRUARY 1999
**A KNIGHT IN RUSTY ARMOR
by Dixie Browning—**
SD #1195 The Lawless Heirs

MARCH 1999
**THE BEST HUSBAND IN TEXAS
by Lass Small—**
SD #1201

APRIL 1999
BLAYLOCK'S BRIDE by Cait London—
SD #1207 The Blaylocks

MAY 1999
LOVE ME TRUE by Ann Major—
SD #1213

Available at your favorite retail outlet, only from

Silhouette®

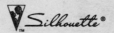

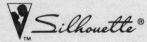

INTIMATE MOMENTS®

™ **Silhouette**®

COMING NEXT MONTH

#925 CATTLEMAN'S PROMISE—Marilyn Pappano
Heartbreak Canyon

Guthrie Harris was shocked when Olivia Miles and her twin daughters showed up on his Oklahoma ranch—with a deed!—and claimed it was *their* home. But since they had nowhere else to go, the longtime loner let them stay. And the longer Olivia stuck around, the less Guthrie wanted her to leave—his home *or* his heart.

#926 CLAY YEAGER'S REDEMPTION—Justine Davis
Trinity Street West

Clay Yeager hadn't meant to trespass on Casey Scott's property—but he was glad he had. The emotions this ex-cop had kept buried for so long were back in full force. Then Casey became a stranger's target, and Clay knew the time had come to protect his woman. He was done with moving on—he was ready to move in!

#927 A FOREVER KIND OF COWBOY—Doreen Roberts
Rodeo Men

Runaway heiress Lori Ashford had little experience when it came to men. So when she fell for rugged rodeo rider Cord McVane, what she felt was something she'd never known existed. But would the brooding cowboy ever see that the night she'd discovered passion in his arms was just the beginning—of forever?

#928 THE TOUGH GUY AND THE TODDLER—Diane Pershing
Men in Blue

Detective Dominic D'Annunzio thought nothing could penetrate his hardened heart—until beautiful but haunted Jordan Carlisle needed his assistance. But Jordan wasn't just looking for help, she was looking for miracles. And the closer they came to the truth, the more Dom began wondering what was in charge of this case—his head or his heart?

#929 HER SECOND CHANCE FAMILY—Christine Scott
Families Are Forever

Maggie Conrad and her son were finally on their own—*and* on the run. But the small town of Wyndchester offered the perfect hideaway. Then the new sheriff, Jason Gallagher, moved in next door, and Maggie feared her secret wouldn't stay that way for long. Could Maggie keep her past hidden while learning that love *was* better the second time around?

#930 KNIGHT IN A WHITE STETSON—Claire King
Way Out West

Calla Bishop was desperate to save her family's ranch. And as the soon-to-be-wife of a wealthy businessman, she was about to secure her birthright. Then she hired Henry Beckett, and it wasn't long before this wrangler had roped himself one feisty cowgirl. But would Henry's well-kept secret cause Calla to hand over her beloved ranch—and her guarded heart?